Ali Blood spent years as a crime reporter in London. He covered murders, terrorist attacks, robberies and riots for various newspapers.

His next career move was into television news as a producer before setting up his own TV production company. He's always had a passion for crime fiction and is now a full-time author living in Hampshire – where he pours blood, sweat and tears into his writing! *The Prisoner's Wife* was his debut novel.

Also by Ali Blood

*The Prisoner's Wife*

# THE OTHER FIANCÉ

## ALI BLOOD

avon.

Published by AVON
A division of HarperCollins*Publishers*
1 London Bridge Street
London SE1 9GF

www.harpercollins.co.uk

HarperCollins*Publishers*
Macken House, 39/40 Mayor Street Upper
Dublin 1
D01 C9W8

www.harpercollins.co.uk

A Paperback Original 2024

1

First published in Great Britain by HarperCollins*Publishers* 2024

A catalogue copy of this book is available from the British Library.

ISBN: 978-0-00-852719-8

This novel is entirely a work of fiction. The names, characters and incidents portrayed in it are the work of the author's imagination. Any resemblance to actual persons, living or dead, events or localities is entirely coincidental.

Typeset in Minion Pro by Palimpsest Book Production Ltd, Falkirk, Stirlingshire

Printed and bound in the UK using 100% Renewable
Electricity by CPI Group (UK) Ltd

This book contains FSC™ certified paper and other controlled sources to ensure responsible forest management.

For more information visit: www.harpercollins.co.uk/green

*To Sonny and Alessia – the latest additions
to our ever-growing family. Wishing them
each a long and happy life.*

# PROLOGUE

I still can't believe what I've been told. The revelations have shaken me to the core.

I can feel sweat beading on my forehead and my heart is banging against my ribs. All I can do is stand in the middle of the room as a riot of emotions tears through me.

'This is all your own fault, Gemma,' he says. 'It didn't have to be like this.'

His words send another cold rush of blood through my veins and I feel vulnerable, helpless, defenceless.

I throw a glance at the door that leads into the hallway and wonder what will happen if I dart towards it. I'm not sure I would even make it. And if I did, what then? No way would I be able to get out of the house. I'm trapped in my own home with a man armed with a knife who wants me dead.

'I've agonised over what to do, Gemma, and I've decided that this is how it has to be. You've done too much and now you know too much. And as I see it, this is the only option open to me. I'm sorry.'

Panic seizes my chest, making it hard to breathe, and as he takes a step towards me, I'm overwhelmed by a gut-churning wave of terror.

There's only one thing I can do, so I throw myself to the side and rush at the door. But I manage only two steps before I collide with a chair that shouldn't be there and stumble face forward onto the carpet.

I roll onto my side and, looking up, I see him standing over me, legs astride mine, knife in hand. He's shaking his head and clenching his jaw.

'I'll make it quick,' he says. 'Just close your eyes.'

# CHAPTER ONE

**GEMMA**

As soon as I exit the dating app on my phone, the blood storms through my veins. It's my body's predictable reaction to what I've just done.

After two weeks of messaging each other, I've agreed to meet up with my latest match and we've even taken the monumental step of exchanging phone numbers.

His name is John Jackman and on his online profile he looks like a young George Clooney. Like me, he lives in South London and apparently works as a financial adviser. And he gives his age as thirty-two. We decided that our first date would be on Friday evening – three days from now – and I suggested a wine bar and restaurant in Balham.

I drop my phone on the sofa and go into the kitchen to pour another glass of chilled white wine. I need it because a wave of unease has settled in my chest. It happens every time I arrange to go on a date. The questions pile up. Is it too soon? Is he as genuine as he sounds? Will I be disappointed yet again?

I ventured into online dating five months ago and have been on nine dates. But, sadly, none of them lived up to my expectations. There was the guy who talked endlessly about himself. The moron who bad-mouthed his ex-wife and made racist comments. And the one who claimed to be thirty when he was clearly at least ten years older.

But it was the cocky Irishman who really took the biscuit. After I told him I worked for a Sunday newspaper as an investigative journalist, he became tongue-tied and then dodged all of my questions before inventing an excuse to leave me in the coffee shop.

Afterwards, I made some enquiries, which, admittedly, I should have done beforehand, and discovered that his profile was a complete fake. His name wasn't Kevin and he didn't run his own computer software company. In fact, to this day, I don't know who he really is or what he does for a living. I can only assume he feared I'd find out before he managed to get me into bed. Or perhaps he suspected that I'd set him up in order to expose him as a fraud on the dating app.

My closest friend, Alice, had warned me that online dating can be a daunting experience, especially for women whose confidence is low. She herself had spent a year dating men through various apps and websites, only to end up in an unhappy marriage with one of them.

Oh well, I tell myself, maybe this time I'll strike lucky and John Jackman will tick all the right boxes and sweep me off my feet. The thought almost makes me smile. But at least I know that he is who he says he is. Since my experience with

'Kevin' I make a point of finding out as much as I can about the men I agree to meet.

I sip at the wine as I head back into the living room. I feel tired, but that's not surprising, since I only returned from one of my regular jogs a short time ago. I'll soon be off to bed, even though it's not yet eight o'clock. Living alone in a small two-bedroom rented house means that most evenings tend to be long and boring, so I rarely stay up late. Plus, I haven't had much of a social life for some time. I could have made more of an effort to develop one after I found myself alone in the world, but I chose not to

I decide to watch TV for a while, but as I reach for the remote, my attention is drawn to the framed photo of Callum on the mantelpiece. It was the last one I took of him. We were out celebrating his birthday and he was wearing the bright blue shirt I'd bought him.

I can't believe it's been three years since he was so suddenly and brutally taken from me. The love of my life, the man I was going to marry, the kindest, gentlest person I had ever known. All I have left of him are the memories and the engagement ring he gave me.

As always, the guilt at having agreed to meet someone new rears its ugly head. I have to tell myself yet again that I can't let that stop me from moving on. I'm now twenty-eight and feel ready to embark on another long-term relationship. Callum wouldn't expect me to remain single for the rest of my life. He'd want me to love again, to have children, to be happy.

We'd been together for just over a year when he proposed. The wedding was going to take place at a register office not far from the flat we shared in Wandsworth, followed by a reception in a nearby pub. Everything was arranged. Everyone had been invited. I'd even bought the dress I was going to wear.

But then, two weeks before the big day, my world fell apart. And I still haven't managed to put it back together.

Half an hour later, I'm still on the sofa, drinking wine and dwelling on the past, when my phone rings.

It makes me jump and I instinctively wonder if John Jackman is calling to check that I've given him my correct number. To my relief, it turns out not to be him.

'I'm sorry to bother you so late, Gemma,' says my editor and boss, Ryan Tapper, who has a habit of calling at all hours. 'Are you free to talk?'

'Of course. What's up?'

'Well, I now need you to come into the office first thing tomorrow morning.'

'But I'm supposed to be attending the press conference in Basingstoke.'

'Not anymore. I'm sending Russell there instead. And he can take over that story.'

'Okay. That saves me a trip. But why the change of plan?'

'Two things have cropped up. We've got wind of another potential exclusive and I want you to take the lead on it.'

'Care to expand?'

'I'll brief you fully when we get together, but it involves an allegation of corruption against a fairly high-ranking copper in the Met.'

'Sounds interesting. What's the other thing that's cropped up?'

He clears his throat before responding. 'That's to do with the interview you've agreed to give to *Capital Crime* magazine. They now want to bring their special edition forward by a month to next Tuesday. Most of it is already in the can and they're asking if they can come in and talk to you tomorrow at eleven instead of next week.'

'D'you know what's prompted them to reschedule?'

'Yes, I do. A woman was found dead earlier this evening in Richmond Park. Police are saying she was murdered.'

I feel a chill wash over me. 'Oh Jesus, not another one.'

'As you can no doubt appreciate, it gives the magazine a good peg to hang their special edition on.'

'It sure does.'

After a brief pause, Ryan adds, 'But are you still up for it, Gem? It's not too late to pull out of the interview. I'm sure they'd understand.'

'No, it's fine,' I tell him. 'I've agreed to do it and this latest killing gives me even more reason not to back out. Tell them I'll be there.'

And with that, the conversation ends.

When I go to bed fifteen minutes later, it's not my next date that keeps me awake. It's wondering how painful it's going to be to tell my story to the magazine reporter when I sit down with them tomorrow.

# CHAPTER TWO

## JACKMAN

As soon as he leaves the pub, it starts to rain. But he's in too much of a good mood to give a toss.

The birthday bash he's just attended for one of his office colleagues was a huge success. Lots of food and drink and a great time had by all.

But that's not the only reason he's feeling so upbeat. The fact that Gemma Morgan agreed to go on a date with him has come as a pleasant surprise. He can't actually believe his luck. He just hopes he'll be able to make a good impression.

Ever since she came up as a match on the app two weeks ago, he hasn't stopped thinking about her. Now, Friday can't come soon enough and he's eager to get up close to those bright blue sparkling eyes, her soft features and thick, lustrous black hair.

He's determined to say and do what he can to win her over. And if he does, then who knows where it will lead.

It's only a fifteen-minute walk from the pub to his home through the well-lit streets of Brixton. On the way, a cold October shower soaks his hair, face and jacket, and thunder rumbles in the distance. But it fails to dampen his mood, because Gemma's face keeps pushing itself into his thoughts. And the more it does, the more excited he's becoming at the prospect of meeting her.

There's just one thing he'll have to bear in mind when the time comes – and that's to be careful not to reveal the truth about himself.

Home is a two-bedroom end-of-terrace house close to St Matthew's Garden. He's been renting it for the past two years and has no plans to move anywhere else anytime soon.

The Tube station is close by, so the journey to his office across the river in the West End is short and quick. In addition, there are plenty of lively bars, pubs and restaurants within walking distance.

And now there's another plus point – Gemma Morgan lives only about two and a half miles away in Balham. It's close to the High Road and not far from where they're going to meet.

It's approaching half ten when he arrives home. After letting himself in, he hangs up his coat and steps into the downstairs loo to dry his hair with a towel. Then he hurries straight upstairs to his bedroom.

Just as he's about to enter it, a voice from inside calls out, 'Is that you, John?'

He can't help but smile as he pushes open the door. He was hoping she'd be here because he's feeling so bloody horny.

'I thought you had other plans,' he says.

Simone is lying seductively on the bed with the sheets pulled back and the side light on. A diminutive figure with a mop of blonde hair, large breasts and full pouty lips. The only thing she's wearing is a wide grin.

'My mate cancelled on me,' she replies. 'I got bored at home so I thought I'd come over and wait for you to get back from your party. Are you pleased to see me?'

'Sure I am. You're just what I need right now.'

Her grin widens. 'Good. I used the spare key you keep under the pot to let myself in.'

'That's what it's there for,' he tells her as he starts to remove his shirt.

He doesn't believe for one minute that her pal let her down. More likely, it was her who cancelled their night out so she could be here when he arrived home to see if he had another woman with him.

But he doesn't intend to raise it as an issue now because he knows it'll spark an argument and she'll bombard him with the same old questions:

*Why won't you let our relationship move to the next level?*

*Why can't I move in with you?*

*Are you cheating on me?*

*Do you really mean it when you say that you love me?*

The truth is, he doesn't love her and as soon as someone better comes along, their four-month relationship will come to an end. But until then he's more than happy to keep her dangling on a string since she's fun to be with and the sex is great.

Her eyes light up when he drops his trousers and she sees that he's already aroused.

'The sooner we get started, the better,' she says as she licks her lips. 'We've both got to get up for work in the morning.'

'Shame it's not the weekend,' he replies as he throws himself onto the bed.

# CHAPTER THREE

## GEMMA

I get up at six on Wednesday morning, having managed only about three hours sleep. When I look in the mirror, I'm a sorry sight, my face lined with emotion and fatigue.

Even before I step into the shower, my mind turns to the interview that I'm due to give to *Capital Crime* magazine later this morning and it provokes a shiver of anxiety. I still don't regret agreeing to do it. I just thought I'd have more time to prepare myself for what is bound to be an upsetting experience.

Talking to a fellow journalist about what happened three years ago is very different to reliving it day after day and night after night in my head. I know because it won't be the first time that I've allowed myself to be interviewed.

Back then, I was a general reporter at the *Daily Mail* and so I knew that as Callum's fiancé the various media outlets would want to hear from me. Despite the state I was in, I felt it was my duty to do what I could to assist the police investigation and help ensure that the story gained as much traction as possible. So, I spoke to newspaper hacks and broadcast journalists and took part in a televised appeal during which I broke down and cried.

Eventually, things moved on and they lost interest in me. There were no more interview requests until two weeks ago when a friend of mine who works at *Capital Crime* magazine rang to tell me they were devoting an entire edition to the sheer number of murders that have taken place in recent years across London's various parks and commons. And he asked me if I'd be willing to tell my story as part of a segment on the impact of the killings on the victims' loved ones. I said yes without a moment's hesitation, in part because I don't want what happened to Callum to ever be forgotten.

By the time I'm showered and dressed, I feel less anxious about the interview. I tell myself that it'll be fine and that I shouldn't have a problem keeping my emotions in check.

After touching up my face with some make-up, I follow the weekday routine of having a mug of coffee and a slice of buttered toast for breakfast. That's all I ever need to get me through the morning.

After that, I sort out my shoulder bag, then stand in front of the hall mirror to check that I'm presentable.

I'm wearing a high-necked lambswool sweater over loose black trousers and I'm happy with the way I look. After I lost Callum, I fell into a deep depression and let myself go. I drank too much and ate too much and put on lots of weight. But over the past eighteen months or so, I've got back to being a size twelve thanks to a healthy diet and regular exercise. I still drink but in moderation.

Before leaving the house, I pull my long hair back into a bun and put on my fleece hooded jacket.

Outside, the new day is draped in billowy grey clouds and a stiff, cold breeze pushes against me as I head for the Tube station. The Northern Line will take me to London Bridge and from there it's just a short walk to the offices of *The Sunday News*, where I've worked since it was launched two years ago. Me and a fellow journalist at The Mail were approached by Ryan and offered jobs as investigative reporters on better terms and conditions. Naturally we both accepted the offer and moved across.

The paper has already managed to gain a readership of around two hundred thousand in what is a very competitive market. It's politically neutral and I'm one of twenty full-time journalists. I enjoy what I do because I'm well paid and every day presents a different challenge.

On the Tube, my thoughts turn to what the boss said about my next assignment. I'm to investigate yet another allegation of corruption against a serving London police officer. It's certainly something I'm keen to get stuck into.

The Met has taken a lot of flak in recent years for what has been described as a 'fundamentally flawed' approach to tackling corruption. Far too many of its officers are bent and not enough has been done to root them out.

When individual coppers are exposed, it always makes for good copy and invariably generates a significant response from readers.

As I step off the Tube at London Bridge, my head is full

of questions that I intend to ask Ryan when he briefs me. But as I emerge from the station, I receive a text that sends my thoughts in a different direction.

*Good morning, Gemma. I just want to tell you that I can't wait to meet you on Friday. I have a good feeling about it and I'm really hoping that it will be the first of many nights out together. Don't hesitate to call me if you fancy a chat over the phone before then. Meanwhile, have a great day and stay safe. John xxx*

The message is totally unexpected and his choice of words makes me smile. Sure, he's jumping the gun in respect of where things might lead, but it sounds like he's got a positive attitude and I like that. I can only hope that it's not an act and he won't prove to be yet another big disappointment.

I start to tap out a response but can't think what to write, so I decide to put it off until later. I'm sure he won't mind.

After shoving the phone back into my bag, I pull up the collar of my coat and head for the office. And on the way, I can't help wondering if John Jackman will turn out to be the man I'll want to spend the rest of my life with.

# CHAPTER FOUR

As usual, the large open-plan office of *The Sunday News* is buzzing. Journalists are tapping away at keyboards and editorial assistants are dashing around clutching files and box folders.

The energy is almost palpable and it'll be ramped up still further as the deadlines approach.

The boss is standing in front of the coffee machine when he spots me heading towards my desk and waves me over.

Ryan Tapper has edited the paper since the launch and has the respect of the whole team. He's very much hands-on and likes to get involved in every aspect of the production process. He's a tall, bespectacled guy in his late forties with a thin, sharp face and sallow skin.

'D'you want a coffee, Gem?' he asks me.

'Yes please. Americano. Milk, no sugar.'

'Coming up.'

One of the things I like about Ryan is that he doesn't act all superior, unlike the other bosses I've worked for. He sees himself as one of us and is more than happy to pitch in when it comes to getting the teas and coffees.

He places a cup on the tray and presses the relevant button.

'I'll brief you on the new investigation in my office in fifteen minutes,' he says. 'But first can you send your notes on the charity story as an email attachment to Russell? He's at the press conference in Basingstoke that you were due to go to.'

'Will do, but as you know I'd only just been assigned to it, so there's not much to pass on.'

'Don't worry. He's aware of that.'

As he hands me my coffee, I ask him why Russell wasn't put on the new story.

'Well, there's a good reason for that, Gem. You see, the copper against whom the corruption allegations are being made is none other than Detective Chief Inspector Elias Cain.'

My heart jumps a beat at the mention of his name.

'The last time I heard from him he called me a fucking bitch,' I say.

Ryan grins. 'And that's why you're perfectly placed to find out if these allegations stand up. You know more about Cain than anyone else on the team.'

I'd never heard of DCI Elias Cain up until a year ago. At the time, he was attached to one of the Met's Major Crime units.

He came to my attention when his wife of five years, Pamela Cain, suddenly disappeared in mysterious circumstances. He claimed she wasn't at home when he returned one evening from a late shift and had no idea where she'd gone. Her car was still on the driveway, but a suitcase and some of her belongings were missing, including her passport and purse.

They'd been having problems in their marriage and she'd apparently threatened to leave him more than once. He assumed that was what she'd done.

They had no children, but his wife's parents refused to believe that their daughter had run away without telling them where she was going. They told Cain's colleagues in the Met that they were convinced he had killed her and hidden the body. According to them, the couple's relationship was strained, partly because they had tried and failed to have children, and also because Cain was apparently addicted to online gambling and had built up considerable debts.

That was when I was assigned to the story and spent weeks looking into it. I spoke to the man himself after a press conference at which he appealed for his wife to let him know that she was safe and well.

I also spoke to his neighbours in Lewisham, his colleagues on the Force and Pamela's parents. I learned, among other things, that the situation got far worse between the couple after Pamela discovered that he'd had a one-night stand with a woman he'd met during a pal's stag weekend in Benidorm. He begged her not to leave him and she didn't, but she made it clear that she could never forgive him.

The story I wrote appeared as a centre-page spread with the headline: *MYSTERY OF DETECTIVE'S MISSING WIFE.* I made sure the piece was accurate and balanced, but it inevitably raised more questions than it answered.

Cain wasn't happy and rang Ryan to complain that I shouldn't have included the quotes from his wife's parents, who were convinced their daughter had been murdered. They were careful not to claim that he must have killed her, but it was implied.

The next day, Cain phoned me on my mobile and threatened to sue me for defamation before launching into an angry rant. He slurred his words, which made me think he was drunk, and insisted yet again that he had no idea what had happened to his wife.

'You should just stick to the facts, you fucking bitch,' he yelled. 'And the facts are that Pam packed a suitcase and left me of her own free will. And she probably thinks it's funny that I'll be living under a cloud of suspicion for the rest of my fucking life.'

He didn't call me again after that, but, oddly enough, I wish he had. Perhaps then I might have prised more information out of him.

A year on, and Pamela Cain still hasn't turned up dead or alive. Her husband kept his job on the Force because no evidence emerged to prove that he had anything to do with her disappearance. However, my journalistic instinct tells me that her parents could well be right and that he did kill her and hide her body somewhere, then made it look as though she'd walked out on him. After all, there are plenty of men in prisons around the world who did exactly that, and some of them are former police officers.

So now DCI Cain is suspected of being a corrupt copper as well as a killer. And I'm being tasked with trying to find out if it's true. I'm looking forward to the briefing when I'll be told more, but first I go to my desk to check my emails. There's nothing that requires my immediate attention, so I set about sending my notes on the charity story to Russell. The investigation is into claims that several prominent charities are squandering public funds on meaningless projects while paying exorbitant salaries to directors, plus undeserved bonuses. The press conference Russell's attending in Basingstoke has been called by one of the charities so that its chief executive can respond to the claims.

Once I've sent the email to Russell, I head straight to Ryan's office. When I get there, he's not alone. He's been joined by one of our researchers, Martin Keenan – the latest member of the editorial team.

He's in his early thirties, always dresses smartly and is by far the best-looking guy in the office. The bad news for all us singletons is that he's in a relationship with a glamourous model who uses her face and body to promote a range of women's clothes on the internet.

'Martin will be your number two on this,' Ryan says when I'm seated. 'He happened to take the call from the bloke who rang in with the tip. And I'm intrigued enough to believe that, for now at least, we should take it seriously and follow it up.' He turns to Martin and asks him to fill me in.

Martin refers to the notebook he's holding and says, 'The guy phoned the switchboard yesterday evening and said he had a story that he thought we'd be interested in. He was put through to me but refused to give his name and his number was withheld. He claimed to work for a criminal gang that operates across London and that Cain has been feeding them information on a regular basis for quite a while. He said that for personal reasons he wants Cain exposed and is prepared to provide us with information that will help us do just that. And he made it clear that he's not after payment. Just revenge.'

'Why doesn't he just pass the information onto the police?'
I ask.

'Well, that's where the story gets even more interesting,'
Martin replies. 'I didn't know until the guy told me that five
months ago Cain was transferred from Major Crimes to the
Anti-Corruption and Abuse Command.'

I raise my brow in surprise. 'That's news to me. Are you
sure?'

He nods. 'I checked and it's true. That's why our mystery
man fears that if he goes through official channels, Cain will
get wind of it and any investigation will be scuppered before it
begins. Plus, his gangster paymasters will probably be tipped
off and he'll end up dead. So, he wants us to take it forward.'

'Then how will he pass the information onto us?'

'He's willing to meet one or two of us at a location of his
choosing, but insisted on remaining anonymous. He claimed
that he'd put together a dossier with incriminating evidence
that will put Cain behind bars. He's going to call me on my
mobile at some point today to find out if we're keen to listen
to what he has to say. If we are, then he'll tell us when and
where to meet him.'

'For now, we assume the guy is genuine and not out to
waste our time,' Ryan says. 'It's possible that we won't hear
from him again, but if we do, then we need to be prepared.'

We then start to discuss how best to approach the story
and who we can call on to help us pull it together.

But the meeting has to be cut short when Ryan's secretary
pops her head in to inform me that the journalist from *Capital
Crime* magazine has arrived.

# CHAPTER FIVE

The journalist turns out to be someone I've heard of but never met. Her name is Kendra Boyle and she's a thirty-something Scottish woman with a warm smile and curly red hair.

I meet her in reception and take her to one of the small conference rooms. On the way, I get us each a coffee from the vending machine.

Once we're facing each other across the table, she tells me that she's worked for *Capital Crime* magazine for five years and that she's a regular reader of *The Sunday News*.

'Thanks so much for agreeing to see me today,' she says. 'As you know, we took the decision to bring our special edition forward as soon as we heard about the murder in Richmond Park. It'll now be published next week.'

'What's the latest on that?' I ask her. 'All I know is that a woman was stabbed to death early yesterday evening, but when I last checked, she hadn't been formally identified.'

'Well, her name was revealed an hour ago: Gillian Ramsay.

A twenty-six-year-old nurse who was returning home from work. She was raped before being stabbed.'

'My God, that's awful.'

'It certainly is. No wonder so many people are so wary of walking alone across this city's parks and commons, especially after dark.'

I'm one of those people and when I jog at night in the winter months, I stick to the streets and paths around Balham. But even then, I don't feel safe, especially when running through poorly lit areas.

'Before we start talking about what happened to your fiancé, can I just say that I can fully appreciate how hard this must be for you, Gemma,' Kendra tells me.

I clear my throat and force myself to smile. 'Thanks, but I'm okay. Your magazine is drawing attention to an important issue and it will clearly help to have input from myself and others like me.'

Kendra nods as she takes out her notebook and places it on the table. 'Then let me start by telling you what I know,' she says. 'It was four years ago when you met Callum Ross at a friend's party. You started dating and moved in together after five months. Then six months after that you were due to get married. But just weeks before the wedding, he took his dog for a walk and never came back.'

I feel tears threaten, so I bite my lip and take a deep breath through my nose.

'That's right,' I say. 'It was the worst night of my life and I've relived it every day since then.'

Kendra then reads from her notes, telling me what I already know about what happened to Callum. And as she speaks, my mind carries me back to that terrible night when Callum took his much-loved bearded collie Sampson for their usual walk across Wandsworth Common, which was just a couple of hundred yards from our rented flat.

It was a dark, damp evening, so the common was almost deserted. But among those who were out and about was the man who attacked Callum on one of the paths and beat him about the head and face with a large stone. Sampson, who it was assumed must have tried to defend him, was also bludgeoned, and they were both left for dead.

Their bodies were discovered by another dog walker, but I didn't find out what had happened until much later when I went looking for them because I was frantic with worry.

I came across the flashing blue lights of police vehicles and officers in their bright yellow vests and knew instinctively that my heart was about to be broken.

As I ran towards the scene, an officer stopped me from getting too close, but not before I glimpsed Callum's bright red waterproof jacket on the ground and started screaming.

'Are you all right, Gemma?' Kendra asks me, her voice raised an octave.

I close my eyes and shake my head, hoping the images from that night will retreat. But they don't and my throat thickens as I try to swallow down my emotions.

'I'm really sorry,' she says. 'It was insensitive of me to just read my notes without even looking up.'

My vision blurs as tears fill my eyes, but I manage not to break down.

'It's not your fault,' I tell her as my heart beats hard and heavy behind my ribs. 'This was bound to happen, but I was prepared for it. So, please carry on.'

After a long pause, she asks me how I coped with the events that followed that night and the question sends a shudder down my spine.

I swipe a knuckle across both eyes before replying. 'It wasn't easy. First, there was the arrest, followed by Callum's funeral, and then what happened inside the prison to the bastard who killed him.'

His name was Chris Tate and he was caught on a CCTV camera fleeing from the common around the time the killings were believed to have taken place. He was arrested two days later and it turned out he was a career criminal with previous convictions for assault, robbery and dealing drugs.

Police found traces of Callum's blood on his shoes. But he denied murder and said he'd stumbled across the bodies and fled because he didn't want to be implicated. He also alleged that as he approached the scene, a man with his face covered by a hood ran past him.

But police didn't believe him and there was no evidence to back up his story about the hooded man. What's more, they learned that Tate had gone to the common that evening to sell drugs. He was charged with murder, but didn't get to stand trial because while on remand in prison, he got involved in a fight with another inmate and was stabbed to death. His killer was a notorious gangster who was already serving a life sentence for murder.

'My family told me to celebrate the fact that Tate had been killed,' I say. 'But I couldn't. Instead, it came as a shocking blow. You see, I was hoping that he'd stand trial and would open up about why he'd attacked Callum. He never told the police and so, to this day, I still don't know. It's meant that since then I've conjured up a whole bunch of wretched scenarios that are trapped inside my head.'

'You're not alone in that respect, Gemma,' Kendra says. 'I interviewed a man two days ago whose wife was murdered while walking her dog across Peckham Rye. She was stabbed several times but not sexually assaulted. The person who did it is still at large so the motive is unknown.'

'I remember reading about that,' I reply.

Kendra then asks me to describe what it's been like for me these past years and whether I've been able to move on.

I swallow hard before responding. 'I wouldn't have been able to cope if it hadn't been for the support of my mother. She's done so much to help me. My dad died when I was thirteen and she wasn't able to start rebuilding her life until she entered into a relationship with another man who is now my stepfather. She found love again and is now happy. And she convinced me to try to do the same, which is why I decided to give it a go and started online dating about five months ago.'

Kendra raises a sceptical brow. 'And how is that working out for you?'

I shrug. 'So far, not very well. I'm beginning to think that I'll never find anyone who will mean as much to me as Callum did.'

Relief surges through me when Kendra tells me she has enough for her feature and thanks me for being so forthcoming.

'Your story and those of the other loved ones I've spoken

to will hopefully raise awareness of a serious problem facing Londoners,' she says. 'And please allow me to wish you luck in your search for love again.'

After I've shown her out of the building, I find a quiet place in the lounge area to gather my thoughts before returning to Ryan and Martin in the newsroom.

I feel a degree of pride in myself for answering all those questions without losing it, but my body is still rigid with tension. The conversation evoked so many bad memories that I know will play on my mind for the rest of the day. I'll just have to put on a brave face and keep telling myself that at least I've managed to claw my way out of that awful pit of despair that I was plunged into. And surely things can only get better from now on.

# CHAPTER SIX

**JACKMAN**

It's almost lunchtime and Gemma still hasn't responded to his text message. He wants to believe that she hasn't yet read it, but what if she has? What if it made her feel uncomfortable and she's decided not to respond?

He fired it off on the spur of the moment as soon as Simone left the house. Now he's wondering if it was a mistake. Perhaps he should have thought it through first and considered how she might react.

It's been a busy morning in the office so he hasn't had time to dwell on it. But now he's on a coffee break and it's all he can think about.

When his phone finally rings, his heart jumps at the thought that it could be Gemma, but disappointment follows when he sees that it's his mum calling. He hears from her at least once a week, so it's not a huge surprise, except that she usually rings in the evening.

'Hi, Mum,' he answers. 'Are you okay?'

'I'm fine, son. I just wanted to have a quick word.'

'Well, I'm at the office, so what's so urgent?'

'Well, your dad and I have been talking and we wondered if you'd like to come over on Saturday,' she says. 'We don't like the thought of you being by yourself.'

He frowns. 'Why, what's so special about Saturday?'

She pauses before answering. 'Please don't tell me you don't know, John. It'll be six years to the day since Lia died.'

He curses himself because he had forgotten, but he's not prepared to admit it.

'Of course, I know,' he lies. 'I just thought it best to try not to think about it. I'll be fine.'

'I don't believe you,' she replies. 'If we're all together, it won't be such a tough day. You can bring the girl you've been seeing if you like. Simone, isn't it? It'd be nice to meet her finally, that's assuming you've told her about Lia and what happened to her.'

He holds his irritation in check and draws a breath. 'I told her soon after we met, Mum, but I'm not sure she'd be up for a get-together to remember a former girlfriend.'

'Well, it won't hurt to ask her. She can only say no.'

'Then let me give it some thought and I'll get back to you later.'

'Fantastic. I'll make a nice roast and you're welcome to stay the night if you want to.'

'That's great. But I've got to go now, so have a nice day, Mum.'

'You too, son.'

After hanging up, he shakes his head and lets out a breath

29

between his teeth. Then his mind takes him back to what happened to Lia and the guilt resurfaces like a flush of acid.

They met at a financial services trade show in London. She was there as part of a team representing an asset management company and when she handed him a flyer, he clocked her name tag: Lia Rainsford.

He couldn't resist telling her that it was his mother's maiden name and it sparked a pleasant conversation that continued for twenty or so minutes. They then met for coffee later that day and it proved to be the start of their relationship.

Lia was pretty, petite and the same age as him. And it was easy for them to get together from the outset because they lived only a couple of miles apart in South London. They often stayed over at each other's flats and after only three months, he couldn't imagine ever being without her.

They had so much in common. A university education. A total lack of interest in politics. A fondness for white wine. Even a fear of spiders. And they were both big fans of songs from the seventies and eighties.

After dating for five months, he proposed and she accepted. They then began discussing moving in together, but it never happened because he let her down badly.

Back then, he worked for a different company and on that day, he and several colleagues attended a conference at a hotel in Southampton. They all travelled down by train on the Friday and stayed over. He had planned to return to London on the Saturday before the conference ended and even made arrangements to take Lia out to dinner to celebrate her new job. It was something she was really looking forward to.

But his colleagues persuaded him to stay the extra night

with them so as to make the most of the all-expenses-paid trip. He told Lia that the conference was going on longer than expected and his boss wanted him to attend a late meeting with a potential client. She was disappointed but didn't kick up a fuss and told him she would go out for a drink with one of her pals instead. He felt bad about lying to her, but that didn't stop him enjoying himself.

He and three of his colleagues had dinner and drinks in the hotel before visiting some local pubs, where they all got slightly drunk. But it didn't stop there. Their night on the town ended with a visit to a local lap dance club and, to his everlasting shame, he did something he'd never done before and paid one of the girls for a private dance, followed by a blow job, in a back room.

Afterwards, the group staggered back to the hotel and when he got to his room, he promptly fell asleep fully clothed on the bed.

Then, at six on the Sunday morning, he was woken by the ringing of his phone. His head throbbed as he rolled over and answered it.

But the pain quickly subsided when he was told that his fiancée was dead.

She was killed when a driver lost control of his car as he swerved to avoid a pedestrian who was crossing the road. The car mounted the pavement and ploughed into Lia and her pal, who were standing on the kerb hoping to hail a taxi. It happened at one in the morning, just minutes after they left a cocktail bar and about the time a lap dancer was giving him a blow job. Both girls suffered multiple injuries. Lia was pronounced dead at the scene, but her friend was rushed to hospital by ambulance and survived.

He didn't own up to what he was doing when it happened, of course, but her father, whom he'd been close to up until then, did make a point of telling him at her funeral that she would still be alive if he'd returned home from Southampton on the Saturday as planned.

The grief was bad enough, but the burden of guilt changed him in so many ways and made him do things during the years that followed that added to the heavy weight on his conscience.

When he allows his mind to carry him back, it's like an act of self-harm. Which is why he's been searching for a way to lessen the pain. Until just over two weeks ago, he feared it would prove to be impossible.

But that was when he was unexpectedly matched with Gemma Morgan on the dating app and her picture planted the seed of an idea in his head.

He knows he can't undo the things he's done, but he now believes that there is a way that he can atone for them.

First, though, he needs to convince Gemma that he's a man she can put her trust in.

# CHAPTER SEVEN

**GEMMA**

'How did it go?' Ryan asks me when I return to his office, and I appreciate the concern. He's now alone, having addressed the team on what he wants from them during the day ahead.

'It wasn't as bad as I thought it would be,' I tell him. 'And I'm glad I didn't back out, even though it's stirred up a lot of bad memories.'

'Well, let's hope that this new investigation will prove to be a welcome distraction. We're still waiting to hear back from the anonymous tipster who's alleging that DCI Cain is a bent copper. I've asked Martin to dig through the files and pull out all the information we have on Cain, the Met's Anti-Corruption and Abuse Command, and the criminal gangs operating across London. I suggest you go and catch up with him. You can brief me later.'

Martin is at his workstation in the newsroom, tapping away at his keyboard. I pull up a chair and sit beside him.

'You're back sooner than I expected,' he says. 'Was it okay?'

'It wasn't pleasant,' I reply.

'Do you want to talk about it?'

'Not now. Let's just get on with the job. How far have you got?'

He points to a folder on his desk. 'It won't surprise you that there's a ton of material for us to go through. The guy on the phone gave no clue as to who he works for, but I got the impression that it's one of the big outfits. So far, I've found nothing in the system that links Cain to any of them.'

'I suppose we shouldn't be surprised. If he is involved in some way, he'll have gone to extreme lengths to keep it under wraps.'

I'm well aware that the two biggest issues facing London's Met Police are organised crime and corruption within its own ranks.

There are believed to be over four hundred criminal gangs operating in the capital. Those most frequently in the news are street crews who peddle drugs and fight turf wars. But away from the headlines are the bigger players who have replaced the old family firms. These gangs are far more powerful and their activities extend across the globe. They're multinational, diversified and tech-savvy, and their operations include cybercrime, money laundering, human trafficking and smuggling.

They continue to prosper thanks, in part, to the widespread corruption within the Force. And it's no longer just about officers accepting £50 bribes and free bottles of whisky for turning a blind eye. These days, it's all about corruption at the top, which is much harder to detect and put a stop to.

'What does your gut tell you about this one, Gemma?' Martin asks me. 'Do you think it has potential?'

I shrug. 'Too soon to say. I've learned from experience not to get overexcited when we're approached by someone claiming to be an underworld snitch. All too often, they chicken out before it comes to actually parting with any incriminating information.'

'Well, I expect we'll know soon enough where we stand if the guy calls me back.'

'And if he does, we need to be prepared. So, let's give some thought to how to go about it.'

Martin continues to print off various archived documents and newspaper cuttings, which I glance through before inserting them in the folder. Among them is the article I wrote about the disappearance of Cain's wife. But no stories about him have appeared in the papers since then, and even his move from Major Crimes to the Anti-Corruption and Abuse Command failed to get a mention.

But there are numerous stories about other police officers who have been found guilty of corruption. They'd taken bribes from crime bosses who wanted them to undermine prosecutions, compromise operations and provide confidential information on investigations.

'One thing's for sure,' I say, looking up from the notes I've been making. 'If Cain is bent, then he'll be a real asset to whoever has him on their payroll. He's well placed within the Force and has been around for years. He's also got access to no end of sensitive information.'

'I wonder what he's done to upset the guy who wants to grass on him,' Martin says.

'That's probably something he won't make known to us in case it blows his cover.'

'Well, it must be something pretty serious if he's taken the trouble to gather evidence and put it together in a dossier.'

We spend the next hour reading through the material and gathering information about DCI Cain from the paper's various contacts. In order not to arouse suspicion, we tell them we're looking to run a story to mark the first anniversary of his wife's mysterious disappearance.

We learn that he's still living in the house he shared with her in Lewisham and that as far as anyone knows he hasn't embarked on a new relationship. We're also told that he's highly regarded by his colleagues and that he himself requested the transfer to anti-corruption when a vacancy arose.

Lunchtime is upon us before we know it and I tell Martin that we should take a break.

'There's no point working ourselves into the ground with all this background research before we even know if we'll be able to make use of it,' I say. 'Let's go to the canteen and talk over what we've learned. I'll then pull together a note for the boss, and hopefully by then, our anonymous whistleblower will have called back.'

## CHAPTER EIGHT

We both opt for a salad and soft drink and Martin insists on paying for it.

'My treat,' he says. 'It's been a while since we last worked together on an investigation and I've been looking forward to catching up.'

The paper employs five full-time researchers and, in my humble opinion, Martin is by far the best. He's smart, hard-working and easy to get along with. We also have something in common, which invariably comes up when we spend time together – online dating.

Shortly after he joined the paper nine months ago, he let it be known that he'd started a relationship with a woman he'd met on a dating app he'd joined a year earlier. Before I took the plunge myself, I asked him about his experiences, which were pretty positive.

But he made a point of warning me, just as Alice did, that I should approach it with caution. His advice was to keep first dates brief, not to give away too much about myself at the start, and to be aware that apps are rife with men who are economical with the truth.

It comes as no surprise that the first thing he says when we're sitting by ourselves at a table is, 'So, how's the search for a soulmate going, Gem? The last time we spoke about it you were due to go on a date with a doctor.'

I grimace as my mind takes me back to that brief encounter. 'That's right. His name was Matt and he was nice enough, but there was no spark between us. He realised it as well as I did, so there was no second date.'

He shrugs. 'That's the way it goes. You just have to stick with it and go on searching for that elusive spark. And keep telling yourself that your perfect match is out there and only a click or swipe away. But I know it's not easy. I was on the verge of giving up myself when I got lucky and was matched with Tracy.'

Most of his female colleagues believe that Tracy was the one who got lucky, and one of them, a fellow researcher, actually said as much to him during an after-work drink in a nearby pub.

It's easy to see why he attracts so much attention, though, with that bright, engaging smile and those wide, blue eyes that have a piercing quality. For me, he ticks all the right boxes and I only wish that I could meet someone like him. Someone who isn't already spoken for.

'Has there been anyone since Matt the doctor?' he asks me, before poking half a tomato into his mouth.

I shake my head. 'No, but there's about to be. I'm going out with a guy on Friday. He's some kind of financial adviser and lives in Brixton. It seems like he has potential.'

I'm suddenly reminded of the text message that John Jackman sent to me earlier and I feel a rush of guilt for not responding to it.

Martin points to my phone, which I've placed on the table. 'Well, come on then. Show me what he looks like. I'll tell you if I think he's good enough for you.'

I can't help but laugh as I grab my phone, log onto the app and pull up John's profile. I've already shown it to Alice and a couple of the girls in the office, so I have no qualms about showing it to Martin.

'He's certainly a handsome hunk,' he says. 'Are you looking forward to meeting him?'

'Of course. I just hope he lives up to my expectations. So many of them don't.'

'Have you spoken to him yet?'

'No. We've only exchanged messages over the past couple of weeks. In fact, he sent me one this morning and said I could give him a call if I want to chat before we meet.'

'Well, since you've exchanged numbers, that sounds like a good idea,' Martin says. 'At least if he gives off a bad vibe, you can cancel the date.'

'I'll think about it,' I say. 'But not before we've given more thought to the investigation that we're both supposed to be focused on. If the guy calls back we need to be clued up and ready to move.'

We go through the documents in the folder again and I make a note of all the points we've raised. When we're back in the newsroom, I type them up and print off copies for Ryan and Martin.

After that's done, I bring up John Jackman's text message

on my phone and I hope that he doesn't think it was rude of me not to have responded sooner.

I quickly tap out a reply:

*Sorry it's taken me so long to respond. I've been really busy. A phone chat sounds like a good idea. You can call me this evening about eight if that suits you.*

Seconds after I send it, my phone rings and I assume it's him calling me back. But it isn't.

'Hi there, Gem,' Alice says and I sense straight away that something is wrong. 'Are you at the office?'

'I am. I wasn't expecting to hear from you today. Everything okay?'

'Not really, no. I just wondered if there's any chance you can pop in on your way home if you have nothing planned. Sean is due back at about seven, so it will have to be before then.'

There's no need for her to tell me what it's about. I've been her shoulder to cry on ever since her marriage started to fall apart, and this isn't the first time she's asked me to come round to her house when her husband's out.

'I can leave early and be there by about half five,' I say. 'Or we could meet up somewhere else.'

'I can't, Gem. I've got things to do here. But are you sure that you don't mind popping in?'

'Of course not. You're my best friend and your problems are my problems. I'll be there as soon as I can.'

Alice met Sean Kelly eighteen months ago through her

40

dating app and she moved into his house just four months later from her rented flat. Then, five months after that, they rushed into marriage, against the advice of her parents and friends. There was a small wedding and he whisked her away on a honeymoon in Greece, which she raved about afterwards.

I was one of those who didn't think he was right for her and told her so. She didn't pay any heed, but it did fracture our relationship for a while. Sean is an abrasive character who has a high opinion of himself, and I've made no secret of the fact that I don't like him. But it wasn't until Alice confided in me two months ago that I learned that he's also a total control freak. He didn't show his true colours apparently until after they had tied the knot. And now Alice is struggling to cope because she says he treats her like a possession rather than a wife.

After I come off the phone, I inform Ryan that I have to leave early. He's fine with that and says, 'I'm beginning to think that maybe the Cain tip was a wind-up after all. It's almost four o'clock and Martin still hasn't heard back from the guy.'

'It could be he's having second thoughts,' I reply. 'It wouldn't be the first time that's happened.'

He nods. 'I know, but it'll be a disappointment just the same. It's been a while since we got our teeth into a major exclusive, and police corruption is a hot topic right now.'

I tell Martin to phone me if he does receive another call and then get ready to leave the office.

Five minutes later, just as I'm about to exit the building, John Jackman replies to my text.

*Delighted to hear from you, Gemma. So glad*
*you think it's a good idea to chat before we meet*
*up on Friday. Will phone you at eight xxx*

I feel a flicker of uncertainty because it'll be the first time I've spoken to a date before meeting up with them. I just hope it goes well and the conversation doesn't put me off him.

# CHAPTER NINE

I've made good time since leaving the office and should be with Alice by five fifteen.

She and Sean live only a couple of miles from me in Tooting. To get there, I just stay on the Tube for two more stops and their house is close to the station.

I'm hoping that my friend isn't in too much of a state, but at the same time, I'm trying to prepare myself mentally for what she's going to tell me.

Her plight is a familiar one. Like millions of other wives, she's found herself in what is termed a coercive relationship. She's told me how Sean constantly puts her down, even though he swears that he loves her. He also monitors her movements, insists on controlling their finances and tells her what and what not to wear. I'm the only one of her friends she's opened up to and I had to promise not to let on to Sean that I know.

It's put me under a lot of pressure because I worry that things will get much worse between them and there's little or nothing I can do about it.

Theirs is a smart detached house in a quiet street and Alice answers the door within seconds of me ringing the bell. She's casually dressed in jeans and a loose sweater, and her dark hair is twisted in a neat knot on top of her head.

'Thanks for coming, Gem,' she says. 'I just needed someone to talk to.'

'It's not a problem,' I tell her as I pull her into a hug. 'I'm guessing the situation with you and Sean is going from bad to worse.'

She nods. 'I'm afraid so. Come in and I'll tell you what's got me worked up this time.'

I follow her into the kitchen, where she asks me if I want a cup of tea or coffee. I opt for tea and then sit on a stool at the breakfast bar as she makes it.

She's the same age as me but a few inches shorter, at five four. Her narrow face is pasty white and the corners of her mouth are turned downwards. She's so very different these days to the happy-go-lucky person she used to be.

We met five years ago when we were members of the same gym and she provided invaluable support to me after Callum's death. She's employed as an IT sales account manager for a firm based in Streatham, often working from home, while Sean runs his own debt collection agency based in Vauxhall.

Once she's sitting opposite me, I see the glistening shine of emotion in her eyes and I fear that something serious has happened.

'So, what is it, Alice?' I ask her. 'Has he hit you?'

She heaves a sigh and shakes her head. 'No, he hasn't, but last night I thought he was going to. He really lost it and he held his fist up against my face and told me that I needed to act like a proper wife.'

'Oh, God, that's awful.'

'What set him off was me telling him that I'm still not ready to try for a baby. We'd previously agreed to leave it for a couple more years and he was happy with that. But now he's changed his mind and is insisting I come off the pill. But the last thing I want right now is to get pregnant with his child. It will tie me to him forever, and if he won't change his ways, that doesn't bear thinking about.'

A surge of anger makes me stiffen and I repeat what I've said to her twice before in the past couple of weeks. 'You need to leave him, Alice, before things get completely out of hand. Men like him rarely change, and from the sound of it, his behaviour is becoming far more coercive and threatening.'

She blinks back tears and her jaw hardens. 'I blame myself for being in this situation. I should have listened to you and my parents and not married him.'

'You didn't see him for what he is, though,' I tell her. 'He pretended to be someone else. It's what a lot of men do.'

'But I still love him. At least I think I do. And I keep telling myself that it's a phase he's going through and it won't last.'

I find it hard to believe that she can be so blind as to what has happened to her and it's so sad that she feels the need to blame herself.

'But the longer it goes on, the more you'll suffer and the harder it will be to end it,' I say. 'You're right to hold off on having his baby. It'd be a big mistake.'

She blows out an exasperated breath. 'You make it sound so easy, Gem. But it isn't. I dread to think how he'll react if

I even threaten to walk out on him. And if I actually find the courage to do so, then I'm scared I'll come to regret it.'

Her anxiety is tangible and I can well understand why. I've written about women who've been in her position and I know that it often ends badly whatever they decide to do.

Her bottom lip quivers and tears pool in her eyes as she struggles to get the words out. 'I've tried to get him to see how unhappy I've become, but he refuses to accept that it's down to him,' she says. 'He just tells me to stop moaning all the time and to be grateful for what I have. And sometimes I even wonder if he's right.'

I'm about to respond when we both hear the sound of the front door being opened.

Alarm shivers in Alice's eyes and my stomach does a flip.

'Oh, shit,' she says as she hurriedly rubs her fingers against her eyes and pushes her shoulders back. 'He wasn't supposed to—'

'It's me, hon,' Sean calls out from the hallway and seconds later walks into the kitchen.

He's wearing a suit that looks too tight on his tall, muscular frame, and his narrow face registers surprise when he sees me sitting at the breakfast bar. As usual I feel uncomfortable in his presence, which is why I've always tried to avoid interacting with him.

'Gemma dropped by on her way home from work,' Alice tells him. 'She was just about to leave.'

'Well, I hope the pair of you had a good catch-up,' Sean says as he crosses the room to give his wife a kiss.

It makes me cringe because he plays the part of the affectionate husband whenever he has an audience.

'I wasn't expecting you back so early,' she replies.

'We weren't very busy, so I thought I would come and take my lovely wife out to dinner. It's ages since I treated you to a slap-up meal.'

Alice smiles at him, but I sense a total lack of enthusiasm in her expression.

He then turns back to me. 'There's no need to rush off on my account, Gem. We won't be leaving here for at least an hour.'

His aim is to project an air of friendliness, but it doesn't fool me. I can tell from the look in his eyes that he resents me being here.

Suddenly, I can't wait to get away and Alice makes it clear that she wants me to go by telling Sean that I've arranged to meet someone.

'Is it a new bloke?' he asks me as he cracks a smile.

I nod. 'It is, as a matter of fact.' It's not actually a fib since I have what could be termed a phone date at eight o'clock with John Jackman.

'Well, let's hope that you stay with this one long enough for us to get to meet him.'

The sarcasm is evident in his voice, but I choose to ignore it and get down off the stool.

'I'll be going then,' I say. 'It was good to see you both.'

Sean has already turned away and is heading for the fridge.

'I'll show you out,' Alice says and follows me into the hallway. 'I'm really sorry, Gem,' she whispers to me as we approach the front door. 'I don't think it's a good idea for you to hang around. I get the impression he wants to do some grovelling.'

'I hope you're right,' I respond. 'But if things get out of hand again, then come straight to my place. You'll be safe there.'

A quick shake of the head. 'I'm sure I won't need to. But thanks so much for coming over and listening to me. You're a true friend.'

We give each other a hug, but as I step outside, I can't help wishing that I could take her with me.

# CHAPTER TEN

When I get home, the first thing I do is pour myself a large vodka and tonic. I feel I need it, because what Alice told me has planted a wedge of dread in my chest.

I keep replaying our short conversation in my head and trying to think of ways I can help her. But, deep down, I know that there's nothing I can do other than try to encourage her to bail out of what has clearly become a toxic relationship.

My friend's well-being is not the only thing that has got me worked up, though. In less than two hours, I'll be speaking on the phone to my next date and the butterflies are already fluttering in my stomach.

I blink away the vision of Alice's anxious face and tell myself that when John Jackman calls, I'll be in a better frame of mind. By then, I will have been for my evening run, had a shower and downed a few more drinks.

It doesn't take me long to change into my thermal hoodie and tights and lace up my running shoes. Soon, I'm pounding the pavement and making a conscious effort to clear my head.

I spend half an hour sprinting through the streets of Balham before returning home, exhausted but refreshed.

After an invigorating shower, I slip into my pyjamas and make myself a bacon sandwich. After I've eaten it, I help myself to another drink. I close my eyes as I fire down the first mouthful of vodka and feel it bite into the back of my throat.

It's now half seven as I sit on the sofa and open up John Jackman's dating app profile on my phone. I need to remind myself of the messages we've exchanged. What have we revealed about each other? What did he say about himself that encouraged me to take things further? Did he include anything that struck me as unconvincing?

It was a question from me about his previous relationships that prompted him to tell me about his fiancée Lia Rainsford, who was killed when a car mounted the pavement and struck her. I felt compelled to make him aware that I understood what he would have gone through because I had also lost my fiancé in tragic circumstances. I didn't go into too much detail, but I did say that Callum was murdered while walking his dog on Wandsworth Common.

'*I'm so sorry to hear that,*' he messaged back. '*I suspect that, like me, you feel the need to move on with your life.*'

After that exchange I typed his girlfriend's name into Google and read about the accident that happened while her boyfriend John Jackman was away on a business trip. I didn't do it purely out of curiosity, of course. I wanted to check that he'd told me the truth, and was relieved to discover that he had.

I have no doubt that he would have checked on me too. He'd have come across the news stories about Callum and seen the photos of us together. But clearly it didn't put him off wanting to meet me.

After another minute or so, I close my phone and go into the kitchen to top up my glass. My pulse is galloping and I didn't realise I'd be this nervous over a bloody phone call. I suspect it's because I haven't had time to prepare myself.

I'm keen to strike the right note and to convey the impression that I'm friendly and open-minded, but not a gullible pushover. And I'm hoping that our chat will break the ice and make our first actual date less stressful.

It's five to eight as I return to the living room and drop back onto the sofa. Two minutes later, my phone rings and a shiver of excitement runs through me.

I take a deep breath and pick up the phone, only to find that it isn't John Jackman who's calling me. It's Martin and he never rings me at home without a good reason.

'I've just heard back from our anonymous tipster and a meeting has been set up for tomorrow morning,' he says.

'Where and when?' I ask him, anxious to keep the conversation short.

'I told him it would be me and another journalist. He wants us to be outside Covent Garden Tube station at eleven. He'll then call me again to tell us that he'll meet us at a venue close by. I had to describe myself and tell him what I'd be wearing.'

'Did you manage to get anything else out of him?'

'I asked him again who he works for, but he wouldn't be drawn. He said he'd tell us tomorrow. But he did repeat that he wants DCI Cain exposed for personal reasons and that the information he has on the guy will cause a shitstorm if and when we publish it.'

'Then we'll see what he says and take it from there,' I say. 'Have you let Ryan know?'

'I have, and he wants us both in at nine sharp for a briefing.'

'Okay. I'll see you then.'

After ending the call, I chug back some more of my vodka and focus on the clock above the mantelpiece as I count down the seconds to eight o'clock.


John Jackman keeps me waiting until four minutes past eight. By then, every muscle in my body is tense, shoulders rigid.

But buoyed by the alcohol, I answer the phone in a voice that I hope sounds cool and confident.

'Hello, John,' I say. 'At least, I trust it's you.'

'It is, Gemma,' he replies, and it strikes me how well spoken he is and how confident he sounds. 'It's good to be able to speak to you at last.'

'You too, although I have been a tad nervous because this is a first for me. I've usually gone from messaging on the app to the first date.'

'I was actually going to suggest we did a video call or Zoom chat. Would you have preferred that?'

'No way. And don't dare suggest it now because I'm wearing pyjamas and look a mess.'

'Oh, I very much doubt that. I'm sure you're looking as good as you do in your profile picture.'

I laugh. 'I appreciate the compliment, but you could not be more wrong. What about you? Did you dress up for this occasion?'

'Of course. I'm wearing my most comfy T-shirt and tracksuit bottoms. I haven't shaved, but then I didn't see the point since I'm straight off to bed after our conversation. It's been a busy day at the office.'

'It's an early night for me too. I didn't get home until fairly late.'

'Have you been working on a big news story then?'

No way can I mention the Cain investigation, so I tell him I've been developing several feature ideas for the paper.

Thankfully, the conversation progresses well and turns out to be much easier than I feared it would be. There are no awkward moments or pregnant pauses. We touch on various subjects, from the weather to some of the negative experiences we've each had with online dating.

John Jackman comes across as friendly and likeable and I find it refreshing that he doesn't keep talking about himself, unlike most of my other dates.

He's the one who suggests we should bring the conversation to an end after twenty minutes. 'If we don't call it quits now, there'll be nothing left for us to talk about on our first date,' he says good-naturedly.

'Fair point,' I reply. 'But it's been really nice talking to you and I'm glad you suggested it.'

'Me too. And I look forward to seeing you at seven on Friday.'

After hanging up, I feel relieved and more than a little pleased with myself. I don't think that could have gone any better than it did. The ice has been broken and I have a much better idea of what to expect on Friday.

He said nothing to disappoint me and I believed him when he told me that since joining the dating app nine months ago, he'd been matched with two dozen women and had met up with fourteen of them. But he hadn't seen any of them beyond the first date.

'The last one was three months ago and she proved to be another disappointment,' he said. 'After that, I gave myself a break and didn't start using the app again until three weeks ago. And that was when you popped up.'

I'm well aware that without making eye contact it's impossible to tell if someone's genuine. But the vibes I'm left with after our chat are pretty positive.

I'm too wired to go straight to bed, so I pour myself another vodka and tonic, even though I know it's one too many. It's been a difficult day, what with the *Capital Crime* magazine interview and then learning how bad things have got for Alice.

At least the phone call has lifted my spirits and I allow myself to believe that Wednesday is going to end on a high note.

But that proves not to be the case, because just minutes later, the doorbell rings and what I see when I peer through the peephole snatches my breath away.

I'm tempted not to answer, but I know I have to, and as I turn the key in the lock, I realise that my hand is shaking.

# CHAPTER ELEVEN

Sean Kelly is standing outside my door and the sight of him alarms me.

I have no idea why he's here. He said he was going to take Alice out to dinner. Did he change his mind? Has something happened? Is she with him? Or is he alone?

'Is everything okay?' I ask him, but I can immediately tell from the angry look on his face that it isn't.

'I need to talk to you,' he snaps, before pushing past me into the hallway without being invited.

I'm too stunned to react and watch as he strides purposefully towards the living room without looking back.

I half expect Alice to appear next, but when she doesn't, I leave the door open and rush after him.

'What the hell is going on?' I yell as I enter the living room. 'Where's Alice?'

He's standing in front of the fireplace, arms crossed, his expression dark and hostile.

'She's at home,' he replies. 'We didn't go out to dinner

because after she told me about the advice you've been giving her, I was in no fucking mood.'

His words send a shiver down my spine, but I manage to meet his gaze and hold it.

'What are you talking about, Sean?' I ask him.

He bares his teeth and draws in a deep breath that inflates his chest. 'You know what I'm talking about. You've been trying to convince her to leave me. And today you told her that she shouldn't have my baby. You want to destroy our marriage because you're jealous that she's got a husband and you haven't.'

'Don't be ridiculous,' I say as a surge of anger fires through me. 'I didn't—'

'Shut it, Gemma, and don't make things worse for yourself by lying. I've always known that you don't think I'm good enough for Alice. But you're wrong. We're meant to be together and I won't let you turn her against me.'

'Does she know you're here?'

Rage burns in his eyes as he unfolds his arms and jabs a finger at me. 'Of course she does. I told her I was coming to tell you to stop fucking with her head. And if you don't, then I'll make sure you come to regret it.'

'Are you serious?' I shoot back. 'Is that a threat?'

'Too bloody right it is. Alice is mine and always will be. And I know what's best for her. You don't.'

He's shouting now from only a few feet away and his demeanour is full of aggression. I suddenly feel vulnerable and my heart starts pumping furiously. I can't help wondering why Alice didn't warn me that he was coming here.

'Look, Sean, you need to calm down,' I say as I hold my hands up, palms out, fingers spread.

His eyes pop out as if on stalks. 'Don't fucking tell me to calm down, you bitch. I've got every right to call you out. My wife is in a bad place because of what her so-called best friend said to her.'

I can feel my face overheating and I want him to know that I was only responding to what Alice revealed to me about his behaviour. But I have to be careful what I say for fear of making the situation much worse for her.

'You should go, Sean,' I tell him. 'You're making me uncomfortable.'

'That's your fault for sticking your nose where it doesn't belong,' he reacts venomously. 'I've told Alice that I don't want her seeing you again. So, stay the fuck away from her. Don't come to the house and don't call her. And don't imagine for a second that there won't be consequences if you do.'

Another threat, and this time I feel compelled to respond. But the words get stuck in my throat as he storms past me and out of the room.

I stand there rooted to the spot, my whole body shaking, for perhaps five seconds. Then I force myself into the hallway and relief surges through me when I see that he's gone.

I quickly lock the door behind him and retreat to the living room, where I slump back onto the sofa, badly shaken.

I find it hard to believe what just happened. The bastard had no right to come into my home and threaten me. I'm tempted to call the police, but I know it would be pointless. It'd be his word against mine.

Closing my eyes, I breathe in deep through my nostrils, the blood pulsing in my ears.

I already knew from what Alice has told me that Sean has

a temper, but I never thought it would be directed at me. Now I've experienced what she must be going through and it's not pleasant. It makes me wonder why she told him that I advised her to end their marriage. It was meant to be in confidence, so did he force it out of her?

My eyes snap open and I grab my phone from on top of the coffee table and tap in her number. I have to find out if she's all right even though he warned me not to call her.

But the call goes to voicemail and I find myself struggling to keep the panic in.

What should I do? Am I worrying unnecessarily? Is she just too embarrassed to pick up the phone?

The ball of anxiety continues to grow in my chest as I get up and start pacing the floor. Then, seconds later, my phone pings and the sound of it fills me with dread. I see that it's a text message from Alice and it goes some way towards steadying my nerves.

*I'm really sorry, Gem. We had a row and I didn't hold back. It all came out and I made the mistake of telling him what you said. He went ballistic. I tried to stop him going to see you, but he wouldn't listen. Please forgive me. I'll call you tomorrow. Love you xx*

I feel so shaken up that I have to pour myself another drink, which I down in one go. But it fails to quell the anger that's raging inside me. And it doesn't stop me from worrying about Alice.

# CHAPTER TWELVE

I haul myself out of bed at five on Thursday morning after lying awake for over an hour. It was a rough night spent twisting and turning beneath the duvet. Sean's brief and brutal visit left me in a state of shock and after he'd gone, I retched into the sink until my throat was dry. Needless to say, I got very little sleep and now feel slightly hungover.

As I make myself a coffee, the words and threats that spilled out of his mouth continue to crash through my head. The man was completely out of order and even if his outburst was fuelled by booze, that's no excuse. I don't think I can ever forgive him and when I see him again, I don't intend to hold back.

I have to wonder, though, where it leaves my friendship with Alice. Is it over? Can she risk staying in touch with me? Am I going to hear from her today or will she be too scared to call?

My mind is leaping all over the place and I feel unsettled. A voice inside is urging me to phone Alice to check that she's okay. But another, louder voice, is telling me not to because it might inflame the situation. And that's the one I listen to. If I leave it a few days perhaps things will calm down and I'll be able to talk to her.

I finish my coffee and jump in the shower, deliberating the day ahead. Martin and I are going to Covent Garden Tube station, where we'll wait to be contacted by the man who wants to expose DCI Cain as a bent copper. All very mysterious and dramatic. But at least it will give me something to think about other than my best friend's vile and abusive husband.

After the shower, I return to the kitchen for another coffee and some toast. And that's when my thoughts turn for the first time this morning to the conversation I had with John Jackman, which has been completely overshadowed by my encounter with Sean.

I'm reminded of how well it went and why I now feel less nervous about our forthcoming date. I'm keen to learn more about the man and to find out if he looks as good as he sounds on the phone. I'm glad we're not meeting up tonight, though, because by the end of the day I'm sure that tiredness will be infusing my bones.

After breakfast, I go back upstairs to get ready. When I look in the mirror, a face I hardly recognise stares back at me. My eyes are dull and ringed with fatigue and my skin appears pale and washed out.

I'm forced to apply make-up more carefully than usual, but I can't conceal the fact that lack of sleep has left its mark.

Before getting dressed, I check the weather. It's going to be cold, but dry, with some sunny periods. And thankfully it's not going to rain. I decide to wear a T-shirt under a jumper and a pair of black jeans.

By seven, I'm ready to roll. I slip on my overcoat, grab my bag and phone, and then just as I'm about to leave the house, I get a message on my phone from Alice.

> *Sean told me what he said to you last night.*
> *I'm really sorry, Gem. Please don't hold it*
> *against me. Will call you when I can xx*

I don't want to dwell on the Alice and Sean saga all the way to the office, so I use my phone to check the morning newspaper headlines. One story jumps out at me and makes my skin prickle. It appears in three papers, but dominates the front page of the *Metro*.

RICHMOND PARK MURDER. MAN ARRESTED.

The man hasn't been named yet, but he's apparently being questioned by detectives at Twickenham police station.

There's a photo of the victim, Gillian Ramsay, who was raped and stabbed to death on Tuesday while walking through the park. I'd already heard that she was a twenty-six-year-old nurse, but now I read that she was engaged to a doctor at the hospital where she worked.

Inevitably, painful memories stir and my heart swells. I know what her fiancé will be going through because I've been there. And I remember that three years ago I read a similar headline to the one in the *Metro*. It appeared just two days after Callum was found dead alongside his dog.

## POLICE QUESTION SUSPECT IN CONNECTION
## WITH WANDSWORTH COMMON KILLING.

The man who murdered Callum, Chris Tate, wasn't named until he was charged days later. So, I suspect that Gillian Ramsay's fiancé will be subjected to the same anxious wait. And his future will now be very different to the one he'd been planning.

It's a chilling reminder of how my own life was knocked off course and why I'm still struggling to find a way forward.

It starts me thinking yet again about how different things would be now if Callum were still alive. We'd probably have at least one child and be living in a quiet suburban street. And I wouldn't be searching on dating apps for another man in the hope that he will help me to escape from the shroud of loneliness that embraces me.

Unsurprisingly, I'm soon feeling a surge of self-pity, and it takes a great deal of effort to keep the tears at bay. But I somehow manage to, and when I arrive at the office, I'm dry-eyed and eager to get stuck into something that will steer my thoughts in a different direction.

# CHAPTER THIRTEEN

The morning editorial meeting kicks off at nine sharp. It's where Ryan briefs the troops on the day's news agenda before assigning tasks.

Two reporters are told to stick with the Richmond Park murder and to dig up everything they can on the man arrested for it.

'He still hasn't been charged, but I've had it on good authority that he will be within a few hours,' Ryan details. 'That will restrict what we can say about the crime, so let's focus on the victim and the guy she was going to marry. Try to come up with an angle that doesn't feature in the coverage between now and Sunday.'

Another big story has broken overnight involving a prominent MP in the Shadow Cabinet who has been accused of assaulting a woman at a constituency event. Ryan instructs a reporter and a photographer to follow it up and gives them the name and phone number of one of his Westminster contacts who he says can provide them with some inside information.

'Next up is a promising tip-off we've received that most of you haven't yet been made aware of,' he continues. 'We'll hopefully know later today whether we should commit people and resources to it.'

He goes on to explain that Martin and I are due to meet a man who claims he wants to expose a corrupt Met detective. It comes as no surprise that the details arouse the interest of everyone in the room. They've all heard of DCI Elias Cain and know that if it can be proved that he's bent it will be a major scoop for the paper.

'It's a big if at the moment, so fingers crossed that the whistleblower is genuine and can come up with concrete evidence,' Ryan says. 'If he can, then we'll throw everything at it.'

After the meeting, I go with Martin to Ryan's office, where he wishes us luck and warns us to be careful.

'When the guy calls, make it clear that you're only prepared to meet him in a public place,' he says. 'If he is part of an organised crime gang, as he claims to be, then we can't discount the possibility that it's not Detective Cain who he has a grudge against – it's this paper. Let's not forget that we've made lots of enemies among the criminal fraternity, especially here in London.'

This is something I haven't considered, but we both assure him that we won't allow ourselves to be lured to some abandoned building or remote location.

'That's good to know,' Ryan replies, as he checks his watch. 'It's after ten, so I suggest you head for Covent Garden.'

Adrenaline is already pumping through my veins as we climb into a taxi.

It's always the same when I set out in pursuit of a potentially explosive story. I can't help wondering where it will take me and how big it will turn out to be.

This one has the ingredients for a front-page shocker if we can stand it up. DCI Cain is a high-profile detective in the Met who has made headlines before because of his wife's strange disappearance. And if he is exposed as a crooked cop soon after joining the Anti-Corruption unit, then the repercussions will be enormous.

It's the sort of thing that really gets my juices flowing and makes me glad that I chose journalism as a career.

We're only seconds into the journey when my phone pings. Instinct tells me that it's another message from Alice, but I'm wrong. It's from John Jackman.

> *I really enjoyed our chat last night, Gemma.*
> *I'm so looking forward to meeting you and*
> *I hope you feel the same about me. In fact,*
> *tomorrow seems a long way off, so is there*
> *any chance we can bring our date forward to*
> *this evening? I'm up for it if you are xxx*

The question throws me and my face folds into a frown.

'Are you okay, Gem?' Martin asks me as I read the message again. 'Only, you look as though you've had a bit of a shock.'

'I suppose you could say that,' I reply. 'It's from the guy I told you about yesterday. I did what you suggested and spoke to him on the phone last night. Well, I must have struck all the right notes because he doesn't want to wait until tomorrow to meet me. He's asking if we can get together tonight for our first date.'

'So, why aren't you smiling? Surely that's a promising start.'

I shrug. 'I suppose it is, except that I don't want to move at a rate of knots with this and I sense that he does. Sure, the conversation went well and I liked the sound of him. But it always makes me slightly uneasy when someone comes across as overeager.'

Martin grins. 'I know exactly what you mean. One of my dates was like that. She kept texting and phoning and it smacked of desperation. And when I ended it after a couple of weeks, she threw a major hissy fit and sent me some vile messages.'

'I've been there, so I know what you mean,' I say. 'But I'm not suggesting that John will turn out to be a stalker. I'd just prefer to take it slowly and not rush things.'

'I don't blame you. That's the sensible approach. Just text back and tell him that you've already made other plans for tonight. I'm sure he'll understand, unless he's a complete psycho, that is.'

Martin teases me with a grin and in response I pull a face and say, 'Very funny.'

Then I write a short reply and I don't feel in the least bit guilty because for all I know I will be working late into the evening if our whistleblower delivers on his promise.

*I'm afraid I can't meet you tonight, John. I'm working late and can't get out of it. See you tomorrow.*

# CHAPTER FOURTEEN

I'm no stranger to Covent Garden, the famous shopping and entertainment hub at the heart of the West End. I visited a couple of the upscale restaurants with Callum and he would always make a point of buying me something from one of the many charming little craft stalls.

I remember on one occasion he bought me a small heart-shaped acrylic keepsake with the inscription: *To my beautiful girlfriend. I will never stop loving you.* It brought tears to my eyes and it still does whenever I look at it now.

It's busy as usual when the taxi drops us outside the Tube station on the corner of Long Acre and James Street.

I'm curious to know why our whistleblower wanted us to come here. Does he live close by? Or is it because he knows that his partners in crime are unlikely to be in the area on a Thursday morning?

'So, we're ten minutes early,' Martin says as we position ourselves in front of the station entrance. 'Do you reckon he's watching us?'

I nod. 'I should think so. He'll want to make sure we haven't come mob-handed. And when he calls to tell us where to go next, I reckon he'll see if we're followed.'

It's a dry, bright day, so there are lots of people walking the pavements, while others are standing around talking or on their phones.

I don't spot any suspicious-looking men paying us undue attention, but then our man might be watching from inside a nearby shop or even from a distance through binoculars. One thing's for sure – he won't have any trouble noticing us, thanks to the distinctive beige overcoat that Martin is wearing.

'This feels really strange,' I say after a few more minutes. 'In all my time as a newspaper hack, I've never done anything like it.'

'It's a first for me too,' Martin responds. 'But I am finding it rather exciting. And it sure beats sitting in the office most of the day staring at a computer screen.'

Eleven o'clock comes and goes and Martin's phone doesn't ring.

At eleven thirty, I call Ryan and tell him that we're still outside the station and the guy hasn't phoned.

'Stick with it for now,' he says. 'It could be that he's just running late. Or maybe as soon as he saw you both standing there, he had second thoughts and made a hasty retreat.'

The next half-hour passes slowly and Martin and I fill the time chatting to each other. I can't resist telling him about Alice's situation and asking for his advice. They don't know each other so I don't feel that I'm betraying her confidence.

'I can understand how you feel as she's your close friend, but I don't think you should get too involved,' he says. 'They have to sort things out between themselves or she needs to leave him. The involvement of someone else often makes a bad situation much worse.'

'I think it already has,' I say and go on to describe what happened last night with Sean.

His brow shoots up. 'Jesus fucking Christ, Gem. That guy sounds like a right nutjob. You should have called the police.'

'I didn't see the point. He would have denied threatening me and I couldn't have proved that he had.'

'Well, his reaction should serve as a warning to you. I know it sounds callous, but it's your friend's problem to solve. And if things are that bad for her, she can get help from the domestic abuse support groups or the police.'

'That's not really what I want to hear, Martin, but I know it makes sense,' I tell him. 'I just wish I knew why some men – a lot of men – have to be so controlling.'

Martin shrugs. 'It's because for them love and loyalty are never enough. Their idea of a perfect relationship is one where they can dominate, manipulate and intimidate. I learned that at an early age from my own father. He was a bastard to my mum, but she couldn't summon up the courage to leave him. Since he died from a heart attack when he was fifty-five, she's enjoyed her life and hasn't had to walk on eggshells every single day.'

I can see the glint of emotion in his eyes, so I give his elbow a gentle tap and abruptly change the subject. 'I can't believe we've been standing here for over an hour,' I say. 'Are you sure that your phone is working?'

He checks it for the umpteenth time and nods. 'Yep, and I'm gutted. I really thought he'd call.'

I take out my own phone and ring Ryan, who is as disappointed as we are that we appear to have been stood up.

'There's no need to rush back,' he tells me. 'Stay in the area for a while and maybe grab some lunch on exes. If he does get in touch, you'll at least be on hand to respond.'

We go to a restaurant just a short walk from the Tube station atop the historic Market Building. Our table has views across the Covent Garden piazza and we help ourselves to a light lunch and a bottle of white wine.

'This definitely beats the canteen,' Martin laughs. 'In fact, it almost feels like we're on a date.'

I laugh back. 'Well, let's hope that Tracy doesn't see us together and get the wrong idea.'

'There's no danger of that. She's on a modelling assignment in Brighton and won't be back until late tonight.'

'And is she the jealous type?'

'She has been since she got with me, but then I suppose that's to be expected.'

I roll my eyes and cluck my tongue, and he laughs even louder.

There are very few people I can enjoy good-natured banter with these days but Martin is one of them. In some ways, he reminds me of Callum and that's probably why I feel comfortable in his company. My ex was also easy to talk to and had a great sense of humour. And just like Callum, Martin doesn't have an inflated opinion of himself.

Waiting around for something to happen is a big part of a journalist's job, but we rarely get to spend it in such pleasant surroundings. For that reason, the next hour passes in what seems like the blink of an eye and I enjoy the food, drink and small talk.

Martin's phone remains silent and at just after one, we both come to the conclusion that our mystery man is unlikely to call. We've been let down by someone who built our hopes up, but it's not the first time and it won't be the last.

We decide to finish the bottle of wine before ringing Ryan to see what he wants us to do. But just as Martin is topping up our glasses, my phone rings with a call from the man himself.

'We've still not heard from the guy,' I say before he gets a word in. 'And we're just about to finish—'

'I don't think you're going to hear from him,' Ryan interrupts me. 'The police have been in touch. A man's body was found early this morning and a murder hunt has been launched. But, get this, the last call the guy made on his mobile was to Martin yesterday evening. So, there's a good chance he was our snitch. You need to come straight back to the office. A detective is on his way here to talk to you both.'

# CHAPTER FIFTEEN

A feeling of unease swells in my chest as we travel back to the office by taxi. Could it really be that the man who stood us up did so because he was murdered?

The news of yet another killing in London has already broken and the story is being carried online. But all that's being reported is that the victim, who has yet to be named, was found shot dead close to his home in Peckham.

'It must be him,' Martin says. 'Nobody else called me yesterday evening on my mobile. Do you reckon his fellow gang members got wind of what he was up to and took steps to protect their asset inside the Met?'

I suppress a shudder. 'That could be what's happened. But most likely it's a coincidence.'

Martin shakes his head. 'Well, it's some bloody coincidence.'

I'm curious to find out how much the police know. Have they identified the man? Do they believe his murder was premeditated or that he was attacked on his way home from somewhere by a gunman who was on the prowl?

Peckham is a South London neighbourhood with one of the highest levels of street crime in the capital. Organised gangs are known to operate there, so it could simply be that the man was the victim of a turf war between rivals.

Traffic is heavy, so it takes us over half an hour to get to London Bridge. As we enter our building, a feeling of dread sits like a brick in my stomach.

We go straight up to the newsroom, where we encounter Ryan coming out through the door clutching two disposable cups of tea or coffee.

'A couple of detectives arrived just before you,' he says. 'I showed them to a conference room and went to get them drinks. I haven't spoken to them other than to confirm that the call you received last evening, Martin, was from a man who didn't give his name. So, let's go and tell them what we know.'

Seconds later, we enter the conference room and as soon as I set eyes on the police officers, I'm in for yet another shock.

It takes a couple of seconds for my face to register with detective Neena Patel and when it does, her jaw drops and she gets straight to her feet, saying, 'It's Miss Morgan, isn't it? Gemma?'

I nod. 'That's right.'

'Well, I wasn't expecting to see you here.'

'This is a surprise for me too,' I reply.

She hasn't changed much since I last saw her three years ago, except for her long black hair, which used to be styled in precise curls, but is now dragged into a low ponytail. She still has the same full face and warm features, with dark eyes that have a piercing quality.

'Detective Inspector Patel was part of the team that investigated Callum's murder,' I say for Ryan and Martin's benefit. 'And she did a lot to help me cope with it all.'

'It's Detective Chief Inspector now,' Patel tells me. 'And I'm really sorry that we're meeting again under such unpleasant circumstances.'

She then introduces her colleague as DC Dave Walsh, a tall man who looks to be in his late thirties. He's dressed in a smart suit, white shirt and navy tie.

'Here are your coffees,' Ryan says as he places the cups on the table.

'Thank you, Mr Tapper,' Patel replies and then gestures for everyone to sit down. 'We'll try not to take up too much of your time. But, as I'm sure you can appreciate, this is a serious matter and it seems likely that you can help us with our enquiries.'

Seeing DCI Patel has caused some bad memories to surface and I'm having to battle with a few vivid images in my mind. There's Callum lying dead on the common surrounded by police officers. Me having to formally identify his body. The face of the man charged with killing him.

I manage to blink them away as Patel starts speaking again, but they leave me feeling as though my insides have been flushed with ice-cold water.

'I'll start by making it clear that what we discuss here is confidential,' she says. 'It will be okay for you to publish the victim's name because that's about to be released. But please don't make anything else public at this stage.'

'You can rest assured we'll play by the rules,' Ryan tells her.

'That's good to know, Mr Tapper. Now, let me begin by reminding you why we're here. The man who was found dead this morning was clearly murdered late last night while on his way home from a pub. He'd been shot in the chest and stomach and his body was left in the doorway of an empty shop. He was discovered by a passer-by who thought at first that he was a homeless man, but then spotted pools of blood. We don't believe the motive was robbery because his wallet and mobile phone were still in his pockets. It took us a while to gain access to the phone and that's when we found that the last call that he made was yesterday evening to Mr Keenan here. Another call was made to this paper's switchboard the previous day. So, we need to know why he called you.'

Ryan explains that the first call to the switchboard was forwarded to Martin. 'The man refused to give his name but said he had a story for us. I'll let Martin tell you exactly what he said.'

Martin opens his notebook and reads from it. 'He told me he worked for a London-based crime gang and alleged that Detective Chief Inspector Elias Cain, who we know works with the Anti-Corruption and Abuse Command, is himself corrupt and feeds the gang with information on a regular basis.'

The shock on the faces of the two detectives is apparent as they exchange looks.

Patel clears her throat and says, 'Please go on, Mr Keenan. What else was said?'

'He told me that for personal reasons he wanted to expose Detective Cain and was prepared to provide us with a dossier containing incriminating evidence so we could run a story,' he says. 'I said we would of course listen to what he had to reveal and it was agreed he'd phone me the next day, yesterday, and we'd set up a meeting. During that second conversation, he said the information he had for us would cause a shitstorm if and when we published it. He told us to be outside Covent Garden Tube station today at eleven and would call again to tell us where to meet him. Gemma and I went there, but he didn't call or show up. And now we know why.'

There's a long, heavy silence before Ryan says, 'So, come on, Inspector. Who was this man and is it possible he was murdered because he was about to become an informer?'

Patel blows out a long breath, then gnaws at her lower lip for a few moments before responding.

'First, let me make it clear that criminals often make false allegations against police officers,' she says. 'And there's no suggestion that Detective Cain is anything other than honest and principled.'

'So, the man who called us was a criminal,' I say.

Patel nods. 'His name was Larry Spooner and he worked for a well-known London crime gang run by two brothers – Lee and Charlie Hagan. I'm sure you've heard of them.'

Their names spark a flash of heat in my chest and I nod. 'I think those guys are familiar to every journalist in London.'

'But I for one haven't heard of Larry Spooner,' Ryan says. 'What else is known about him?'

After a short hesitation, Patel says, 'He was released from prison nine months ago after serving five years for dealing drugs.' She pauses there and throws out a sigh. 'And since you're bound to look into it, I might as well make you aware of the fact that it was Detective Cain who arrested him and was instrumental in securing that conviction.'

# CHAPTER SIXTEEN

My eyes stretch wide and I let my breath escape in a low whistle. The story is getting bigger by the minute.

'This whole thing needs to be carefully handled by all of us,' DCI Patel says, breaking the silence.

'I agree,' Ryan replies. 'But do you believe it's possible that Larry Spooner decided to seek revenge against Detective Cain for getting him sent down by making false allegations against him?'

'That's pure speculation, Mr Tapper,' Patel says. 'And it may well have had nothing to do with his murder.'

'But surely it's also possible that the allegation that Cain is on a gang's payroll isn't false,' Ryan persists. 'And that Spooner was killed because the Hagans found out that he'd approached us with the aim of exposing him.'

Patel is looking unsure as to how to react, but we all know she can't allow herself to be drawn into making a judgement call on a fellow police officer, who she may well know personally.

'We obviously can't discount Spooner's claim out of hand and will treat it as a serious line of enquiry,' she says. 'In the meantime, I would ask you to hold fire and not to disclose this aspect of the case.'

'But it's a legitimate news story, Inspector, and you can't expect us to ignore it,' Ryan replies. 'However, I do accept that we would have to withhold Detective Cain's name. But there's something else to consider, which is that Spooner may well have approached other tabloids or broadcast news outlets. If so, they might already have teams digging into it.'

Ryan's response doesn't seem to surprise either of the detectives. They give each other a resigned look and Patel heaves a sigh.

'I realise that we can't stop you from pursuing the story, Mr Tapper, but I don't want you to make things more difficult for us. In view of what we've been told, we will have to speak to Detective Cain and also to the Hagan brothers. And where it will go from there is anybody's guess, especially if Detective Cain's identity is leaked. It will certainly damage his reputation, even if he's totally innocent of any wrongdoing, which I don't doubt that he is.'

'But it won't be the first time his reputation has been called into question,' I point out. 'There are still those who are convinced that he had something to do with his wife's disappearance.'

Patel narrows her eyes at me. 'That's an entirely different matter, Gemma, and you know yourself that there was no evidence to suggest that he was in any way involved. But once it gets out that you're looking to carry another story on him, it will spread like wildfire and he'll be tried once again by the court of public opinion.'

I feel obliged to let her know that we've already made enquiries in respect of Detective Cain.

'For your information, we've spoken to a number of our contacts in the Met about him,' I say. 'In order not to arouse suspicion, we told them we're pulling together a story about his wife's disappearance a year on.'

Patel's colleague, DC Walsh, is the first to respond. 'So does that mean you didn't mention the call from Spooner and the allegation he made?'

I nod. 'Martin and I were instructed not to. Our aim was to update ourselves on the man, and we discovered that he's highly regarded by his colleagues.'

'We also learned that he'd transferred from Major Crimes to Anti-Corruption some months ago,' Martin adds. 'That was news to us.'

Patel takes a sip from her coffee and then gives a thoughtful nod.

'I think we'll leave it at that for now,' she says, putting her notebook in her bag. 'But please do bear in mind that the murder of Mr Spooner is likely to attract a lot of attention. And if you report what he told you, it could create serious problems for us. I'll leave you my card and I'll be grateful if you would let me know what you intend to publish and when. In return, I'll make sure to keep you informed of what progress we make.'

That seems fair to me. A quid pro quo arrangement with the police usually works well on the big, sensitive stories.

And with that, Patel and Walsh stand up, thank us for our

help, and Ryan shows them out of the conference room and down to reception.

When he returns, the three of us discuss what we heard and the boss makes it clear that we're to stick with the story.

'This is even bigger now, so I'll assign more people to work on it,' he says. 'Let's find out all we can about Larry Spooner and the Hagans. And, Gemma, I want you to concentrate on Detective Cain. I've decided that we should actually run a piece on the anniversary of his wife's disappearance. Not only will it be of interest to our readers, it will also give you a reason to approach him.'

A cold shiver washes over me. 'Are you serious? You want me to talk to the guy?'

Ryan nods. 'Absolutely. Detective Patel didn't tell us not to, and now that we're pulling together a feature on his wife, then it's only fair that we involve him. Of course, at the same time, I want you to see if you can establish a link between him and the Hagan brothers.'

He goes on to concede that the task he's set me will not be an easy one.

And I have to agree with him. For starters, it's unlikely that Cain will want to engage with me or anyone else from the paper. And I doubt he'll be keen to see the story of his missing wife resurrected.

A year ago, he claimed he had no idea where she'd gone, but said that he was convinced she'd simply walked out on him due to problems in their marriage following the one-night stand he had with another woman. But her parents didn't believe him and told police they were convinced he had murdered her and dumped her body.

I'm reminded yet again of what he said to me after we ran the interview that I did with them.

'*You should stick to the facts, you fucking bitch. And the facts are that Pam packed her suitcase and left me of her own free will.*'

I find it hard to imagine that he'll be pleased to hear from me again. But the thought of contacting him has stirred up mixed emotions. The journalist in me relishes the challenge. And I'm excited at the prospect of seeing how he'll react to whatever questions I throw at him.

But, at the same time, I feel uneasy because my gut tells me that Detective Elias Cain is a man with secrets, and that could mean he's unpredictable and even dangerous.

## CHAPTER SEVENTEEN

We spend the rest of the afternoon in the newsroom gathering information and discussing the way forward.

Ryan has assigned two more reporters and a researcher to work with Martin and me.

I have to decide how and when to approach Detective Cain. Do I go through formal channels and try to set up a meeting with him? Or do I just turn up at his home or office and put him on the spot? Alternatively, I could simply ring him on his mobile phone.

But before contacting Cain, I need to get in touch with his wife's parents, Marion and Nigel Owen. Now that Ryan has decided the paper should mark the fact that their daughter Pamela has been missing for a year, they have to be brought on board.

I still have Marion's number, but when I ring it, there's no answer, so I leave a voice message telling her what we're planning and asking her to call me back.

When I come off the phone, Martin draws my attention to some of the information the team has gathered.

Forty-two-year-old Larry Spooner has now been officially named as the man found dead on a street in Peckham. And it's been confirmed that he had a criminal record and was linked to organised crime in the capital.

The paper has sent a reporter and photographer to his home in Peckham and to the crime scene. They'll speak to neighbours and visit the pub where it's believed he spent his final hours. They'll also try to contact close family members if he has any.

'Lee and Charlie Hagan have both done time and have been on the Met's watch list for years,' Martin informs me. 'They live in Bermondsey, and word has it, they head up one of the biggest and most violent gangs in London. They're involved in drugs, illegal weapons and people trafficking. Spooner was working for them when he was arrested by Cain and sent down. And when he came out, they welcomed him back into the fold. As yet, we haven't come up with anything connecting Cain to the gang.'

It's almost five o'clock when I finally decide to make contact with Cain via a direct call on his mobile phone. It's not something I'm looking forward to and a jolt of unease makes me shudder. I've half convinced myself that he won't answer, so when he does after just a couple of seconds, I'm taken aback.

But my surprise turns to shock when he says, 'Well, if it isn't the tabloid troublemaker, Gemma Morgan. I'm glad you've called because I was going to get in touch with you later to find out why the fuck you and your fellow hacks have been ringing around all sorts of people to ask questions about me.'

I have to swallow down the lump that forms in my throat before I can respond.

'How did you know it was me?'

'Surely you remember that I called you once before. Your number is stored on my phone. But forget about that. Just tell me what's going on and why you rang a bunch of my colleagues in the Met before ringing me.'

'We're intending to run a story to mark the first anniversary of your wife's disappearance, Mr Cain,' I say. 'But we thought that it would be sensible to find out what you're up to and how you are before approaching you.'

'Do you expect me to believe that?' he snaps. 'It sounds like total bollocks and that you're using it as an excuse to stir up trouble for me again.'

I'd love to tell him that we're investigating a claim that he's a corrupt copper, but I know I can't. So, I say, 'It's the truth, Mr Cain. I thought you'd welcome us drawing attention to your missing wife. It might actually lead to solving the mystery of her disappearance.'

'I've told you before. It's not a mystery. She packed her bags and left me.'

'But surely if that were the case, she would have been in touch with her parents.'

There's a long, awkward pause before he responds.

'Look, as far as I'm concerned, you can publish your story, but don't expect me to co-operate. And be warned. I'll come down on you like a ton of fucking bricks if what you write infers that I did something to Pamela.'

He abruptly ends the call and it occurs to me that he's the second man to lob a threat at me in the past twenty-four hours. Granted, Sean's words came across as more sinister, but even so, I'm left with a bad taste in my mouth. I find myself wanting to believe that he is indeed a bent copper and will soon be exposed, even though Larry Spooner is dead.

I pass on what Cain told me to the team and Ryan says, 'We don't need his input to run with the update on his wife. We'll talk to her parents and the detective who was in charge of the case. And, at the same time, let's go full steam on the corruption thing.'

I feel mentally fried by the time I leave the office at six and I'm hoping I'll be able to switch off when I get home. I'm just glad that I didn't agree to bring forward my date with John Jackman to this evening. I'm in no mood to socialise, especially with someone I've never met.

It's been one of those days when I've had too much to think about. First the Alice and Sean drama. Then learning that the man we had been expecting to hear from had been murdered. Followed by an encounter with the detective who investigated Callum's murder.

On the way to the Tube station, my phone rings. It's Marion Owen returning my call. She tells me that she and her husband have been struggling to deal with the fact that their beloved daughter has been missing for a year.

'We're happy for you to interview us,' she says. 'We know it won't bring Pamela back, but we want to make sure that everyone remembers her. And hopefully it will put pressure on the police to reopen the investigation and get to the truth about what happened to her.'

She then asks me if her son-in-law will also be interviewed.

'I'm afraid not,' I answer. 'He told me he wants no part of it.'

'That doesn't surprise me. Elias Cain wants the world to forget that our daughter even existed. And he'll be wary of giving away any clues as to where he hid her body. I just wish to God that Pamela had never married him. Some men are monsters, Gemma, and he's one of them.'

# CHAPTER EIGHTEEN

## JACKMAN

It's now seven in the evening and his eyes feel like they're burning at the edges. He's been here for two hours already, sitting in his car across the road from the modest terraced house that's home to Gemma Morgan.

It's a quiet street with poor lighting and, so far, no one has paid him any attention. A few people have walked past, but they didn't appear to have noticed him slumped down behind the wheel of his Hyundai Kona.

Gemma hasn't appeared yet, so he's hoping that means she told him the truth and is working late. But he knows that might not be the case. Perhaps she has a date with another bloke and will go straight from her office to where they've arranged to meet.

He should know soon enough. And then he'll either be able to relax or once again find himself struggling to suppress those negative emotions that he's always found so hard to control – namely, anger, jealousy, guilt, frustration and rejection.

They've blighted his life since he was a boy, which was why he gave his parents so much grief. Nothing was ever done about it and so the onus has always been on him to keep it in check. And most of the time he's managed to. But it's always been there, beneath the surface, waiting to be triggered by something that makes him feel angry or threatened.

After Lia's untimely death, it got much harder to manage and too often his responses to events were totally over the top. Sitting here in the car reminds him of one of the worst episodes – the night he decided to punish Amanda Dewsbury. She was one of the women he dated via the app. She was beautiful, funny and highly intelligent. He was smitten from the moment he met her in the coffee shop on the first date. But after six weeks and five more dates, she dumped him.

She actually told him by phone that she was ending their relationship, but denied she'd met someone else.

'It's just that I no longer think we're right for each other,' she said.

He got so worked up over the next twenty-four hours that he decided to drive to her house to see if there was any way he could get her to change her mind.

When there was no answer, he waited nearby in his car, and at just before midnight, she returned home. But she wasn't alone. She was holding hands with a man who went inside with her.

Seconds later, the light went on in the upstairs bedroom, where he himself had made love to Amanda numerous times. His heart then lurched when he watched her close the curtain.

Another minute passed before the light went out again and the thought that they were in bed together felt like a blow to the gut.

He wanted desperately to cross the road, ring the bell and get Amanda to come to the door so that he could confront the two-timing bitch. But he managed to resist the temptation by telling himself that she wasn't worth it.

Instead, he decided to go home and drink himself to sleep. But just as he was about to pull away, something caught his eye. It was Amanda's beloved pet Poppy, stepping outside through the cat flap in the front door.

The sight of her gave him an idea, a way to get revenge on the woman who had broken his heart without getting himself into trouble.

He'd met the cat a few times and had even held her in his arms, so she didn't run away when he approached her in the small front garden. He picked her up after making sure he wasn't being watched and took her to the car, where he placed her on the passenger seat.

She spent that night in his garden shed and the next day he placed her on a bin bag and stabbed her in the heart with a kitchen knife. He found it immensely satisfying and it even made him smile. He then took her wrapped-up body to a secluded spot in nearby Brockwell Park, where he dropped her on the grass and took a photo.

Back home, he printed off the picture and deleted it from his phone. A week later, he posted it to Amanda and his only regret back then was that he wasn't able to see her reaction when she opened the envelope.

The memory of what he did rages in his head with

heart-stopping clarity. He should have known that it would come rushing back if he staked out Gemma's house.

But this is an entirely different situation. He isn't in a relationship with Gemma and hasn't yet had the opportunity to fall in love with her. And, unlike Amanda, she has never made him believe that she wants to spend the rest of her life with him.

Despite that, he's becoming more anxious with every passing minute and he can feel the heat rising from his neck to his temples.

If only he could . . .

The thought suddenly stalls in his mind when he spots a woman walking towards him along the pavement on the other side of the road. He holds his breath until she's close enough for him to be sure that it's her.

He feels an instant swell of relief when he sees that she's carrying a shoulder bag and a briefcase. That's enough to convince him that she's come straight from her office and that she told him the truth.

She doesn't look his way as she approaches the house and as she steps up to the front door and lets herself in, a smile forms on his face.

The lights go on both upstairs and downstairs and he's still watching the house two hours later when they finally go off.

She hasn't gone out and no one has paid her a visit. But just the same, he hangs around for another hour. And when he drives away at 10 p.m., he's keener than ever to strike up a relationship with the woman who he hopes is going to give his life new meaning and purpose.

# CHAPTER NINETEEN

**GEMMA**

I'm up early on Friday morning after another restless night. My mind struggled to relax because I couldn't stop thinking about the events of the previous day.

Learning about the death of Larry Spooner. Being threatened by Elias Cain. Seeing the detective who investigated Callum's murder. It was a lot to process, and still is. Then, when I check my phone, there's a message that gives me something else to think about.

> *I hope you have a good day, Gemma.*
> *For me, tonight can't come soon*
> *enough. See you at seven xxx*

I've yet to meet John Jackman, but I get the impression that he already believes I tick all his boxes. None of the men I've dated since Callum have been so expressive in their messages before the first date. It's making me wonder what it says about the man. Is he an impatient person? Does he believe it will help me warm to him? Is it something he does with all the women he engages with online?

To be honest, I find it slightly off-putting, but it doesn't stop me looking forward to our date. I'm still keen to meet him.

I feel I have to reply, but I don't know what to say, so I send him three thumbs-up emojis.

Having been reminded of our date tonight, it sits at the forefront of my mind as I shower, dress and have breakfast. I need to make sure I get home on time and decide what to wear.

The wine bar and restaurant I've chosen only opened a few months ago and I haven't been there yet. But I've walked past it often enough and it looks tastefully furnished and cosy, but not pretentious. And from what I've seen of the customers, the dress code appears to be smart casual.

It's the sort of place that should be perfect for a first date, but that's not why I chose it. When John and I agreed to meet up, he asked me to pick the venue, which came as a surprise since all the other men I went out with took it upon themselves to arrange things. The bar sprang to mind because it's only a ten-minute walk away and so it'll be a quick trip home if the evening doesn't go so well.

I catch up with the news on my way to the office and it shifts my mind away from tonight. There's extensive coverage of the murders of both Larry Spooner and nurse Gillian Ramsay.

Police have released a photo of Spooner and issued an

appeal for witnesses. He had the face of a typical villain. Shaved head and an ugly scar across his left cheek.

There are photos too of the spot where he was shot and the pub where he downed his last pint. Police have established that he left the pub at closing time and was a little drunk as he headed home. Apparently, nobody heard the shot and it's thought the killer may have used a pistol with a silencer attached.

Unnamed sources are quoted as saying it was widely known that he worked for a notorious crime gang, but there's no mention of the Hagan brothers or Detective Elias Cain.

The man arrested in connection with the rape and stabbing of nurse Ramsay in Richmond Park has now been named and charged with murder. And her fiancé has released a statement saying she was a wonderful woman and her death has left him devastated.

It's a stark reminder of how dangerous London has become, especially for women. And it inevitably triggers a frisson of disquiet in me, because this very evening I'll be hooking up with a virtual stranger. A man I have never met and know very little about.

I arrive at the office fifteen minutes before the morning editorial meeting gets under way. It means I have time to grab a coffee and check my emails before getting together with the rest of the team.

Friday is always a busy day as the deadlines for the next edition approach and the paper starts to take shape.

Ryan begins by confirming that unless another major story

breaks, the front page will be dominated by our exclusive angle on the murder of Larry Spooner.

'We'll reveal that he called us shortly before he was shot and that he claimed he wanted to expose a crooked detective in the Met,' he says. 'We won't mention Detective Cain by name, of course, but we will make it clear the allegation relates to an officer in the Anti-Corruption and Abuse Command.'

My task is to write an inside-page story marking the first anniversary of Pamela Cain's disappearance. It's a straightforward assignment that entails speaking to various people and revisiting the coverage we gave it at the time.

I'll ensure that everything I include is accurate and hopefully the article won't antagonise Detective Cain again.

'But don't forget that the real purpose of running the story is that it gives us a reason to dig up as much info as we can on her husband,' Ryan reminds me.

I grin. 'I don't have a problem with that. If anything it makes the task far more interesting.'

I set to work straight after the meeting and the first call I make is to the detective who investigated the disappearance. He hasn't got any updates to pass on, but he does insist that there's still no evidence to suggest that Detective Cain was in any way involved.

I speak again to Pamela's mother, who gives me some moving quotes, and I arrange for a photographer to visit her and her husband. What I write will focus on how hard it's been for them this past year not knowing what has happened to their daughter.

I don't make much headway in respect of Detective Cain,

though, and neither do the rest of the team. The only feedback we're getting is that he's an honest, hard-working copper, which we strongly suspect he isn't.

We've only got until tomorrow to pull everything together for Sunday, but pressure is something we're all used to.

I touch base with Martin a couple of times and I notice that he's more subdued than usual. He's wearing a sombre expression and it strikes me that he appears somewhat detached, which isn't like him.

'Are you okay?' I ask him at one point. 'You're not usually this quiet.'

He gives a little shrug. 'I'm fine. It's just that the day got off to a bad start because Tracy and me had a silly row. But it's all sorted and I don't know why I've told you.'

I give his arm a gentle nudge. 'It probably just slipped out. But don't worry, I'm not going to ask you if you want to talk about it.'

He grins at me. 'You're a gem, Gem. And, trust me, it would bore you anyway.'

I'm not convinced about that and I'm left to wonder if what's happened between them is just a minor domestic or if there is actually trouble in paradise.

But it's not a matter for me to dwell on now, so I crack on with the job at hand. I'm determined to get as much done as I can because I want to leave earlier than usual so I can get ready for my date with John Jackman.

I doubt very much that it will be a late one, so I'll be in early tomorrow to wrap up the anniversary story and help put together our front-page exclusive on Larry Spooner.

The afternoon is spent making phone calls, discussing

things with my colleagues and rummaging through files. Ryan is happy for me to take off at four and as soon as I leave the office, I switch my thoughts to what I'm going to wear tonight.

And I start to feel the excitement build.

# CHAPTER TWENTY

When I get home just before five, I can feel the panic rising inside me. Pre-date nerves have kicked in for sure.

In two hours, I'll have to be at the wine bar, which doesn't give me much time to get showered, dressed and put on my make-up.

I'm looking forward to meeting John Jackman and I hope we hit it off. I just wish the whole process of striking up a new relationship wasn't so stressful. With Callum, it was easy because we met at a party and were immediately attracted to one another. It was the old-fashioned way of doing things, without the app, the exchange of messages or the big build-up to that first awkward face-to-face.

It doesn't help that deep down I still have reservations about committing to another relationship. Sure, I feel ready after three years without Callum, but that doesn't silence the nagging voice inside that keeps casting doubt as to whether I'm emotionally and mentally prepared.

I won't know for sure, of course, until I take the plunge,

which is what I've been trying to do for the past five months. John Jackman is my tenth date and although the signs so far are positive, I'm certainly not going to build my hopes up. That would be a mistake.

I don't want to overdress for the occasion, so I opt for black trousers and an elegant long-sleeved blouse with a bow tie front. And I spend a fair bit of time on the make-up to ensure it's flawless.

I'm eventually happy with the way I look and feel quite glamourous, attractive and confident. After tucking myself into my overcoat, I grab my bag and head for the venue with the fizz of anticipation in my stomach.

I recognise him the moment I step into the wine bar and it comes as a huge relief that John Jackman didn't catfish me on the dating app with fake photos. He's sitting at the table I've reserved and when he sees me, he switches on a smile and stands up.

My heart quickens as I approach him and I feel the initial stir of attraction. He's tall and athletic-looking, with broad shoulders and a narrow waist. He's wearing a pale blue shirt tucked into dark trousers and his posture is straight and confident. He's also unquestionably good-looking, with prominent cheekbones, a strong jaw and large, intelligent eyes.

'We meet at last,' he says when I reach the table.

I assume we're just going to shake hands, but he leans in for a first kiss on the cheek and his lips almost touch mine, which I find uncomfortably forward of him.

I detect the scent of spicy aftershave and note the flecks of grey in his dark, wavy hair.

'You look amazing, Gemma,' he says, his voice strong and steady. 'Ever since we met online two weeks ago, I've been praying that this moment would come.'

It strikes me as an odd thing to say as soon as we meet and it takes me a couple of seconds to come up with a response that is somewhat stilted and not entirely genuine.

'It feels to me as though we've been engaging with each other for much longer,' I say.

He nods. 'I know what you mean. Please, sit down and tell me what you'd like to drink.'

'I'm happy to share a bottle of wine.'

'Perfect. Red or white?'

'I prefer white.'

'Me too. And I'm sure we're going to find we have a lot more in common before the end of the evening.'

Despite the slightly awkward start, the date soon feels easy and relaxed. We talk about each other's jobs and our families as we tuck into a selection of bread, olives and a bowl of fries.

John has an expressive face and his eyes hold steadily on mine while we eat and drink. We cover a lot of the ground we've already covered in our messages and phone call, but it actually helps to make things flow. And I'm pleased that he doesn't keep bringing the conversation around to himself, unlike most of my other dates. But he does ask lots of questions about me and once again it makes me feel slightly uncomfortable.

Inevitably, we get around to the subject of our previous long-term relationships and I tell him about my interview with *Capital Crime* magazine.

'That must have been very difficult,' he says.

I shrug. 'It wasn't easy, but I'm glad I did it.'

I then see the emotion on his face when he tells me that tomorrow will be six years to the day since his girlfriend Lia was killed by a car that mounted the pavement.

'I can't believe it's been so long,' he says. 'It took me quite a while to get over it and find the strength to move on.'

I know how he feels because I've been there and the fact that he's still thinking about her six years on endears me to him.

We choose not to dwell on the subject of our exes and move on to our likes and dislikes and where in the world we've been.

By half nine, we're finished eating and have polished off two bottles of wine and I'm ready to go home.

'I'm afraid I have to work tomorrow,' I say. 'But thank you for a really pleasant evening.'

'I've enjoyed it too,' he replies. 'Would you be up for seeing me again?'

I've already decided that it's worth taking things to a second date, so I respond with a smile and a nod. 'Of course. When are you—'

'What about tomorrow night? We could have another meal or just a drink?'

I instinctively shake my head. 'That won't work for me, John. There's a good chance I'll be in the office till late helping to put the paper to bed.'

I see a flicker of disappointment on his face. 'Then let's have lunch on Sunday. You decide the time and place and I'll be there.'

I'm tempted to say no because I feel it's too soon, and

because I'm slightly put out by the fact that he wants me to organise it again. But at the same time, I find myself not wanting to disappoint him.

'That would be nice,' I say. 'I'll have a think about the venue and let you know.'

I then take my purse out of my bag, believing we're going to split the bill.

'Put it back, Gemma,' he says. 'This is on me.'

'But—'

'No buts. I insist.'

'Well, that's kind of you. Thanks. I'll get lunch on Sunday.'

He pays the bill and we exit the bar after he calls for a taxi for himself. I've already told him that I intend to make my own way home.

'Are you sure you don't want the cab to drop you off?' he says. 'I don't like the idea of you walking home alone at this time.'

'I'm positive, John. I don't live far and the streets are fairly busy.'

The truth is, I feel it's too soon to let him know where I live.

'Take care then, Gemma,' he says as his taxi pulls into the kerb. 'And I'll see you on Sunday.'

We touch cheeks and each kiss the air before he climbs into the cab and I watch it drive away before heading towards home. I'm pleased that it turned out to be a fairly pleasant first date. At least John Jackman was not a huge disappointment. Granted, he didn't sweep me off my feet, but he did make a reasonably good impression and who knows how I'll feel after our lunch on Sunday?

# CHAPTER TWENTY-ONE

**JACKMAN**

He can't stop smiling as the taxi heads for Brixton. His first date with Gemma Morgan went far better than he could possibly have hoped for.

He can feel a warm glow in his chest and he's not ashamed to admit to himself that he's completely besotted with her. That sexy smile, her unblemished skin, those glossy lips that look as though they're naturally pursed. He closes his eyes, visualising himself kissing her while caressing her naked body.

There's no doubt in his mind that he played a blinder and charmed the hell out of her. The chemistry between them positively sizzled and she clearly enjoyed herself. He's confident it will only take a few more dates to convince her that she wants to spend the rest of her life with him.

Sure, he's disappointed that she didn't jump at the chance to see him again tomorrow, but she can't help having to work, and hopefully after lunch on Sunday, he'll be able to persuade her to spend the rest of the day, or even the night, with him.

He told quite a few lies, of course, but he chooses to ignore them. Having met Gemma, he's more determined than ever to win her over and that means he'll have to neutralise any negative thoughts. He knows for sure now that with her by his side, he'll become a better person. A more honest person. The person he would be now if Lia hadn't died.

He can already see them living together, getting married, having children. She's the answer to his prayers, the only person who can help him right the wrongs of his past. Meeting her for the first time has made him believe that fate brought them together for a reason. And no way is he ever going to let her go.

It's not until he's halfway home that he remembers he switched his phone off before he entered the wine bar. He didn't want to have to answer any calls or respond to any messages while with Gemma.

Now, as he turns it on, he's glad that he did. There are three missed calls from Simone, plus a voice message that infuriates him.

'*You told me you were going to be working from home this evening. I dropped by to keep you company. So where the fuck are you?*'

It's not the first time he's used WFH as an excuse to avoid meeting up with her. But it is the first time she's turned up despite that.

He knows she doesn't trust him and up until now that

hasn't bothered him. But this time she's overstepped the mark and the tone and content of her message has made his blood boil. Who the hell does she think she is?

He'll be home soon, so he's not going to ring her back. Instead, he turns his mind to what he's going to do about it, and it doesn't take long for him to decide that it's time to dump her. It makes sense anyway now that he's hooked up with Gemma.

A suspicious, unhinged Simone will pose a serious threat to this new and far more important relationship, and he's not prepared to let that happen.

She's served her purpose and he's had fun with her. But there's no real connection. For him, it's just been about the sex and it's not his fault that she convinced herself there was more to it than that.

She must have heard him get out of the taxi because when he approaches the front door, it opens and there she is, fully dressed and looking none too happy.

'You don't seem surprised to see me, John,' she says and he can smell the alcohol on her breath. 'Does that mean you eventually turned your phone on and heard my message?'

She stares at him, frost in her eyes, and he feels a rush of anger.

He responds with a derisive snort before pushing her out of the way and stepping inside.

It takes the wind out of her sails, and as he strides along the hall towards the living room, she calls out, 'You lied to me about working tonight, didn't you? Is it because you're cheating on me and you don't love me? Is that it?'

They're the same old accusations which until now he's denied or deflected. But not any more. Sexy Simone has reached her sell-by date. He's at last upgraded to a newer and fitter model and she can now be consigned to history, along with all those others who provided him with temporary satisfaction.

As he enters the living room, he sees an almost empty bottle of wine on the coffee table and next to it a half-empty glass.

Seconds later, she rushes in after him, the breath wheezing in her chest.

He's standing with his back to the wall-mounted TV, his body rigid as a board, hands balled into fists at his sides.

She comes to an abrupt halt and says, 'Well, aren't you going to tell me that I'm wrong? Or else admit that the game is up? I want the truth, John. I can't go on like this.'

He listens with mounting irritation until the anger bursts out of him and he lunges forward, grabbing her arms and pulling her towards him.

A small, startled cry flies out of her mouth and he sees the sheen of fear in her eyes.

'Listen to me, you pathetic drunk,' he growls. 'I don't have to explain myself to you, so I won't. I'm not your bloody husband and never will be. Whatever we had is over. You've gone too far and I'm sick of it.'

She shakes her head. 'I can't believe this. I'm the one who should be ending it.'

He releases his grip on her arms and pushes her back. 'Just go, Simone, before this turns really ugly. And don't ever come back here. If you do, I'll make you wish you'd never been born.'

She thrusts her jaw at him and bares her teeth. 'I always suspected there was another side to you, John Jackman. And now I know that there is. You're a nasty bastard and I feel sorry for the next woman who gets lured into your trap.'

The heat burns in his chest and he's strongly tempted to punch her in the face like he did to the last woman who hurled a volley of abuse at him. But he holds back because the last thing he needs is to get arrested, which would surely ruin any hope of taking things forward with Gemma.

Her coat and bag are lying on the sofa. After picking them up, she gives him a hard look and says, 'Your front door key is on the table in the hall. If I were you, I wouldn't put it back under the pot out front. If you do, I might be tempted to let myself in while you're out so that I can start a fucking fire.'

She turns on her heels then and storms out of the room. When he hears the front door slam shut, he closes his eyes and exhales a slow breath, willing himself to relax.

Five minutes later, he sends a text message to Gemma.

> *Please let me know that you got home safely. And thanks again for making our first date so memorable xxx*

She responds almost immediately.

> *I'm back and getting ready for bed. Sleep well, John, and I'll let you know about Sunday.*

Her words make him smile and convince him that Simone's dramatic departure could not have been better timed. Now he can move on to the next chapter in his life and build a relationship with a woman he really wants to be with.

# CHAPTER TWENTY-TWO

**GEMMA**

I wake up at six on Saturday morning after a troubled night. I had so much on my mind. The job. The future. Alice. And the latest man to enter my life. The same thoughts and concerns are still raging in my head.

Thankfully, I won't have to dwell on them because working for a Sunday newspaper means that I don't get Saturdays off. And there will be a lot going on today to keep me busy and distracted.

I check my phone before jumping in the shower and find yet another text from John Jackman sent barely an hour ago.

*Good morning, gorgeous. I hope you had a comfortable night. Enjoy the day ahead and don't work too hard. If you fancy a chat, then give me a call at any time. I'm already missing you xxx*

Once again it strikes me that he's being too familiar too soon. Perhaps I wouldn't react this way if I already sensed a strong connection between us, but I don't. To me, our date was just okay. Not amazing. On the plus side, he ticked a lot of boxes. He had good table manners. He didn't harp on about politics. And not once did he check his phone.

But I didn't feel a spark of electricity.

The problem for him and the other men I've been out with is that Callum is a tough act to follow. From the moment we started speaking at the party, I knew that if we stayed together he would make me happy. I felt instinctively that we were right for each other.

At the end of our first date, I wanted him to hug me, kiss me and even take me to bed. With John, it was different. Even though he's undoubtedly attractive, I'm so far not turned on by the prospect of having sex with him.

I reply the same way I did before, with three thumbs-up emojis, and I hope that makes it clear to him that I'm not yet ready to be all lovey-dovey.

After that, I shower and get dressed before making myself a coffee and slice of toast.

When I leave the house at seven, it's still dark outside and there's a sharp chill in the air. The journey to work is uneventful and I arrive just before Ryan kicks off the morning meeting. He has a couple of updates for us.

'I've talked to DCI Patel and she told me that a thorough search of Spooner's home has been carried out, but no dossier of any kind has been found,' he says. 'She also confirmed that Detective Cain has been asked about the man's allegation and has categorically denied it. He's still on duty for the time being and there's no evidence yet to back up what Spooner said to Martin.'

'Do you think that's all true?' I ask him.

'I reckon so. Unless, of course, it's the beginning of a cover-up.'

I nod. 'That really wouldn't surprise me given all that goes on inside the Met.'

The team then crack on with pulling together what we have while I start by writing up the piece on Pamela Cain's disappearance a year ago.

As usual, on the day before publication, things move forward at a frenetic pace. But that doesn't stop me from noticing how downcast Martin still is.

'Would I be right in assuming that you and your good lady still have some issues?' I ask him when we get a moment together.

'I didn't realise that you were such a nosy bugger,' he says, and I can tell from his expression that he's teasing me.

I shrug. 'You're more than just a colleague, Martin. You're a mate. And I don't like it when you're not your usual chirpy self.'

He smiles. 'Well, okay. I'll tell you, but I don't want it to become a subject for gossip.'

'Whatever you confide to me stays with me,' I assure him.

He takes a breath and says, 'The fact is, we're both coming to realise that we're not getting on as well as we should be. We had a long talk about it last night and have agreed to make more of an effort. But it's difficult because too often we don't seem to be on the same page.'

'I'm sorry to hear that, but I'm sure you'll work things out,' I tell him and he responds with a shrug.

'Enough about me,' he says. 'How did your date go last night?'

'It went well,' I reply. 'He seems like a nice guy and we're meeting up again for lunch tomorrow.'

'Sounds promising.'

'We'll see. I got the feeling he was keener on me than I was on him, but that could be because I was expecting too much. That's why I thought it was only fair to agree to a second date.'

'That makes perfect sense,' Martin says. 'Good luck with it.'

The conversation gets cut short when Ryan calls everyone together for an afternoon briefing. He wants to know what progress we've made and gives us an idea of what the paper is going to look like.

The Spooner story will be on the front page and my piece on Pamela Cain's disappearance will be on page three. The rest of the paper will be filled with doom-laden stories about ever-growing hospital waiting lists, house prices nose-diving, businesses collapsing and ugly spats between politicians. It's all very depressing, but it's the kind of information that our readers lap up and can't get enough of.

By five o'clock, it's all come together. The stories and features have been written and edited and page layouts finalised. But until the presses start to roll, there will be scope to make room for any late breaking news.

Some of the team are going for the usual after-work drink and I plan to go with them. But just minutes before we're due to set out, my phone rings and I'm tempted not to answer it until I see it's from Alice and I fear it might be an emergency.

She begins with another apology for what Sean subjected me to the other night and then asks me if it's possible for us to meet up. 'I'm supposed to be working late but have just been told that I can leave early,' she says.

'What about Sean?' I ask. 'Where is he?'

'He'll soon be home from the football and he's not expecting me back until about eight. But look, if you'd rather not because of what he said to you, then I'll understand. I just don't want to lose you as a friend and if I can see you and explain, I'll—'

'Of course, I can meet you,' I cut in. 'Luckily, I'm about to knock off myself. Where do you want to get together?'

'What about our favourite coffee shop? That stays open late. I can be there in under an hour.'

'Me too. I'll see you then.'

# CHAPTER TWENTY-THREE

I have serious reservations about meeting up with Alice behind Sean's back. If he finds out, then I fear he may harm her. But there was no way I was going to turn her down. She's my best friend and she's going through hell, so I need to be there for her, even if it incurs the wrath of her husband.

I'm not prepared to let the brute come between us if that's not what Alice wants. I realise that by ignoring his warning to stay away from her I might worsen the situation between them, but turning my back on her is not an option. She needs me by her side now more than ever.

My mind returns to when he came to the house and recalling what he said makes my heart rate step up a notch.

'I've told Alice I don't want her seeing you again. So, stay the fuck away from her. Don't come to the house and don't call her. And don't imagine for a second that there won't be consequences if you do.'

Was it an empty threat? Or is the man capable of doing something reckless? I know he has a fierce temper and I suspect that there are times when he can't control it. But does that mean he'd resort to physical violence? Instinct tells me he would, and it scares me to think what he could do to Alice if he really loses it. I really do worry about her and I know that her situation is a difficult one. She's married to the guy and has to set her own boundaries. And it can't be easy being trapped in a coercive relationship and having to walk on eggshells all the time.

I can perfectly understand why she doesn't want to start a family with him, but at the same time, I think she needs to accept that he's unlikely to change. Men like him rarely do. They just go on subjecting their women to various forms of physical and mental abuse.

I just wish there was more I could do other than to urge her to call time on their relationship. But that in itself could place her at risk, as statistics show that many women are murdered by their former partners soon after leaving them.

Right now it feels like a lose-lose situation, but I'm determined to be there for Alice wherever things go from here.


The coffee shop is in a quiet street between Balham and Tooting, within walking distance of both our homes. When I arrive there, Alice is waiting for me, one of about half a dozen customers.

As I approach the table next to the window, she stands up and gives me a hug.

'It's so good to see you, Gem,' she says. 'Thanks for coming.'

'I'm glad you called,' I reply. 'I've been worried I might never see you again.'

I take a step back and she offers me a tight, unconvincing smile. 'I've already ordered our usual Americanos and Helen said she'd bring them over when you came in.'

As we sit down, I notice her swollen eyes, tousled hair and streaked foundation, and my heart goes out to her.

'Do I take it that we're meeting in secret and that Sean doesn't know?' I ask her.

A guilty look crosses her face and she starts to speak, but then stops herself when Helen arrives with the coffees.

'Nice to see you both again,' Helen says. 'It's been a while. Enjoy.'

When Helen walks away, Alice picks up her cup and sips at her coffee. The sleeves of her sweater are rolled up and so I'm able to see two dark bruises on her right arm. They send a bolt of alarm tearing through me and I jab a finger at them as the words tumble unbidden out of my mouth.

'My God, Alice. Did he do that to you?'

It takes her a second to realise what I'm referring to and she shakes her head vigorously as she replaces her cup on the table. 'Of course not,' she says and it's obvious to me that she's lying. 'I knocked it against a . . . a door at work.'

I roll my eyes. 'Come off it, Alice. I'm not stupid. I've seen bruises like that before.'

She heaves a breath and starts blinking furiously. 'All right, he did grab me, but it was my own fault because I was screaming at him. He didn't mean to hurt me and he apologised when he saw what he'd done.'

I raise a sceptical brow. 'You can't just shrug it off, Alice. When we last spoke, you told me that things had got really bad and since then they've clearly got much worse. He came to my house to threaten me and he's got physical with you. And if nothing is done about it, then Christ only knows where it will lead.'

'But I'm not ignoring it, Gem, and neither is he,' she replies. 'That's why I wanted to see you. To explain.'

'Explain what?'

'That we're going to do all we can to put things right between us and I want you to bear with me until it's sorted. We had a long, constructive talk and I now realise that he's turned into the man he is partly because I've made him feel insecure.'

I'm gobsmacked. 'Are you serious? Is that what he told you?'

'Yes, I am serious. It made sense. I accept now that I've not been a particularly good wife. And when I said I didn't want to try for a baby, it really hurt him. I then made things much worse by telling him that I had talked to you about it. He felt betrayed and because of that he overreacted. But he's acknowledged to me that it was a mistake and now I want us to move on from that. For all our sakes.'

I can hardly believe what I'm hearing and I'm about to tell her how naïve I think she is when she continues with, 'I can tell from the look on your face that you're not convinced, Gem. You probably think I've been brainwashed. But I haven't. I sincerely believe that Sean and I can mend our relationship. And when things calm down, I'm sure I'll be able to persuade him that you aren't determined to pull us apart. Then things can get back to how they were.'

I'm speechless, but it's clear to me what has happened and I feel a pulsing sense of unease. Alice is doing what too many women do in her position, which is to take it upon themselves to make relationships work by changing their perception of their partner's behaviour. She's going to emphasise the beliefs that support her decision to stay with him. And that means seeking to justify what he says and does to her.

I could try to make her see sense, but I really don't think she's in the right frame of mind to listen to me. So, instead, I say, 'I'm not clear where that leaves us, Alice. Do I keep my distance until he says you can start speaking to me again?'

The guilty look returns and there's a long silence between us, awkward and unnerving.

Then: 'You'll have to, Gem, but it won't be for long, I promise. He just needs time to accept that you and I aren't conspiring against him. I know it's a lot to ask, but please be patient, for my sake. I don't want to lose my husband and my best friend. And if I can't sort this mess out, then I fear I will.'

## CHAPTER TWENTY-FOUR

As I head home from the coffee shop, my concern for Alice's well-being is causing the blood to beat in my ears.

We were forced to make a hasty retreat after she decided to check her phone. It had been in her bag and on silent mode and when she opened it, she saw two missed calls from Sean, plus a text asking where she was.

Panic seized her features as she said, 'He got home early and when he couldn't get through to me, he rang work and found I wasn't there.'

The tears welled up in her eyes and I feared she might break down, so I suggested we get going.

Once outside, I asked her if she felt it would be safe to go home to him.

She dabbed at her eyes with a tissue and gave a sharp nod. 'Of course, it will. I've just got myself all worked up. Sean's not upset. He's just worried about me.'

I didn't bother to tell her that she was crazy to think that because I knew she wouldn't listen, so I threw my arms around her and said, 'You know where I am if you need me, Alice. Just take care and don't do anything you don't want to.'

'You've got to stop worrying about me, Gemma,' she replied. 'I can look after myself.'

I find it impossible not to worry about her, though, especially as she'd be no match for Sean if he decided to do his talking with his fists. As a result, I feel guilty for not staying with her, even though I know she wouldn't have let me. It's a situation I don't have any control over, but that does nothing to ease my anxiety.

I can't get those bruises on her arm out of my head and I hate to think what he might do to her when she gets home. This is not something I've ever been through, so I can't draw on experience. I can only react as I see fit and hope and pray that my best friend comes to her senses and leaves the bastard before it's too late. But I fear that's not going to happen and it's a hard pill to swallow.

The closer I get to home, the more my mind rages in all directions. I can feel a headache forming behind my tired eyes and the urge to turn around and go to Alice's house is hard to resist. But I know I have to because she's given me no choice.

The first thing I do when I get in is take a couple of paracetamol to keep the headache at bay.

It's still early, so I intend to go for a run, but not before I've called my mother. I check up on her and my stepdad at least a couple of times a month. They retired to Spain five years ago and I don't often get to see them.

As expected, they're doing fine and loving the fact that the country is basking in unusually high temperatures for October.

Speaking to Mum brings to mind the only time I visited their villa on the Costa Blanca with Callum. We had such a great time and spent most of it in the pool and on the beach. My parents adored having him there and one night when we were all out having dinner in a restaurant, Mum sidled up to me and said: 'He's a keeper, Gem. And it's as clear as day that he loves you dearly.'

I've only been back there twice since his death and it proved quite upsetting to be reminded of what we did and where we went.

Inevitably, more memories of our time together are suddenly racing through my mind and they bring a lump to my throat. I go to pour myself a stiff drink but decide to wait until I return from the run. Instead, I sit back on the sofa and close my eyes, allowing the weight of everything to hit me.

I'm still sitting there ten minutes later, unable to relax, when I hear the familiar ping of my phone. I'm not surprised when I open up another message from John Jackman. But I am slightly annoyed, and two questions pop into my head. Doesn't the man have anything better to do with his time than fire off text messages and is he already more than a little obsessive?

*Hi Gemma. I hope you had a constructive day at work. Mine's been pretty boring. The highlight was popping out to buy a new shirt for our date tomorrow. Don't forget to let me know where we're meeting. I'm now watching telly with a glass of wine. Would love a catch-up call if you're not too tired xxx*

It's almost as though he knows I'm already at home even though I told him I'd probably be working until late. Of course, that's not possible since he doesn't know where I live. So he's clearly just taking a punt in the hope that if I did finish early, I'll give him a call.

But I'm certainly in no mood for a conversation with him, so my reply is short and sweet.

> *Still at the office, John. I'll let you know later or tomorrow morning where we can have lunch. Enjoy your evening.*

# CHAPTER TWENTY-FIVE

## JACKMAN

As he reads Gemma's reply to his message, his heart plummets. She's told him she's still at her office and yet it's an outright lie. He knows because he saw her arrive home less than an hour ago.

His car is parked in the same place as before and he's been here since four o'clock. He came to make sure that she didn't turn down his invitation to meet up tonight because she was going out with someone else. He's now wondering if she's planning to do exactly that.

Unless, of course, she just doesn't want him to know she's home for an entirely different reason. Perhaps she's just knackered after a hard day at work and the last thing she wants is to be drawn into a conversation on the phone. So she decided to fib to him rather than hurt his feelings.

He'll give her the benefit of the doubt for now and will know the truth soon enough since he has no intention of driving away.

He's not proud of what he's doing because he promised himself that he wouldn't stalk a woman again after what he did to Amanda Dewsbury. But Gemma Morgan is in his head now and in his heart, and paranoia is growing inside him. He needs to know where she goes and what she does while he works towards getting his emotional grapple hooks into her.

But being here this evening has certainly added to the weight on his conscience at the end of what has been a difficult day. It was always going to be after his mum reminded him that it was the sixth anniversary of Lia's death. He spent it trying not to think about it, which was why he turned down the invitation from his parents to go to their house. They would have talked about it non-stop and got out the many photos they have of her, and it would have piled on the guilt. He would have also had to explain why Simone wasn't with him and that would have meant coming up with a story that they probably wouldn't have believed.

Instead, he chose to stay at home by himself and went out only once to get a paper and a new shirt, making sure he was back in time to come to Balham.

He's been here for almost three hours already and before receiving Gemma's text, he was fairly relaxed. But now he feels tense, wired, agitated, and he keeps drumming his fingers impatiently on the steering wheel.

He's wondering if she's in her bedroom getting all dolled up. One of the upstairs lights is on, but he's trying not to imagine her applying make-up or trying on a sexy dress.

The mere thought of her getting ready to impress another man is making his blood run cold. She belongs to him now, even though she doesn't yet know it and there's no way he will—

His heart suddenly shunts up a gear when he sees her front door open. Then she steps out clad in a bright green jacket, tight black pants, a woollen hat and a pair of white trainers. He watches her close the door behind her, walk onto the pavement and start running.

He wants to believe that it's a good sign, that she would be unlikely to go for a jog this late in the evening if she has a date. But he intends to hang around just the same. He doesn't reckon she'll be long and he's got nothing to rush home for.

The street remains relatively quiet with only a few pedestrians and passing cars.

But five minutes after she set out, a car pulls up in front of her house. The lights go off and a man steps out. He's of medium height and wearing a dark overcoat. He then walks straight up to the front door and rings the bell.

When there's no answer, he returns to his car and gets back in. But he doesn't start the engine. Instead, he just sits there behind the wheel and that's where he stays, presumably watching and waiting for Gemma to arrive home. John's mind spirals with fresh fears and questions. Does this mean he was right to be suspicious? Has the guy turned up to spend a pre-planned evening with Gemma? Or will his arrival come as a surprise to her when she returns from her run?

He inhales deeply, trying to calm his racing heart. But he can feel the panic rising inside him and he knows that it's going to take all his willpower to remain where he is and just watch as things play out.

# CHAPTER TWENTY-SIX

**GEMMA**

I'm on my way back now, sweaty and exhausted, but with a clearer head.

I feel the run has done me the world of good. I'm more relaxed and have even decided to give John Jackman a call to tell him where I think we should have lunch tomorrow.

I regret my little white lie earlier about still being at work, but I won't fret over it because he will never know. It's not like me to be dishonest, but when the pressure builds, it sometimes happens because it offers a way to avoid difficult situations.

Before Callum was killed, my life was so different and much less stressful. My future was mapped out, so I didn't have to agonise over who I would spend it with. And because of that I was able to live in the moment while enjoying a positive mindset. Engaging with people rarely made me anxious or suspicious and I was a very trusting person. Now

I'm on edge much of the time and running has proven to be a godsend when it comes to perking me up both inside and out.

As I turn into my street, I start to look forward to a warm shower and a cold glass of wine.

Just fifty more yards to go.

Then twenty.

Then ten.

As I approach my house, I notice that there's now a car parked right outside. And it's familiar to me.

When I draw level with it, the driver's side door is thrown open and a man leaps out.

I stop running and a rush of heat burns in my chest.

'I thought you'd probably gone for a jog so I decided to wait,' Sean Kelly says as he stares at me with undisguised hostility. 'And I'm glad I did because we need to talk.'

'What about?' I ask him.

'I gather you ignored my warning and met up with my wife for a coffee. That was a big fucking mistake.'

His words cause my body to stiffen, but more out of anger than fear, and a smouldering rage rips through me.

'You're the one who's made a mistake by coming here again,' I shout at him. 'You might think you scare me with your threats, but you don't. And I won't let you bully me like you bully Alice.'

His gaze drills into me as he grits his teeth. 'I told you to stay away from her, Gemma. She's upset again and it's because of you. You're on a mission to destroy our marriage and I won't let you.'

'You're the one destroying the marriage,' I say. 'You obviously don't love her. You just want to control her. I saw the bruises on her arm and it's clear you assaulted her again after she told you we met up.'

He takes a step towards me, the veins bulging out of his neck. But I stand my ground and get ready to defend myself if he attacks me.

'This is your last warning, Gemma,' he says, then leans forward, lowering his voice to a steely whisper. 'If you don't stay away from my wife, I'll take matters into my own hands. And, believe me, you won't be left with just a few bruises.'

By now, every nerve in my body is jumping, but I don't let that stop me from responding.

'You've just made another mistake by thinking I'll let you get away with threatening me again,' I say. 'As soon as I step through the door, I'm going to call the police. I'm not prepared to put up with your shit.'

Without waiting for him to react, I turn and rush up to my front door. Before opening it, I look back to make sure he isn't behind me.

He isn't. But he is still standing there on the pavement staring at me.

'I'd think twice before calling the cops,' he calls out. 'For one thing, there's no way you'll make 'em believe you. And for another, it'll be Alice who'll suffer more than me.'

I take out my key and quickly let myself in. After I've closed the door, I look through the living-room window and watch Sean get back into his car and drive away.

# CHAPTER TWENTY-SEVEN

My shoulders slump with relief when I know Sean's gone, but my heart continues to thump relentlessly in my chest. The bastard has subjected me to another unsettling experience and I hate him for it.

I go and sit on the sofa to try to calm myself, closing my eyes and breathing in deep through my nostrils. But despite the warmth of the room, my mind soon becomes a jumble of senseless thoughts and boiling emotions, and I really don't know what to do next.

I told him I was going to call the police and that's what I want to do. But what's holding me back is fearing what it will do to Alice.

If I make a formal complaint and accuse him of threatening behaviour, it will have a huge impact on her, even if he's not charged because it can't be proved. He'll deny it and I have no doubt that she'll back him up. She'll be too scared not to.

But if I let him get away with it, what then? Will it be only a matter of time before he turns up here again with more threats? And perhaps next time he'll be worked up enough to attack me.

And what if he takes abusing his wife to the next level and hurts her? Or perhaps he'll get carried away enough and kill her.

I've seen the statistics and I know that a disturbing number of women are murdered every year by their abusive partners or exes. And I know that if I keep schtum and it happens to Alice, I will never be able to forgive myself.

Oh fuck.

I swallow down the lump in my throat before I make a snap decision.

Seconds later, I pick up my phone and dial 999.

Their quick response surprises me. Two uniformed officers arrive in a patrol car within fifteen minutes. A man and a woman, both somewhere between thirty and forty.

It's the woman who does the talking, a PC Matlock. She has a long, sharp face and offers me a warm smile before asking me to provide details about myself. Am I married? Do I live alone? What is my job? Is this the first time I've contacted the police in respect of this man?

Then she wants me to expand on what I told the emergency operator.

I start by explaining my relationship with Alice and what she said to me when I went to see her on Wednesday.

'Later that evening, her husband turned up here ranting and raving and accusing me of trying to break them up,' I say. 'He told me to stay away from her and that if I didn't there would be consequences.'

I then explain in detail what happened today. How Alice invited me for a coffee. The bruises I saw on her arm. Then how Sean had turned up here and threatened me again.

'This time it was even more alarming,' I say. 'He told me that if I remained in contact with his wife, he would take matters into his own hands and leave me with more than a few bruises.'

I have to pause there because emotion is threatening to overwhelm me.

PC Matlock reaches out and pats my knee. 'Take your time, Miss Morgan. We know this isn't easy for you,' she says.

I take a breath to regain my composure and continue. 'Alice has been my best friend for years and I care for her. The man is treating her terribly. I fear he will really hurt her if he isn't stopped.'

'Have you heard from her since Mr Kelly came here?' she asks.

I shake my head. 'I don't suppose he'll let her ring me and I didn't want to call her because it might make things worse. But I wouldn't be surprised if he's been physically abusive to her again. That's why I called you. My main concern is her well-being and so I didn't think I had a choice.'

I'm then asked to provide Alice's contact details and I show them the text messages she sent to me after Sean's first visit here.

PC Matlock says they will pay the couple a visit and goes on to tell me something I already know – that the use of threatening and abusive behaviour towards another person can amount to a criminal offence if words are intended to cause alarm, distress or harassment.

'We take such things very seriously, Miss Morgan,' she adds. 'But I suspect it won't surprise you to hear that it's often very difficult to secure a conviction, especially in cases like this where there are no independent witnesses.'

'I realise that and I'm sure he'll deny that he threatened me,' I respond. 'But hopefully a visit from you will stop him abusing his wife and threatening me.'

After the police have gone, my mind resolutely refuses to switch off. I pour myself a glass of wine and drop onto the sofa.

I just hope I've done the right thing and that I won't come to regret it. I'm sure that Alice will understand why I felt compelled to involve the police. She'll probably blame herself for asking me to meet up with her in the coffee shop. But I doubt she'll tell me that for fear of upsetting her husband.

The man doesn't deserve her. He's an aggressive control freak and he deserves to be locked up. It's as clear as day that he regards me as a threat and wants me out of her life. That way, she'll have no one to confide in, to seek advice from, to tell her that she should get out before it's too late.

I don't care that I've made Sean Kelly my enemy. But I do care about my best friend. She's married to a monster and he appears to have a stranglehold over her.

I finish the glass of wine and decide to have another before shedding my running clothes and going for a shower.

But as I'm heading for the kitchen, my phone rings, causing my heart to leap.

I jump to the conclusion that it's Alice, but it turns out not to be.

It's John Jackman, and I stare at the phone for several long seconds trying to decide whether or not to answer it.

# CHAPTER TWENTY-EIGHT

**JACKMAN**

If she doesn't answer the bloody phone, he's not sure what he'll do.

First, the guy turned up in his car and when he discovered Gemma wasn't in, he got back in it to wait for her. Then when she returned from the jog, he jumped out and confronted her. After what looked like an angry exchange of words, he drove off.

It came as a relief that she didn't go with him, but the urge to call her then was strong. He held back, though, because he wanted to see if the guy would come back or if she would go out. Instead, the police arrived after about fifteen minutes, which came as another shock.

A dark unease has pushed its way into his mind and now he can't—

'Hello.'

Oh fuck.

He feels a stab of panic at the sound of her voice and suddenly realises he hasn't worked out what he's going to say to her.

'Hello,' she repeats. 'Is that you, John?'

'Oh yes, it's me,' he responds awkwardly. 'I didn't think you were going to answer, so I was about to hang up.'

'I'm sorry. I was in the other room, but I did intend to ring you before going to bed.'

'Well, that's what I'm about to do, so I just thought I would call to check that all is well and see if you've decided where we're having lunch tomorrow.'

'Have you heard of The Bugle just off Brixton Hill? It's nearer to you than me.'

'Yes, I know it well. Are you sure you don't mind coming over this way?'

'I think it's only fair since you came here yesterday. Shall we say one o'clock?'

'That's fine with me. I'm really looking forward to seeing you again.'

'And I'm looking forward to seeing your new shirt.'

He can't believe she's so calm after what has happened. He wants to prise it out of her, but at the same time he has to be careful not to make her think that he knows something.

'So, how has your evening been?' he asks her. 'Did you get home very late?'

'It wasn't too late, thankfully. I've had time for a jog and I'm just about to jump in the shower.'

Clearly, she's not going to tell him what else happened and he's forced to close his eyes and exhale slowly, willing his body to relax.

He wants to prolong the conversation in the hope that she'll open up, but just as he's about to ask her what story she worked on today, she gets in first.

'Well, I'd better go, John,' she says. 'The later I go to bed, the less likely it is that I'll get to have a good night's sleep.'

'Oh, of course. It was good to talk and will see you tomorrow.'

'Goodnight then.'

'And goodnight to you.'

After she hangs up, he has to straighten his back to release the tension between his shoulders. So many questions are dancing through his head. Who was the man who came to the house? Is he an ex-lover or someone she's currently seeing? What did he want with her and what did they argue about? And was it her who called the police?

He stares across the road at her house, wishing he could just go over there and get her to provide him with the answers. But he can't. She must never know that he's been spying on her. That would bring their relationship to an end before it's got started.

His heart continues to pound as he watches lights go on and off, and he even catches a glimpse of her as she closes the curtains across an upstairs window.

He doesn't drive away until the house is in complete darkness and he's sure that she's gone to bed.

By then it's almost midnight.

# CHAPTER TWENTY-NINE

**GEMMA**

I hear back from the police at ten o'clock on Sunday morning, just as I'm about to leave the house to go and get a copy of my paper.

'I hope I didn't wake you,' PC Matlock says.

'I've been up since seven,' I tell her. 'I didn't have a very good night.'

'That doesn't surprise me, Miss Morgan, given the circumstances.'

'Are you ringing to update me?'

'Indeed, I am. But first can you tell me if you've had contact with Mr Kelly since we spoke?'

'No, I haven't. But fearing that he might turn up here again is why I struggled to sleep. Plus, I was worried for Alice and I half expected her to call me.'

'Well, as promised, we paid him a visit and spoke to both him and his wife.'

'And let me guess. He denied threatening me.'

'Yes, he did, but we expected as much. He told us he went to your house to ask you politely to stay away from his wife because she's emotionally fragile at the moment. He claimed that it was you who lost your temper and started shouting and making unfounded allegations against him, just as you did when he visited you on Wednesday.'

A bolt of anger surges through me. 'That's complete rubbish.'

'Off the record, Miss Morgan, I really don't doubt it. But the problem is, it's your word against his and as there are no—'

'What about Alice, his wife? What did she say?'

'She said to tell you that she's sorry she asked you to join her for a coffee. That it was a mistake on her part.'

'Did you ask her about the bruises on her arm?'

'She claims they were the result of an accident she had with a door at work.'

Her words slice like razor blades through my mind, but I don't know why, since this is more or less what I expected would happen.

'I'm sorry to disappoint you, Miss Morgan,' the officer goes on. 'You were right to call us, but based on what has been said, we are not in a position to take this forward. However, we have strongly advised him not to go to your home again. And I think it would be sensible for you to stay away from his wife, at least for the time being.'

I feel a spike of alarm and shake my head. 'But what if he does something to her? She's not safe with him.'

'She insists that she is and we therefore have no option but to take her word for it. But if anything else happens, please don't hesitate to contact us.'

I have to wonder if calling the police was a waste of time. Sure, there's now a red flag against Sean's name, but will that stop him from abusing his wife and threatening me? I very much doubt it.

It could help him to achieve his aim, though, which is to keep Alice and me apart. I've been advised not to engage with her and it's likely that she will keep her distance from me even if she doesn't want to.

No more visiting each other's homes. No more meeting in coffee shops and pubs. No more long, friendly chats over the phone in the evenings. He will have put a stop to her seeking my advice and me giving it.

Put simply, he's won.

I have to sit down for a few minutes, consumed by a rage borne of injustice and frustration, but I can't let it rattle me for the rest of the day. I've got things to do before my lunch with John.

It requires a bit of an effort to get up and put my coat on. But as soon as I step outside, I feel marginally better. It's a beautiful Sunday morning for a change, with the sun out and the sky bleached a pale blue.

I'm reminded of the very last Sunday with Callum before he was murdered. That was a bright day too and we went to a barbecue at his parents' home in Bromley. The conversation was all about our upcoming wedding and his mum told me that she had never seen her son so happy.

'I'm so glad he met you, Gemma,' she said. 'You really were

meant for each other. And I know that you're going to make each other very happy.'

It only takes me ten minutes to get to the store, where I buy a copy of *The Sunday News*, along with three other rival papers. Checking the competition is something I have never been able to resist.

As soon as I'm back home, I make myself a coffee and sit at the breakfast bar. The front page of my paper really stands out.

## EXCLUSIVE: WAS LARRY SPOONER MURDERED TO STOP HIM TALKING TO US?

Reporting team: Gemma Morgan, Martin Keenan, Phil Jacks and Mary Wood.

There has been a dramatic development in the hunt for the killer of London mobster Larry Spooner.

We can reveal that only hours before he was shot dead in a Peckham Street on Wednesday night, he contacted this newspaper. He said he wanted to expose a corrupt and high-ranking Metropolitan Police detective who had been providing information to his criminal gang.

We're not at liberty to disclose the name of the officer who is the subject of the allegation, but it has been passed onto the police.

Two of our journalists arranged to meet Mr Spooner at a central London location on Thursday morning, but unbeknown to them, he had been killed the night before while walking home from a pub.

The story goes on to explain that *The Sunday News* will continue to work with the investigating officers and that the detective named by Spooner will be spoken to.

The other papers I've bought have the story about his murder, but nothing on our exclusive angle.

I then check out my story about the one-year anniversary of Pamela Cain's disappearance. It dominates page three with an eye-catching headline.

## THE WHEREABOUTS OF DETECTIVE'S WIFE STILL NOT KNOWN

By Gemma Morgan

It's almost a year since Pamela Cain disappeared and her parents are using the anniversary to make a fresh appeal for information.

Mrs Cain hasn't been seen or heard from since her police officer husband left for work one morning in October last year.

Detective Chief Inspector Elias Cain, who works with the Met's Anti-Corruption and Abuse Command, says he returned home to find that she had vanished along with a suitcase and some of her belongings, including her purse and passport.

He has always believed that she left because of problems in their marriage. But her parents are convinced that something has happened to her and that she may even have been murdered.

'If she were alive, she would have let us know,' her

mother told this newspaper. 'We just need to be put out of our misery.'

I'm still going through the paper when I receive a call from Ryan, who always makes a point of being in the office on publication day.

'Hello, boss,' I say. 'I wasn't expecting to hear from you.'

'Hi, Gem. I just want to bring you up to date with some developments.'

'Sounds intriguing. The paper looks great, by the way.'

'We've had a good response so far to our Spooner exclusive. I've been told that the rest of the mainstream media are clamouring to follow it up and have been inundating the Scotland Yard press office.'

'That's what I like to hear.'

'But that's not all. I've just come off the phone to Cain himself. He's not happy about your piece on his missing wife. He reckons that the underlying message once again is that he did something to her. He's now accusing you of being unprofessional and he's also got it into his head that this paper wants to bring him down.'

'That's nonsense.'

'I know it is, but the piece has generated a lot of noise online, with people speculating that he probably killed his wife and that he's got away with it because he's a copper. I've seen some of the stuff myself and it's pretty nasty. And there are calls for the investigation into her disappearance to be reopened.'

'As it should be.'

'That's exactly what I told him.'

'And how did he respond?'

'He said he was going to consult his lawyer and then hung up on me.'

'He's in a panic,' I say. 'I'm guessing the last thing he wants is for the investigation to get off the ground again and he's put right back in the frame. In addition, he's got the Larry Spooner allegation on his plate now, and that could go on for a while. He must be really feeling the heat.'

'Absolutely, but look, the guy is extremely angry, so if he contacts you, then I want you to let me know. If he wants to have a go at the paper, that's fair enough, but I won't have him approaching individual members of staff. And if he goes so far as to use any threatening language, then don't hesitate to call the police.'

# CHAPTER THIRTY

So now I've made enemies of two extremely unpleasant men, Sean Kelly and Elias Cain, and I'm mindful of the threats they pose.

I'd be stupid not to take them seriously. I've reported on enough alarming incidents where angry men went from threats and intimidation to committing extreme acts of violence against people who they had it in for.

I can't possibly know what those two are capable of, but I will have to be on my guard until I'm confident that I am no longer in their sights.

Detective Cain must have given Ryan cause for concern with what he said about my article and how he's convinced that *The Sunday News* wants to destroy him. And I'm reminded of what he said to me after I phoned him about the piece I was writing on his missing wife.

'*Be warned. I'll come down on you like a ton of bricks if what you write infers that I did something to Pamela.*'

My mind then leaps back to what his wife's mother said about him when I spoke to her on the phone.

'*Some men are monsters, Gemma, and he's one of them.*'

As I sit there, my body as rigid as a tent peg, unsettling questions start screaming in my head. Did Elias Cain kill his wife? Is he on the payroll of a notorious criminal gang? Did he know that Larry Spooner was going to be murdered? If the answer to each of those questions is yes, then he is a man to be feared.

It's tempting to believe that because he's a senior police officer in the Met he must be innocent on all three counts. But, of course, we've learned over recent years that even highly respected cops can be cruel, callous killers.

As cold goosebumps ripple across my flesh, I realise I'm overthinking the situation in respect of Sean and Cain. However abhorrent the pair are, it's unlikely they would risk everything just to punish me for a perceived wrongdoing. They surely have more important things to worry about.

At least that's what I tell myself in the hope it will stop the jitters from getting their claws into me.


I really don't want to go out to lunch and I'm in no mood for light conversation with a man I hardly know. But I'm not prepared to let John down this late in the day. Besides, it might be just what I need to cheer me up and free my mind of troubled thoughts.

I intend to make an effort to look shiny and polished, but I don't want to overdo it for a lunchtime date. After a quick look through my wardrobe, I settle on a safe option – red top, black trousers and navy Puffa jacket.

The Bugle is only just over two miles away, so I decide to walk there. The sky is still a flawless blue and there's no wind to speak of. And I'm hoping that a dose of clear, fresh air will help to liven me up.

The pub is an old-fashioned, cosy establishment and I arrive at five minutes after one. As I enter, I spot John at the bar ordering himself a drink. He greets me with a full-wattage smile as I approach him and we air-kiss each other on the cheek.

'I've ordered a pint of beer,' he says. 'What would you like?'

'A glass of white wine for me, please.'

While at the bar, we check the menu, but for both of us it's a no-brainer. We choose a Sunday roast.

Once ordered, we go to a table. The place is not very busy so we have a wide choice.

Before he sits down, John removes his coat and I give an approving nod.

'Nice shirt. Is that the new one?'

He grins. 'It is. Not too bright, I hope.'

'No way. It suits you.'

It doesn't actually, but I see no point in saying so. It's too tight and too bright for my liking and would probably look better on a younger, thinner guy.

But at least it's broken the ice and got the conversation going. We start by exchanging comments on the weather and how nice it is. Then he tells me he bought a copy of *The Sunday News* this morning for the first time.

'I don't normally buy papers, but I went to the store specifically to get yours,' he says. 'And I'm glad I did. I saw your by-line on the front page and then again inside. I was very impressed and it made me realise I'm dating a top journalist.'

I feel my cheeks flush. 'It's not always like that. Some big stories have broken this week and it's kept me busy.'

'Is that why you sounded a little stressed when we spoke on the phone last night?'

The question surprises me and I suddenly feel awkward, self-conscious even. 'I didn't realise that I did,' I respond.

John gives a little shrug. 'It wasn't that obvious. Just something I picked up in your voice and it made me wonder.'

My first instinct is to say that it was probably because I was tired. But, instead, I seize the opportunity to share with someone what happened last night. I suppose it's because my subconscious believes that it will help me to deal with it.

John listens intently as I tell him about Sean and his waiting for me when I returned from my run.

'He was so threatening that I was compelled to call the police,' I say. 'They came and then went to question him. You called me shortly after they left and so I was still a bit shaken.'

The look on his face is one of sheer relief and I take that to mean he's glad that nothing more serious happened to me.

'It must have been awful,' he says. 'Your friend's husband is clearly not a nice guy.'

The food arrives then and although I try to change the subject, he keeps bringing it back to my traumatic experience.

'Do you know if the police arrested him?' he asks.

I have to swallow a slice of carrot before responding. 'No, they didn't. He denied threatening me and said I was verbally abusive to him.'

He pulls a face. 'That's disgraceful. What about his wife? Has she got back to you?'

'Not yet, and I'm not sure she will.'

More questions about Sean and Alice follow before he moves on to ask me about my wider circle of friends. Who do I usually socialise with? Do I mix with work colleagues outside office hours? Have I any close relatives living nearby?

They're questions that did not arise during our phone call and first date in the wine bar. His manner is casual and friendly, but it feels like the tables have turned on me and I'm being probed by an eager journalist.

As I chug back more wine, I realise that the date is not going as well as I'd hoped it would. He's coming across as more serious than before and I'm finding it hard to get a word in.

As a result, I suddenly lose my appetite before I've cleared half my plate and begin to wish that the time would move more quickly.

'Are you sure you can't eat any more?' he asks me.

'I'm full to bursting,' I answer.

'I guess you won't want a dessert then.'

'You guessed right.'

After our plates are taken away, he orders another drink for each of us and says, 'Do forgive me if I'm coming across as too inquisitive, Gemma. It's just that I really like you and I want to find out as much about you as I can.'

I pull my mouth into a smile. 'No need to apologise. I take it as a compliment.'

'That's a relief. And I can assure you that I wouldn't be half as curious if I didn't want to go on seeing you.'

I recoil at his words because I know he's eager for me to respond in a positive way and I don't want to.

Luckily, the waiter comes to my rescue by turning up at our table to ask if we want desserts. I say no and John opts for apple pie and custard. The distraction allows me to excuse myself for a toilet visit.

I take my time and think about what I'm going to say when he asks me to go on a third date with him. Once again, I don't sense a spark between us and I haven't been comfortable with all the questions. Plus, when I imagine us kissing, cuddling and even making love, it doesn't cause my pulse to speed up and surely that's quite telling.

I return from the toilet to find John tucking into his apple pie.

'It's delicious,' he says. 'Are you sure you don't want any?'

'Positive. I'm full up.'

I ask him then what he's got planned for this afternoon.

'That depends on you, Gemma,' he replies. 'I'm free and I'd love to spend it with you if you're not going to be busy.'

This is something I'd anticipated, so I'm ready with a fictitious response.

'I'm afraid I can't, John. I have to take part in an editorial meeting via Zoom as soon as I get home. And the rest of the day will be taken up with all the feedback generated by today's edition of the paper. It's the same every Sunday.'

I can see from his expression that he's disappointed.

'Never mind,' he says. 'What about tomorrow night? Are you free then?'

'I'll need to check and get back to you.' It's the response I decided on in the toilet and I hope it didn't come across as too cold and clinical.

He puts down his spoon and reaches across the table to place his hand on my arm. 'There's no rush, Gemma. Whatever day suits you. Maybe next time we can take in a movie or even a West End show.'

'That sounds good,' I reply and try to make it sound convincing.

John then excuses himself to go to the toilet and when he returns, he tells me he's settled the bill.

'But it was my turn,' I say.

He smiles down at me. 'I'll let you pay next time. Okay?'

'Okay,' I reply and smile back at him while trying not to let him see that his apparent desperation to have a third date has unsettled me.

When we leave the pub, he offers to walk me home, but I tell him there's no need and I see another flash of disappointment on his face.

'You take care of yourself then,' he says before kissing my cheek.

'You too, John,' I reply.

He turns and walks north along Brixton Hill and I head south towards Balham.

# CHAPTER THIRTY-ONE

It takes me just over half an hour to get home and by then, I feel like a flat battery, all my energy sapped.

I haven't stopped thinking about John Jackman and trying to decide whether to see him again. In fairness to him, I need to make up my mind as soon as possible.

Once inside, I step out of my clothes and into my pyjamas and dressing gown, then make myself a cup of tea. Everything is dancing around in my head and I can feel the pressure forming behind my eyes.

I take the tea into the living room and settle down to watch the news on the TV. But I find it impossible to concentrate on anything other than my own woes, which seem to be mounting by the hour.

There's my deep concern for Alice, the vitriol directed at me by her beast of a husband and the fact that Detective Elias Cain has got it into his head that my colleagues and I are out to make life difficult for him.

Right now, there's nothing I can do about all that, but what

I can do is resolve the issue of whether or not to pursue a relationship with John.

Unfortunately, today's lunch date was disappointing, but that wasn't just down to him. My heart wasn't really in it and I struggled to enter into the spirit of the occasion.

That said, I didn't feel that he drew me any closer to him, and at times it seemed like he was conducting an interview with me.

I now have a choice – go on a third date and see if my feelings towards him change, which is unlikely. Or end it now and save us both a lot of time and anguish.

The fact is, I don't believe that there's a romantic future for us. I felt the same with my previous dates over the past five months. For sure, John is ahead of all the others on points, but he's still falling short of the magic number that would encourage me to invest in an emotional relationship with him.

It soon becomes clear what I'm going to have to do and that's to cut ties with him, just as I did with the other men I met through the app. There were nine of them and all except the Irishman who left me in the coffee shop received a tactful text. Five of them didn't bother to respond. Two of them told me they were sorry but wished me well. And one of them messaged back to tell me I was an ugly bitch and he had only wanted to meet me for a second date so that he could try to get into my knickers.

I don't expect a nasty reaction from John. He strikes me as a gentleman who will appreciate that it's just part of the dating game.

Nonetheless, I spend the next half an hour playing with

words and finally come up with what I regard as an acceptable rejection note.

A pang of guilt tugs at my conscience as I tap the send button and I really do hope that John is not too disappointed.

# CHAPTER THIRTY-TWO

## JACKMAN

It's after 4 p.m. and he's on his second whisky as he ponders how to fill the rest of his day. He had hoped to spend it with Gemma, but yet again she went and disappointed him.

To be fair to her, though, she did offer up a plausible excuse and he doesn't doubt that she was telling the truth.

He came to his local pub because he didn't feel like going home to an empty house. It's much busier than The Bugle was, but he's got a small table to himself close to the bar.

Seeing Gemma again has reinforced his belief that she's the woman for him, especially now that he knows the full story about what happened at her house yesterday.

She's unaware that he watched it all unfold from his car, so there would have been no need for her to make it up. He's immensely relieved that the bloke who threatened her isn't an ex or someone she's been seeing.

All he knows about the guy is that his name is Sean and

he's married to Gemma's best friend. But as he gets closer to Gemma, he'll make it his business to find out more about him, including where he lives. Then he'll ensure that the piece of shit will come to regret his actions.

He drains his glass and is about to get up and order another when his phone pings. He tugs it from his pocket and sees it's a message from Gemma, which makes his face break into a smile.

But as he starts to read it, the smile vanishes and he gasps in disbelief.

*Hi John. Thanks so much for lunch today and dinner on Friday. I really enjoyed meeting you and I feel bad for not paying my share. There's no easy way for me to say this, but I respect you enough to be honest. I'm afraid I don't feel that there's a strong connection between us and so I won't be seeing you again. It's no reflection on you, John, and I know there will be many women out there who will jump at the chance to be with you. For me, the spark just isn't there. My very best, Gemma.*

He feels the air leave his lungs as though he's been kicked in the chest and a bout of trembling grips him.

He has to read the message again just to make sure that his eyes are not deceiving him. They're not, and her words are like poison darts striking his heart.

This is totally unexpected and he just doesn't understand it. He knows she likes him. It was so bloody obvious from the moment they met. And during their lunch, she didn't convey the impression that she was about to dump him. And he's sure he didn't say anything to upset her.

It makes him wonder if something has happened in the last hour. Something that has prompted her to send this rotten message.

A wave of impotent rage sweeps through him as he jumps to his feet and heads for the door. He's not going to call her until he gets home and calms down. And if she doesn't answer the phone, then he'll drive straight to her place to find out what the hell she's playing at.

Even though he can feel the acid churning in his stomach, it doesn't stop him from pouring himself another whisky when he gets home. He needs it to help him cope with the shock of what happened.

He takes a swig as he drops down onto his favourite armchair.

His mind is a maelstrom of conflicting thoughts and his heart is racing, thumping in his chest. He needs to get a grip before he calls her and that entails keeping his anger in check. But it's not going to be easy after being dealt such a crushing blow.

He opens his phone and reads the message again, and this time two lines stand out.

*I'm afraid I don't feel that there's a strong connection between us.* And *for me the spark just isn't there.*

He just doesn't get it. There's most definitely a strong connection between them and she's simply not seeing it yet. And if he felt the spark, then he can't believe that she hasn't felt it as well.

Another ten minutes pass before he's ready to make the

call. But when he does, there's no answer. He tries several times, letting it ring for ages, but she doesn't pick up and he feels the anger build inside him.

Next, he taps out a message with trembling fingers:

*Please let me talk to you, Gemma. I'm sure I can persuade you not to give up on us. If you think that things are moving too fast, then we can slow them down. The feelings I have for you are so very strong and despite what you say, I truly believe we're meant to be together xxx.*

He has to wait another five minutes before she responds.

*I'm sorry, John, but I've made up my mind and would kindly ask you not to contact me again.*

Her words sit cold inside him and it suddenly feels as though the room is shrinking, the walls closing in.

He downs some more whisky and closes his eyes as he contemplates his next move. There's no way he's going to lose her, not now that he's fallen head over heels in love with her. He'll just have to convince her that they're right together and that what she's feeling is a fear of commitment, which is something she can overcome with his help.

He's had too much to drink and is feeling woozy, so he can't drive to her house straight away. He'll go later, after he's had a couple of coffees and something to eat.

He's determined not to let her get away, for her sake as well as his own.

# CHAPTER THIRTY-THREE

**GEMMA**

I'm finding it hard not to feel a degree of sympathy for John. His last message came as quite a surprise. I had no idea that he had already developed such strong feelings for me.

He obviously believes that I'm someone he can build a relationship with and the tone of his message smacked of desperation.

I'm so glad that I didn't answer the phone when he called. I feared that it might encourage him to think that he'd be able to change my mind.

I was tempted, of course, but after only two dates I don't feel I owe him a full explanation as to why I've decided to call it quits.

I know that the search for love can be a difficult and painful journey. There are countless books, websites and magazines that offer tips and advice to women on all aspects of it, including how and when to end it if you know instinctively that he's not 'the one'. They all urge you to be upfront and not to drag things out. And if you've only been on a couple of dates, then a friendly, concise text message is quite appropriate.

But even though I've ended this relationship before it had even got off the ground, I still feel like I've let the guy down.

It's made me wonder yet again if I'm ever going to find someone to fill the vacuum in my heart left by Callum. It could be that I'm setting the bar too high. He was a perfect match for me and I just can't imagine meeting anyone who'll compare with him. I still find it hard to believe that we were together for just under a year. It was a fairytale romance that I wanted to last forever. I still cherish every day and night I spent with him and there's a part of me that doesn't want to create new memories with someone else. I have to wonder if that's why my dates never progress to something more meaningful.

With so much going on in my head, I find it impossible to relax. As the evening progresses, I drink half a bottle of wine in front of the television, but I can't be bothered to cook anything for dinner, so I munch on crisps and fruit.

I'm well aware that I'm back to drinking too much to help me cope with the stress, and I know it's something I will have to address. But not just yet.

Tomorrow is the start of a new week, so I decide to have an early night. I switch off all the downstairs lights at seven and go upstairs. Before getting into bed, I need to shake the stiffness from my bones, so I have a shower and stand under the hot water for endless minutes. It helps, and when I crawl beneath the duvet, I feel much better.

I close my eyes and try to relax by thinking of Callum. What comes to mind is the night he proposed to me. We were at his flat and had just finished a meal he'd cooked. I had no clue as to what he was about to do, so when he suddenly got off his chair and took to one knee it came as a complete surprise.

'Before I go and get the desserts there's something I want to ask you,' he said and produced a small box from his pocket.

I stopped breathing and my jaw dropped as he opened the box and showed me the ring.

'Gemma Morgan,' he continued, nerves distorting his voice. 'You've captured my heart and I love you so much. I want to be with you forever, through the thick and thin of life. Give me a chance to be the luckiest man alive. Please will you marry me?'

A smile exploded on my face and before I fell into his arms, I said, 'Yes, yes and yes.'

I'm awake thinking about that evening when the sound of the doorbell startles me. I'm not expecting anyone, so my first thought is that Sean has returned to threaten me again and a ripple of unease snakes up my back.

As I climb out of bed, the bell rings again and whoever is at the door leaves their finger on the button so it doesn't stop.

My stomach twists in an anxious knot and I stop myself from switching on the light. Before I reveal that I'm home, I want to know who it is and whether it'll be safe for me to go downstairs and open the door.

My bedroom window faces the road and although the curtains are closed, there's a gap of about an inch between them, which allows me to peer outside.

The path is almost directly below and I can see a shadowy figure in front of the door.

Suddenly, the bell stops ringing and the figure steps back. That's when I see that it isn't Sean Kelly.

My visitor is John Jackman.

I should feel relieved, but I'm not. The fact that he has turned up here has creeped me out.

I never gave him my address, so how did he know where I lived? Could it be that he followed me after lunch today? Or did he make it his business to find out before we even met?

I fully expect him to look up at the window, so I'm prepared to move my head quickly behind the curtains.

But he doesn't. Instead, he turns around and marches back along the path to the pavement. I then watch him cross the road and get into a dark-coloured SUV. Seconds later, he drives off, leaving me wondering what would have happened if I had opened the door to him.

I draw in a deep, steadying breath, but it doesn't stop my insides from shaking. I return to the bed and sit on it.

It's not just the fact that he knew where I lived that has deeply disturbed me. It's also that he ignored my plea for him not to contact me again.

So, did he come here to politely beg me to reconsider my decision to end it or was his intention to cause me harm?

I don't know what to believe because I don't know him well enough to be sure either way. I'm tempted to ring him now, but then he'll know I'm in and he could well come back.

He might have suspected I was in anyway and realised that

I wasn't going to answer the door. Or perhaps he assumed that since it was not yet eight o'clock, I'd gone out.

There's a dull beat thudding in my chest and the rest of my body is rigid with tension. I have to wonder if I've seen the last of him. Or will he turn out to be one of those blokes who refuse to let go until they're made to?

I'm reminded of the guy who stalked me for a month and kept on phoning and texting until I threatened to report him to the police. It was a very unsettling experience and I wouldn't want to go through it again.

I've read no end of articles about the risks of online dating. The stories about other women who've had serious problems with men who took rejection badly. How they too were stalked and harassed and, in some cases, physically abused.

I don't want to believe that John Jackman is one of those men, but have I missed crucial signs in his behaviour? Red flags?

We've only been out together twice and had one phone conversation, and yet he already appears to be fixated on me. The clue is in what he wrote in his message.

*The feelings I have for you are so very strong . . . and I truly believe we're meant to be together.*

And before that, I felt he came across as overeager. He wanted to bring our first date forward after our phone chat and it felt like he was trying to move things ahead too quickly. And I was uncomfortable with the way he fired questions at me. The lunch date felt almost like an interrogation.

But coming here tonight trumps everything else. It's unnerving to think he knew where I lived, since I made a point of not telling him, just as I never told any of my previous dates.

He also knew that I didn't want to see him, but that didn't stop him from suddenly showing up, which in itself is pretty alarming.

All I can do now is wait and see what transpires. Will he see sense and leave me alone or is he in the grip of an unhealthy obsession?

I shake my head and exhale a long, hard breath. It was bad enough having to worry about Sean Kelly and Elias Cain.

Now I've got to add John fucking Jackman to the list.

# CHAPTER THIRTY-FOUR

It's Monday morning and as I haul myself out of bed at five o'clock, my body feels sluggish and syrupy. Lack of sleep has worn me out before the day has even begun.

No surprise really, considering all the disruptive thoughts that preyed on my mind throughout the night. They're still there, of course, like a heavy burden that I'm going to be lumbered with for God only knows how long.

Before I head for the shower, I look out of the window to see if any familiar cars are parked on the road. It's still dark, but I'm pretty sure that John isn't out there waiting for me to emerge from the house.

I then check my phone and feel a rush of relief that I haven't received any more text messages overnight.

It's so hard to believe that this is happening to me. In the space of a few days, my life has suddenly become more complicated. And it's thanks to three men, who, for different reasons, are making me feel uncomfortable. Each of them has got into my head and I don't like it.

I want them to leave me alone so that I can return to my normal self. I don't want to get anxious when there's someone at the door or when my phone pings with an incoming text message. And I resent having to accept that there's very little I can do about my situation other than to keep my wits about me and ride it out.

But at the same time, I'm determined not to let it all get to me. I'm not helpless and I don't see myself as vulnerable. So, I will do my best to stay strong and confront whatever I'm faced with.

In the shower, the steaming-hot water has a calming effect and afterwards I feel more ready to face the day ahead.

I stick to the routine of coffee and toast while watching the news on the TV. Fresh stories have broken overnight and there's no mention of the Larry Spooner murder. That doesn't surprise me since the news cycle moves at a rapid rate and has to reflect what's going on around the world.

The cold air bites into my skin when I leave the house and the emptiness in the street echoes what I feel inside. But at least John Jackman doesn't make an unwelcome appearance, which encourages me to believe that he might not be a problem going forward after all.

Staff shifts on *The Sunday News* are staggered, but most of us journos come in on Mondays and take Tuesdays and Wednesdays off. That's because it's always a busy day dealing with feedback and follow-ups generated by the last edition.

I turn up at the office at just after eight and before I've had time to switch on my computer, Ryan approaches my desk.

'Morning, Gem,' he says. 'I'm glad you're in bright and early.'

'Why is that, boss?' I reply.

'Well, it means you'll have plenty of time to think about an interview you'll be doing later.'

'And who is it with?'

He presses out a grin. 'The man himself, would you believe? Detective Chief Inspector Elias Cain.'

My heart skips a beat. 'Are you kidding me?'

A shake of the head. 'I had him on the phone again just before you got here. He's intending to give several interviews today, including one with us that we can run online. He says he wants to put the record straight regarding his missing wife.'

'He had a chance to do that when I spoke to him a few days ago.'

'I know. And he says he regrets not talking to you then. But he's been blindsided by all the wild speculation that our story sparked on social media.'

'I'm not sure why. It's been going on ever since his wife vanished.'

'But up until yesterday the comments and accusations were few and far between. It wasn't even like this after we published our first piece.'

'I'm sure that was because most people assumed that his wife would turn up safe and well after a few weeks despite the fears expressed by her parents.'

'I suspect you're right. Anyway, when he offered to be interviewed by us, I jumped at the chance.'

'Does he know you're getting me to do it?'

Another smile. 'He insisted it was you.'

I feel a spike of adrenaline. 'Jesus. The guy is a glutton for punishment.'

'But there is one condition I agreed to,' Ryan adds. 'If you discuss Larry Spooner's murder and the allegation that he made, it has to be entirely off the record. Very few people in the Met know that he's the officer in question and he doesn't want his name out there.'

'I can understand that. So, when and where do I interview him?'

'He's coming here at twelve. After the morning meeting, you can revisit the first story you wrote and reacquaint yourself with all the information that we have on him and his wife.'

My forthcoming interview with Detective Cain is the first item on the agenda when the editorial meeting gets started.

Ryan briefs the team, who all express surprise, but a few of them groan when he tells them that we can't get an on-the-record response to Larry Spooner's claim that he's a corrupt copper.

'And it's important that we don't leak his name at this stage,' Ryan says. 'I've given him the same undertaking I gave to the detective investigating Spooner's murder and to the Met's press office.'

Ryan then draws our attention to what some people have posted about Cain online.

'One post on Twitter included a photo of his wife and the question: "*Am I the only one who doesn't believe that she just ran away?*"' Ryan informs us. 'And on another site, someone wrote: "*The woman's parents have said they believe she's dead.*

*And they've also made it clear that they think her husband killed her.'"*

He goes on to mention several other posts:

*I don't understand why the police have stopped looking for the poor woman.*

*The cops should be digging up the couple's back garden.*

*Pamela Cain would surely have contacted her distraught parents if she was still alive. They only have her husband's word for it that she packed her bags and left him.*

It's obvious to everyone why Cain feels it necessary to allow himself to be interviewed rather than simply issue a statement.

'It could backfire on him, though,' Martin points out. 'If he doesn't come across as genuine, then it's bound to stir up an even bigger storm.'

Ryan then makes it clear that the paper is going to pursue both angles of the Larry Spooner story – his murder and the allegation he made about Cain being corrupt.

'You'll be the lead on it, Gemma,' he says, looking at me. 'See what you can get out of him today and then draw up a plan for going forward. Who should we talk to? What info can we dig up on the Hagan crime gang? It'll be great if we can come up with another exclusive for next Sunday.'

'Do you want me to come in tomorrow and Wednesday?' I ask him.

'If you can, that'll be terrific,' he answers. 'If you can't, then dish out the assignments and keep across things as best you can from home.'

'I think I'd rather come in, boss,' I say. 'I've got nothing else planned.'

Ryan nods. 'I hoped you'd say that. Keep a note of the days you're owed and then you can take a well-deserved extended break at some point.'

After the meeting, I return to my desk and look back at the story I wrote a year ago shortly after Pamela Cain vanished, the one that prompted her husband to call me up and say: *'You should stick to the facts, you fucking bitch. And the facts are that Pam packed a suitcase and left of her own free will. And she probably thinks it's funny that I'll be living under a cloud of suspicion for the rest of my life.'*

In the article, I pointed out that the couple were having problems in their marriage, but I didn't include the fact that she had threatened to leave him after he had a one-night stand with another woman while on a friend's stag weekend in Benidorm.

I'm still wading through all the notes I took back then when I'm told that Detective Cain has arrived in the building and Ryan asks me to go down and greet him.

'I informed him that a colleague will sit in on the interview and he didn't object,' Ryan says. 'I want it to be Martin, so he'll be waiting for you in the small conference room.'

# CHAPTER THIRTY-FIVE

It's been about a year since I last saw Cain and when I set eyes on him in reception, he looks very different.

He's lost weight and his once bushy dark hair is now almost completely grey.

He's still a tall, commanding presence, in a sharp blue suit and open-neck white shirt, though, and if I didn't know that he was fifty-one, I'd think he was much younger.

My body is tight with tension as I approach him, but I manage to plaster a smile onto my face. He doesn't smile back, but he does offer his hand for me to shake.

'Long time, no see, Miss Morgan,' he says, his expression composed and neutral. 'Just so you know, I can only spare you about half an hour. My next appointment is with the *Daily Mail* at one.'

'Then we had best get straight to it,' I say. 'A room has been set aside upstairs and my colleague is waiting there. He'll be taking the notes. I understand from my editor that you're happy for us to get a single head-and-shoulders photograph of you.'

'I am,' he replies. 'And did your boss also make it clear that this interview is about my wife? Not Larry Spooner.'

'He did.'

'Good. Then I'm ready when you are.'

I take him straight up to the small conference room, where I introduce him to Martin and Tony, our photographer. After declining the offer of a hot drink, Cain sits down at the table to have his picture taken. Tony then leaves us and I get straight down to business.

'I'd like to start by thanking you for coming here to talk to us, Detective Cain,' I say. 'I fully appreciate that it can't be easy for you.'

His pale, wolfish eyes drill into me. 'You need to understand that I'm not here out of choice, Miss Morgan. The powers that be in the Met insisted that I put out my side of the story today. They didn't want me to remain silent following the online reaction to your article in yesterday's paper. The sickos came out in force to lay into me, but then it wasn't really a surprise since you once again implied that I must have had something to do with my wife's disappearance.'

I feel my face heat up. 'I can assure you that was not my intention. I just reported the facts. And to be fair, I did invite you to contribute and you turned me down.'

His expression shows irritation. 'But I didn't want to. What I want is for this whole thing to be left alone. I've told you and everyone else that Pam walked out on me. I did nothing to her. And it's not my fault that she hasn't been in contact with her parents to let them know that she's okay. But what they haven't told you is that she never got on with them. She rarely spoke to them and they always made it clear to her that they didn't like me.'

He spots Martin scribbling notes and his eyes tighten into a grimace.

'Don't you dare use what I just said as a direct quote,' he snaps through gritted teeth. 'I didn't come here to make things worse for myself by slagging off my wife's family.'

'Then what is it you want to tell us?' I ask him.

He exhales a slow, stilted breath. 'I want to reiterate what I've said many times that I loved Pamela and still do. A year ago, we were going through a rough patch. We weren't getting on as well as we used to. But when I returned home that night and found she'd gone, along with some of her belongings and passport, I was devastated. I naturally assumed she had left me, perhaps for someone else. I also think now that she probably moved abroad and is settled into another life.

'I made several appeals through the media for her to let me and her parents know that she was all right, but there was no response. There's not much else I can do. None of her friends or workmates knew where she'd gone.

'My colleagues on the Force carried out a missing persons investigation, but found no evidence to indicate that she had come to any harm. They naturally interviewed me, just as they would any husband in such circumstances, and quickly came to the conclusion that I was as much in the dark as everyone else.'

He rubs a knuckle under his nose and sits back in the chair, crossing his arms.

'You must know yourself, Miss Morgan, that when wives go missing suspicion always falls on the husband,' he goes on. 'And because I'm a police officer there are a lot of people out there who want to believe that I killed her.'

The muscles in his jaw are twitching now and I can tell he's struggling to control the tremor in his voice.

'So, what would you say to those people who are posting inflammatory remarks about you online?' I ask.

He gives me a hard, unblinking stare. 'I would ask them to please stop. It's very hurtful and I don't deserve it because I've done nothing wrong. I don't want it to get to the point where I'm forced to consider taking legal action against them.'

I ask a few more questions, but wrap things up after fifteen minutes so that I can squeeze in a couple about Larry Spooner.

'Before you go, Detective Cain, I just need to make sure that you don't want to say something to us on the record regarding Larry Spooner and the allegation he made against you,' I say.

He sits bolt upright and sticks his chin out. 'I knew you wouldn't be able to resist moving onto that. But I made it clear to your boss that I'm saying nothing on the record. But, between us, I will say that it's total bollocks. The guy was trying to trash my reputation. You must know that I got him sent down and he wanted to get his own back. I'm not bent and I've never had any dealings with the Hagan brothers. His absurd claim has prompted an internal investigation and if my name is leaked, it'll be used as another stick to bash me with.

'Larry Spooner was a low life, nasty piece of work and he had lots of enemies. He was winding you guys up and whatever he was planning to tell you would have been a pile of bullshit.'

173

As he stands up, I can feel his steely gaze burrowing into me.

'And that brings us to the end of the interview,' he says. 'No more questions. But know that everything I've told you is the truth. And when it comes to my missing wife, I would ask you to stick to the facts and don't try to make me sound like a man who's hiding something. Because I'm not.'

# CHAPTER FORTY-SIX

Martin returns to the newsroom while I go with Cain down to reception.

In the lift, he turns to me, his eyebrows arched inquisitively, and says, 'So, did I manage to convince you that I'm innocent on both counts, Miss Morgan?'

The question catches me off guard and makes my jaw stiffen.

'It's not my job to judge you, Detective,' I reply. 'I report the facts, and in the case of your wife, that's all I've ever done. I'm sorry that what I wrote last year upset you. But nothing I included in that article was untrue.'

He curls his mouth into a wry smile. 'And I'm sorry I got so uptight back then and called you a fucking bitch. I should have apologised afterwards.'

There's a total lack of sincerity in his voice, but I push down the impulse to respond with a sarcastic remark and mouth a silent thank you.

The lift arrives on the ground floor and we both step out.

But rather than head straight for the swing doors, he stops and says, 'What about Larry Spooner's allegation? Are you inclined to believe him or me?'

I shrug. 'Well, I didn't get a chance to speak to the man, so I don't know what he would have said to me. But I do accept that if his aim was to damage your reputation, then all he had to do was give rise to suspicion by putting your name out there.'

He nods, teeth tugging at his bottom lip. 'That's exactly right. But you just said that you didn't speak to him. I've been told that he spoke to a *Sunday News* reporter and assumed it was you because you've been calling my colleagues to find out stuff about me.'

'It was a fellow journalist who had a brief conversation with him,' I explain. 'I was then assigned to the story.'

'And I understand that Spooner arranged to meet you on Thursday morning.'

'That's correct. But he didn't show and we later learned why from the officer in charge of the investigation into his murder.'

'DCI Patel came to see me as well,' he says. 'She told me that the last two calls Spooner made on his phone were to this paper.'

'They were. And that's why one line of enquiry for Detective Patel is that he was shot to stop him passing on information to us.'

The muscles around his eyes tighten. 'Or it could be that the murder was completely unrelated to that. The guy was a villain. A career criminal. I've no doubt that he had far more enemies than I've got.'

'I can well believe it,' I say. 'But now that he's dead I don't suppose we will ever know what he was going to tell us.'

He's about to ask another question, but changes his mind and says, 'I'll be off then. Have a good day, Miss Morgan. I look forward to seeing how you frame the interview. And I really hope that you don't give me a reason to complain.'

He doesn't wait for me to respond, just turns and strides towards the exit.

A bolt of anger shoots through me as I watch him leave the building.

And that's when it occurs to me that he didn't mention the dossier that Spooner said he had compiled and had been planning to hand over to us. I wonder if that means that DCI Patel didn't tell him about it.

It might not exist, of course, but if it does, then it could well contain evidence to prove that DCI Cain is a lying bastard and actually is one of the Met's legion of crooked coppers.

I replay the man's words over in my mind as I go back up to the newsroom. I'm not convinced he was honest with me, but I will stick to the brief when I write up the interview, thus allowing him to defend himself.

It's impossible to know if it will evoke much sympathy and stop him from being maligned on social media. But there's one thing I do know, and it's that I intend to put my all into trying to find out what Larry Spooner was going to reveal to us.

When I enter the newsroom, I learn that Martin has already briefed the boss on how the interview went.

'So, all Detective Cain offered up were denials,' Ryan says to me.

I nod. 'It was to be expected. He's launched a counteroffensive and I got the impression that he's confident that nothing will come of Spooner's allegation.'

'It'll be hard for the Met to prove anything if there's no evidence.'

'But there could be if Spooner did compile a dossier and the police unearth it,' I say.

Ryan purses his lips. 'I reckon if he was murdered to stop him exposing Cain and if there is a dossier, then it's now in the hands of whoever killed him.'

It's one of the points we will have to consider as we endeavour to bring the various threads together into another front-page exclusive. But I know it's not going to be easy.

Stories that involve organised crime and possible police corruption always present a particular challenge. People are reluctant to speak out for obvious reasons. The cops are less co-operative because they have to guard against reputational damage. And the journalists involved are more likely to encounter resistance and even serious threats.

None of this is going to stop a hack like me from wanting to get stuck into it, though.

Ryan asks me to write up the Cain interview straight away so that it can be posted online, and minutes later, my fingers are flying over the keyboard.

It doesn't take me long and I set the tone in the first paragraph.

The top London detective whose wife has been missing for a year is still hopeful that she's alive and today he made another emotional appeal for her to contact him or her parents.

I make a point of saying that he remains convinced that she walked out on him because they were going through a rough patch in their marriage and that he strongly denies harming her. I also use the quotes where he says he still loves her and pleads with people to stop trashing him online.

Once it's done, I forward it to Ryan and the subeditors and then decide to see if Martin wants to join me in the canteen for some lunch.

But just as I'm about to get up, my phone rings and when I check it, I feel a flush of heat in my chest.

It's John Jackman calling. For a split second, I consider answering it. But common sense prevails and I tap the button to cut him off.

I then take a deep breath and let it out in a long, tuneful sigh. I should have known that he would try to contact me today, having failed to find me at home last night. Nevertheless, it still comes as a shock and I feel a flutter of nerves as I get up from my desk and go in search of Martin.

# CHAPTER THIRTY-SEVEN

I feel the need to talk to someone, to offload on them. Since Callum's death, it's always been Alice. But she's not here for me right now and so it will have to be Martin. He's my colleague and my friend, and one of the few people I'm prepared to confide in.

Over lunch in the canteen, I tell him about my shit weekend, beginning with how Sean came to my house and why I called the police.

'I felt I had no choice,' I say. 'He really made my blood boil and I was concerned that he might go back home and lay into Alice again.'

His face registers alarm. 'That must have been awful, Gem. The bloke should be locked up, especially if he's already harmed his wife.'

'Well, he lied to the police and told them I'd made it all up. And Alice told them her bruises were caused by an accident with a door. The officer who came said she believed me, but that the most they could do was warn him to stay away from me. And they don't want me to contact him or Alice. But that's bloody hard because I'm worried about her.'

'Well now that he's on the police radar, they're bound to keep an eye on the situation,' Martin says.

I really can't believe that, but I decide to leave it and go on to tell him about John Jackman and my decision to end it with him yesterday.

'I just didn't feel we were right for each other and so I thought it best to bail out before things became too complicated,' I say. 'I explained myself in a text, but it turns out he's one of those guys who won't accept rejection. He responded by basically pleading with me to reconsider. And last night he came to my house, but I didn't answer the door to him. Then just now he phoned again.'

'And what did he say?'

'I didn't answer.'

'Well, the next step should be to block his number.'

'That's what I did when the other bloke I told you about stalked me. But he carried on calling using different numbers.'

Martin then tells me that Tracy had a similar experience with a man she met on a dating app.

'She ended things with him after six weeks, but he wouldn't leave her alone for a couple of months after that,' he says. 'He kept phoning, texting and turning up at her place. It stopped suddenly and she reckons he must have simply grown tired of it. But it really upset her and she didn't start using the dating app again for another six months.'

'I don't blame her,' I reply. 'And, since you've mentioned Tracy, how are things going between the pair of you? Last time we spoke, you were really down.'

Martin shrugs. 'We had a good talk yesterday and I'm confident we're okay now. You know what it's like in any relationship. Some days and weeks go better than others.'

He fails to convince me that it's all sorted between them, but it's not my place to question what he's told me, so I move the conversation away from ourselves and say, 'Time to turn our thoughts to the Spooner story and come up with a plan of action. I expect Ryan will want to know what progress we're making before the day is out.'

When we return to the newsroom, we assemble the team who are working on the story with us.

Quite a lot of information has already been gathered. A list has been drawn up of people we need to approach, including a few of the guys who Larry Spooner hung out with. We've also established that his widowed mother resides in a care home in Camberwell, which isn't far from where he lived.

His nearest neighbours in Peckham have already been interviewed and described him as a flash but pleasant bloke who kept very much to himself.

He'd lived alone since being released from prison nine months ago and the house had been passed onto him by his parents. It was where his mother had lived before she was moved into care a year ago for health reasons.

Clive Bridger, *The Sunday News*'s crime reporter who's working with us, lets it be known that he's been fishing for information among his police and underworld contacts.

'Word on the street is that the Hagan brothers rated Spooner highly and he worked closely with them across their South London manor,' he says. 'If Detective Cain is on their firm's payroll, then there's a good chance that Spooner was told or found out. And a possible scenario is that he then set about gathering evidence to bring down the man who got him sent to prison.'

Clive will be the one liaising with the Met's press office and he also happens to be on first-name terms with the officer in charge of the Anti-Corruption and Abuse Command.

'I can tell you that they're not happy that an allegation has been made against one of their own officers,' he continues. 'But it's not the first time it's happened, so there's a procedure in place to deal with it. I've also had it pointed out to me that since the Met stepped up its fight against corruption within its own ranks several years ago, there's been a significant increase in the number of false and malicious allegations made against serving officers.'

'I seem to recall we ran a story on that a while back,' I say.

Clive nods. 'That's right. The Police Commissioner raised the issue during a press conference. He said a great deal of time and money had been wasted during the previous year on investigating spurious claims of corruption and misconduct.'

I wheeze out a breath. 'For what it's worth, I find it hard to believe that Larry Spooner would have arranged to meet us if he didn't have a pile of real dirt to dish out on Detective Cain. He'd have known that whatever he handed over would be subjected to a thorough examination – whether it be photographs, documents or recordings of conversations. And that if we couldn't stand it all up, we wouldn't publish it. So, for now we work on the assumption that what he said was true and we'll see if we can prove it.'

\* \* \*

I spend the next hour scouring the internet and our own digital files for stories that mention Larry Spooner and the Hagan brothers.

Spooner's trial and conviction for dealing drugs attracted limited coverage six years ago, but his name didn't appear in the news again until he was murdered. And it seems he never had a presence on social media, or if he did, it's been deleted.

Lee and Charlie Hagan, on the other hand, have featured numerous times over the years. They have both served short jail terms: Lee for assaulting a man and Charlie for burglary. And it has become an open secret that they are now a pair of hardcore villains with their fingers in lots of illicit pies.

Their criminal enterprise stretches across much of South London and into the West End, and it's therefore generally assumed that there are more than a few bent coppers on their payroll. Coppers who are prepared to drop charges, destroy evidence and turn a blind eye to all manner of nefarious activities. And the question being asked now is whether Detective Elias Cain is among them.

I'm just about to see how much exposure they've had across social media when my phone rings.

Alice's number appears on the screen and causes my insides to contract. She's the last person I expected to hear from today and it makes me wonder if something has happened.

'Alice, are you okay?'

'Yes, I'm fine and I'm so relieved that you've accepted my call,' she responds in a voice that's low and quivering.

'What do you mean? Why did you think I might not?'

'Well, because of all the grief I've caused you – Sean, the police. I just feared that you would never want to hear from me again. And I wouldn't have blamed you. I feel so guilty.'

'No, you shouldn't feel guilty. That bastard husband of yours is the guilty one. Has he hurt you again?'

She gives a little cough before answering. 'No, he hasn't. But things are even more tense between us now and I'm really not sure how long I can put up with it. But look, I rang to tell you that I'm so sorry. I should have been honest with the police when they came here. I was in shock, though, and Sean begged me not to contradict what he told them. I know he lied and that he did threaten you. And I know I let you down badly. It was my fault he came to your house and I should never have involved you in what I'm having to deal with.'

'I'm your best friend, Alice. I want you to involve me. I've been so worried about you. But the police told me not to make contact. And I feared that if I ignored them, it would make things even harder for you.'

'I'm not supposed to be ringing you either, Gem, but it's been playing on my mind so much that I just had to.'

The desperation in her voice makes my stomach twist and drop. It's heartbreaking and I feel so helpless because there's nothing that I can do to make things better for her.

'What are you planning to do then?' I ask her. 'It's surely time you took control of your own life. And if he won't let you, then you'll have no choice but to leave him.' I'm aware that what I'm saying to her is what her husband doesn't want me to say. And if it gets back to him, he'll most likely feel that he has just cause to threaten me again. But if he stops her contacting me, I won't get another chance so I feel I have to take this opportunity.

'But it's complicated, Gem,' she replies. 'I really want our marriage to work and I keep telling myself that it will once he accepts that he's the one in the wrong. Not me.'

I huff out a breath. 'Do you really believe that will happen, Alice? It's who he is and you're kidding yourself if you think he'll change. He won't, and as I said to you before, the longer you stay with him, the worse things will get for you.'

'This is why he doesn't want me talking to you, Gem,' she responds, and I detect a note of irritation in her voice. 'He knows what you'll say to me and he's afraid you'll persuade me to walk out on him.'

'I shouldn't need to persuade you. Surely you realise by now that he's not the man you thought you'd married. And you shouldn't let him convince you that he behaves the way he does because he's insecure. That's ridiculous.'

'I appreciate that you're . . .' She suddenly stops mid-sentence and draws in a sharp, audible breath.

'What is it, Alice?' I say to her. 'What's wrong?'

She clears her throat and lowers her voice so it becomes even more conspiratorial. 'He's back, Gem. I'll have to go. Sorry. We'll talk again soon. I promise.'

And with that, she abruptly hangs up and a knot tightens in my throat.

I close my eyes and pray to God that she doesn't let on to Sean that she phoned me – for both our sakes.

# CHAPTER THIRTY-EIGHT

I sit at my desk for a minute breathing in shallow gulps of air. I want to know what's going on with Alice, but there's no way I can find out.

I can't chance ringing her straight back now that Sean has returned, for fear of setting him off. It makes me feel helpless and anxious and a cold weight settles in my chest. I just hope that I'm worrying unnecessarily, that she's not being subjected to any mental or physical abuse.

I close my eyes and try to stop my thoughts spinning out of control. But my friend's face pushes itself into my head and she's wearing a fearful expression.

It's enough to force my eyes back open and to prompt me to seek a distraction. I can't allow myself to become consumed by something I have no control over.

Looking out across the newsroom, I spot Ryan outside his office in a huddle with Clive and Martin. I quickly get up and go and join them.

'Am I missing something?' I ask.

It's Ryan who answers. 'I was going to call you over, but you were on the phone. I was just passing on some feedback from your online interview with Cain.'

I give a tight-lipped smile. 'Don't tell me he's called in to complain about it.'

'No, I haven't heard from him. I'm on about the reaction from readers. When I last checked, there were fifty comments and all but five of them were unimpressed by what he told us. Several of the remarks are close to being libellous. They're convinced he knows where his wife is – or where she's buried – and they want the police to reopen the investigation into her disappearance.'

'Then it looks as though his attempt to attract some sympathy has failed,' I say. 'But I'm not really surprised.'

'Me neither,' Clive says. 'As long as his wife stays missing, he'll have to live under a cloud of suspicion.'

'And it won't get any easier for him when he's publicly identified as the copper accused by Larry Spooner of being corrupt,' Martin points out.

'That might never happen,' Clive responds. 'Very few people in the Met know it's him and the brass are hoping he can be cleared before it gets to the point where he has to be named.'

'I reckon that's wishful thinking on their part considering that half the people in this building are in on the secret,' Ryan says. 'Plus, these things are never resolved quickly. Internal investigations tend to move at a frustratingly slow pace.'

Off the back of our chat, Ryan convenes a team catch-up, which I welcome because it steers my thoughts away from Alice and her plight.

I'm asked to outline how I think we should approach our follow-up to the Spooner exclusive. It's fairly straightforward and no one is expecting much this early on.

'But make no mistake this is a delicate story to pursue,' I say. 'Trying to establish a link between Detective Cain and Larry Spooner without revealing that Cain is the unnamed officer at the centre of it won't be easy. It'll restrict what we can report and what questions we can ask.'

It's a tricky one, but I've been here before, and so have the rest of the team. We therefore know how to navigate the obstacles and how not to overstretch ourselves.

I then invite Clive to update us on the investigation into Larry Spooner's murder.

Referring to his notes, he says, 'DCI Patel has spoken to the Hagan brothers and it will come as no surprise that they both have alibis for Wednesday night. They confirmed that Spooner worked for them, but in a legitimate capacity as a minder. And they claim not to know who shot him or why.'

'And I assume she told them what Spooner was planning to do,' Ryan says.

Clive nods his head. 'She revealed that he contacted this newspaper and was going to spill the beans on a corrupt Met officer who was allegedly working for them. They asked her who he was, but she declined to give them Cain's name for obvious reasons. If she had, it would be all over town by now, and they would most certainly have denied having any connection with him. Anyway, they reckoned they had no idea what Spooner was playing at, but that he was probably intent on trashing the copper's name over some personal grievance which had nothing to do with them.'

'And did she believe what they told her?' I ask.

Clive shrugs. 'She wouldn't be drawn on that. But she did say they're pulling out all the stops to find out if there's a link between the Hagan firm and Cain. It includes accessing bank accounts, phone records and electronic devices.'

It's clear to me that the cops are going to have their work cut out. Organised crime gangs go to great lengths to protect the bad apples in the police service who feed them information. And if Spooner was murdered because he was about to grass on one of them, then he'd have known that he was taking a huge risk. If he'd let slip his intentions and the Hagans had found out, then it would have been like signing his own death warrant.

Ryan rounds off the briefing by reminding us that we're facing stiff competition.

'I'm fairly certain that we're the only media outfit that Spooner approached,' he says. 'But all the others are now chasing the story and it wouldn't surprise me if at least some of them have already got wind of Cain's name.'

That was bound to happen. These days, it's virtually impossible for individuals at the centre of a major story or scandal to retain their anonymity. In the age of social media platforms and instant-messaging apps, keeping secrets is positively discouraged.

It's bad news for Detective Cain, of course, even if he is the victim of a false allegation by a well-known reprobate. The trolls will insist that there's no smoke without fire and his enemies, both inside and outside the Force, will put pressure on the Met to demote or sack him.

Before we return to our desks, Ryan makes a point of

reminding everyone that tomorrow will see the publication of the latest edition of *Capital Crime* magazine.

'I advise you all to check it out, and not just because it will feature Gemma's own tragic story,' he says with a nod towards me. 'For those of you who don't already know, this month it'll be entirely devoted to the high numbers of murders that have been committed across London's parks and commons in recent years. There's sure to be a wealth of material that we can follow up.'

I hadn't forgotten that the magazine is going to hit the streets tomorrow, but being reminded of it makes my heart jump. I'm not sure how I'm going to feel when I read my own story and see Callum's face staring out at me from the pages.

But I still don't regret giving the interview. The issue of violent attacks against both men and women in the capital's open spaces deserves as much coverage as possible.

Back at my desk, I go through my notes and type up a list of action points. The working day is drawing to an end so these won't get under way until tomorrow.

I'm still trying to decide what task to assign myself when my phone rings, provoking yet another spurt of anxiety.

Alice's name appears on the screen again, so I'm quick to answer it.

'Hi, Alice,' I say. 'I didn't expect to hear back from you so—'

'It's not Alice, Gemma,' Sean responds and his words hit me like a cattle prod. 'When I told you not to talk to her, I meant over the phone as well as face to face. Now she's fucking upset again over what you said to her.'

I feel a flash of anger. 'I don't believe this. I didn't ring her. She rang me.'

'That's no excuse. You should have hung up on her.'

'How the fuck do you know anyway?'

'Because I'm having to check her phone and monitor her calls. She's in a bad place thanks to you playing with her mind. And I won't let you make things worse.'

'You bastard. You're the one who's making her life unbearable. You need to—'

'Shut the fuck up, Gemma,' he snaps. 'We both know you're desperate to see our marriage fall apart and I've told you that I won't let that happen. I've also warned you to stay out of our lives. And if you think that involving the police will help you, then I suggest you think again. They won't come between Alice and me and they won't stop me from destroying your life if you carry on trying to destroy mine.'

Every nerve in my body is vibrating and I want to scream into the phone, but I hold back because I don't want to draw the attention of my colleagues in the newsroom.

Keeping my voice low and steady, I say, 'Do you get off on threatening women, Sean? Is that it?'

There's a long, strained pause, before he splutters out a reply.

'You're really pushing it, Gemma, and it's getting to the point where I'll need to resort to more than just threats in order to get you to listen.'

Before I can respond, the line goes dead and I'm left holding the phone to my ear as a fierce rage runs rampant in my mind.

# CHAPTER THIRTY-NINE

As I place my phone on the desk, a chill settles over me and my heart feels like it's about to crash out of my body.

For a third time, Sean Kelly has threatened me and he's made it clear yet again that he will hurt me if I don't do as he says. The involvement of the police appears not to have impacted on his behaviour. He's still prepared to act like a raving psychopath to ensure that he doesn't lose control of his wife. He fears that if she develops a mind of her own, she'll leave him, and he's making it known that he'll do whatever it takes to stop that happening. I hate to think what he's doing to Alice behind closed doors.

For a few minutes, my thoughts swim in feverish circles as I try to decide whether or not to call the police again. Is there any point? Would they be able to do anything? Once again, it would be his word against mine and it's unlikely that Alice will take my side. The cops might even tell me that it was unwise to have taken her call since I'd been advised not to have any contact with her.

It doesn't help that I keep hearing Sean's voice in my head and it makes it hard for me to refocus. But eventually I decide that I shouldn't rush into calling the police. That if I do so it would be like pouring petrol onto a raging fire.

'You look as though you're lost within yourself,' Ryan says, breaking into my thoughts.

I stretch my face into a smile for his benefit. 'Just thinking about how and where to kick things off tomorrow, boss,' I lie.

He smiles back at me. 'Well, why don't you leave that until the morning? I came over to tell you that I'm knocking off, so you ought to as well. It's been a long shift for all of us and since you're coming in tomorrow, you should leave now and have a relaxing evening.'

There's no denying I feel really tired, so I'm more than happy to take his advice and knock off. I shove the notes I've made into my bag and put on my coat. When I glance at my watch, I'm surprised to see that it's 6 p.m. already. Later than I thought.

Martin is also calling it a day, so we go down in the lift together.

'I couldn't help noticing that you didn't seem to be enjoying the conversation you were having on the phone earlier,' he says. 'Would I be right in thinking that you were talking to one of the two blokes you told me about over lunch? Your friend's disagreeable husband or the guy you dumped yesterday?'

My eyebrows slide upwards. 'Was it that bloody obvious?'

The ghost of a smile touches his lips. 'Not to anyone else in the room.'

I take a deep breath and blow out through puckered lips.

'As a matter of fact, it was Sean. He tried to do his best again to scare me.'

The lift judders to a stop and as the doors open, Martin says, 'I can see that he's wound you up good and proper. So, if you're not in a hurry to go home, then how about going for a quick drink? You can tell me about it over a glass of wine and get it off your chest.'

It's an offer I can't refuse. I'm sure it will do me good and help to release the tension that is now sitting inside me like a ball of muscle.

'That sounds good,' I tell him. 'Where do you suggest?'

'How about the Rose and Crown?' he replies. 'It's only a short walk and it'll be quiet.'

I give a sharp nod. 'Fine by me.'

The London rush hour is well under way and the street outside is heaving with traffic and pedestrians. As we head for the pub, it occurs to me that Martin very rarely goes for an after-work drink with anyone. He always makes a point of going straight home to the flat he shares in Islington with Tracy.

'Are you sure you're up for this?' I ask him. 'Won't Tracy be expecting you?'

He shakes his head. 'She's on a modelling job until eight. A photo shoot at a clothes store in Kensington. They're using her to help promote a new range of women's winter coats. I'll aim to get home before she does.'

'Sounds like she's doing well.'

'She is. The work has been flooding in for months and she gets so many freebies that she's created another income stream by selling the stuff online.'

'That is impressive.'

'I know, but I just wish it didn't take up so much of her time,' he says. 'She works non-stop and hardly ever takes a break. It's not good for her.'

I wrestle down the urge to ask him if that's one of the reasons they've been having problems in their relationship. I'm sure that if he wants me to know, he'll tell me. Just as I'm about to tell him why it feels like I've suddenly been lobbed onto an emotional rollercoaster.

The Rose and Crown is quieter than usual and Martin insists on paying for a bottle of wine for us to share.

'No way am I letting you do that,' I say. 'You've been kind enough to invite me here so that I can harp on about my problems. The least I can do is foot the bill.'

He starts to argue, but I jab a stiff finger at one of the booths and tell him to go and sit down.

He gives me a playful salute and heads over there while I order a bottle of the house white wine at the bar.

When I join him, I shrug off my coat and try to act as though I don't mind being here. But I do. It's not like me to seek any emotional support from anyone other than Alice. Yet that's what I'm doing because I've been badly shaken by what's happened over the past few days. And, of course, I don't have Alice to turn to. It's made me realise yet again how quickly and easily your life can be knocked off track.

'So, what did this Sean fella say to you then, Gem?' Martin asks me.

Just as I'm about to answer, the barman arrives with our wine. He sets the bottle down on the table between us and fills two glasses.

I take a sip of mine before responding to Martin's question.

Once again, he's appalled at Sean's behaviour and his eyes grow wide in their sockets.

'You need to call the police,' he says. 'The guy is clearly unstable and that makes him dangerous.'

I shrug. 'But he'll just deny it like he did before and there will be nothing they can do.'

'In that case, you ought to heed the advice I gave you before, which is to step back from it. Let your friend sort things out for herself.'

'That's easier said than done.'

'I realise that, but you shouldn't put your own life on the line in what is essentially a domestic dispute that doesn't involve you.'

We talk about Alice and Sean for perhaps another half an hour, during which time the wine makes its way into my bloodstream. The sensation is welcome. It makes me feel more at ease and encourages me to keep on talking.

I decide to widen the conversation by explaining to Martin that it's not just Sean's threats that have so unsettled me.

'It started with the *Capital Crime* magazine interview,' I say. 'I wasn't expecting it to be brought forward and it stirred up so many painful memories. Then came the stuff with Larry Spooner which brought me back into contact with Elias Cain which hasn't exactly been a pleasant experience. And while all this was going on, I got involved with a guy who appears to have developed an unhealthy obsession with me after only two dates.'

He listens patiently as I go on to explain how it's all come as a big shock to my system. And how, because of what happened to Callum, it doesn't take much to undermine my confidence.

Putting it all into words triggers a fierce tide of emotion and I feel my composure deserting me. The last thing I want to do is lose it in front of Martin and as a sob swells up inside me, I quickly swallow it down.

'I can tell that it's really got to you, Gem,' he says. 'But I'm sure it will all sort itself out pretty quickly.'

I push out a sigh. 'I bloody hope so.'

'And don't hesitate to call me out of hours if you want my advice on something – anything – or if you just want to talk.'

I reach across the table and pat the back of his hand. 'I appreciate that, Martin, I really do. And can I ask you not to share all the stuff we've talked about with anyone else in the office? There's no need for them to know.'

'You don't have to worry about that.'

Having got through all the heavy stuff, I'm up for sharing another bottle of wine and a bit of light-hearted banter. But after checking his watch, Martin says he has to make a move so that he can be home when Tracy arrives.

I try not to let my disappointment show and thank him for listening to my woes.

As we get up from the table, I can't resist giving him a kiss on the cheek. I've never done it before and he responds by giving me a hug.

Not for the first time after I've had a drink, I find myself wishing that Martin Keenan wasn't spoken for. And that he and I were more than just friends and colleagues. But it's a thought I dare not give a voice to. My life is complicated enough, and from the sound of it, so is his.

Martin is in a hurry to get home, so once we're outside he goes off in search of a taxi while I head for the Underground.

I'm so glad I went to the pub and I feel that it's done me the world of good. With half a bottle of wine sloshing around inside me, my problems don't seem so intense. The alcohol has given me a sense of perspective and that's just what I needed.

I start to feel the hunger pangs when I'm on the Tube and regret not having had something to eat at the Rose and Crown. But I won't bother grabbing a bite of anything until I get home. There are plenty of snacky bits in the fridge and that will do me.

It's just after half eight when I turn into my street, which is narrow and poorly lit, with crew-cut verges and small, neatly spaced trees.

And it's from behind one of those trees that a man suddenly appears as I'm approaching my house.

'Hello, Gemma,' he says and I'm close enough to see John Jackman pull his mouth into a hesitant smile.

I come to an abrupt halt on the pavement and my heart slams against my chest.

'What the fuck are you doing here?' I say to him.

He takes a step towards me. 'Isn't that obvious? We need to talk, and since you won't answer my calls, I had no choice but to pay you a visit.'

# CHAPTER FORTY

I feel a twist of panic in my gut and every nerve in my body is suddenly taut.

'There's no need to be scared, babe,' John says. 'I just want to explain how I feel about you, and why I'm convinced we're meant to be together.'

I can't believe he thinks it's acceptable to suddenly confront me in the street and in the dark.

Or that he called me babe!

'Have you lost your fucking mind?' I shriek at him. 'You nearly gave me a heart attack. And how the hell did you know where I lived? I didn't give my address to you.'

He shrugs as though it's not a big deal. 'I made it my business to find out soon after we were matched on the app. It wasn't that difficult. But, look, I'm so sorry that I frightened you. I was waiting in my car when I saw you. So, I rushed across the road to—'

I raise my hands to stop him talking. 'Please, just go. You're freaking me out. You shouldn't have come here and I've got nothing to say to you.'

I go to walk around him, but he moves to block my path, which sends a shiver through my body.

'Just talk to me, Gemma,' he pleads, and I can see that his eyes are burning with intensity. 'I don't understand why you suddenly went cold on me. I thought you liked me and things were going so well. When we had lunch yesterday, you gave me the impression that there would be more dates.'

I hold his gaze and feel the veins in my temples start to pulse.

As I see it, there are three options open to me. Scream in a bid to attract attention and hope he'll run off. Push him out of the way and make a dash for my front door. Or respond to his questions in the hope that it will put an end to this madness.

My inner voice prompts me to go for the third option, so I release a breath in a violent gasp, and say, 'I explained myself in the message I sent to you yesterday. You now need to respect my decision so that we can both move on. I'm sorry if it's not what you wanted or expected to happen, but I just don't feel that we gel. And that should be the end of it.'

He shakes his head. 'But I can't just ignore my feelings, babe. I'm in love with you. I know it sounds ridiculous after only meeting up twice, but that's how it is and I'm sure you'll eventually feel the same way about me if we can just have some more time together.'

He comes closer, reaching for my shoulder, but I knock his hand away.

'For God's sake, don't touch me. And stop calling me babe.

I'm not your babe. And you need to stop stalking me and accept that we don't have a future together.'

'I'm not stalking you. All I've done is to try to get you to talk to me over the phone and to respond to my messages.'

'That's not true, though, is it? You came here last night and kept ringing the bell. That was totally out of order and you're lucky I didn't call the police.'

He gives a short, caustic laugh. 'So, you were in. I bloody well knew it. Why didn't you come to the door?'

'Because I wasn't expecting you to just show up like that and I didn't know what you were going to do.'

'I just wanted to make sure that you were all right. I was worried.'

'But why? What was there to worry about?'

He stares at me, blinking hard, and I suddenly realise that I was right to end it with this man. It would have been a huge mistake to have carried on seeing him.

'I feared that something might have happened,' he responds. 'Something that made you cut me off like that. Your message was unexpected and brutal, and it sent me into a panic.'

By now, every molecule in my body is screaming and I have to get away from him.

'I've had enough of this,' I say. 'I've answered your questions and now I'm going into my house. If you dare try to stop me, I'll cause a scene and have you arrested.'

His face breaks into a wide, but unconvincing smile. 'I'm not going to stop you, Gemma. I'm just glad that I got to speak to you and I want you to give serious consideration to what I said. I'm not going to give up on us. I can't. I truly believe that we're meant to be together. The problem is you just don't see it yet. But you will, given time. I'm sure of it.'

I half expect him to try to touch me again and so it comes as a huge relief when he turns and walks across the road to where his SUV is parked and doesn't look back.

I stand there rooted to the spot, shaking like a leaf in a storm, until he drives away. Then I rush towards my front door.

# CHAPTER FORTY-ONE

As I enter my house, the silence envelops me. I have to slow down my breathing to get the air into my lungs. And there's a roar in my head louder than a jet engine.

I feel like drinking myself into oblivion, so the first thing I do is go to the fridge and take out a bottle of wine. After filling a glass and chugging it back in one go, I carry both bottle and glass into the living room and sink onto the sofa.

I then drink more wine as I try to process what just happened.

John Jackman's words echo in my head and part of what he said has my stomach churning with dread.

'*I'm not going to give up on us. I can't.*'

Did he really mean that? Will he carry on stalking me? And keep appearing out of nowhere in the hope that he can persuade me to change my mind?

The man is totally deluded if he thinks I'll come to realise that I've made a mistake, especially with how he's acting now. I just wish I'd spotted that something was wrong about him during our online chats. Sure, I felt he asked too many questions and was overeager. But he seemed normal. Nice. Friendly. Attractive. And although I decided after our two dates that he wasn't right for me, he didn't strike me as an oddball.

Now I'm faced with the daunting prospect of being harassed by him. It's not what I need right now on top of everything else. It's as though life has suddenly turned against me. Again.

I pick up my glass and, clutching it by the stem, start pacing the room like a caged animal.

What have I done to deserve this? Why are so many bad things happening all at once? A man I was due to meet on Thursday was shot dead in the street the night before. My best friend's husband has started threatening me. And a man I hardly know has developed an intense and disturbing infatuation for me.

A feeling of despair claws at me and I consider phoning Martin to tell him about John. But I quickly dismiss it as a bad idea. Why spoil his evening with his girlfriend? I can speak to him about it tomorrow, and it's not as if he could say anything to me that would ease the tension in my bones.

I empty my glass and go into the kitchen to get something to eat. But that's when I realise that I've lost my appetite. I'm pretty sure that if I force something down it will come straight back up. So I return to the sofa and pour another drink.

And it's then I suddenly decide to phone my mother. She has always been there for me and I'm sure that whatever advice she can offer will give me strength.

But as I reach for my phone, I change my mind. It just

wouldn't be fair to offload my problems onto her. She'd only worry. It'd be different if she lived close by. Then I could go and spend time with her and my stepdad. But she doesn't.

The rest of the evening passes in a blur and I go upstairs at ten o'clock feeling shaky and light-headed.

I shed my clothes and have a long, soothing shower. But when I come out of it, I don't feel any better. I'm still in the grip of a creeping sense of dread and when I turn out the lights, the darkness feels oppressive, as though it has weight.

I climb into bed in the hope that I will drop off pretty quickly. But troubled thoughts manage to keep me awake for much of the night despite the copious amounts of wine I've drunk.

# CHAPTER FORTY-TWO

**JACKMAN**

He's awake early on Tuesday morning, but he doesn't get straight out of bed. He lies there with his eyes open, thinking about the awkward conversation he had with Gemma.

It's clear that he's got his work cut out, but there's nothing he likes more than a challenge.

He's faced many over the years and has always come out on top. And he's determined to do so yet again.

He's under no illusion that winning Gemma over will be easy. She's got it into her head that he's not the man for her. That she can do better.

But she's wrong on both counts and she'd come to realise that if only she would let him spend more time with her.

However, she's like so many of the women who look for love online. They're impatient. Expect everything to fall into place from the start. Every box has to be ticked after only a couple of dates or they opt out, saying that there's no spark or chemistry. Then they move on to the next guy.

It's what is known in the dating world as the 'paradox of choice,' where having so many options can make it harder to reach a decision and commit to one person. It means they're forever dating, but avoiding the deeper, more meaningful stages of a relationship.

He knows from experience and from what he's read that feeling the 'spark' at the outset doesn't always mean that you're romantically compatible with your companion. Most successful relationships are not built on instant chemistry and instead develop over time. The slow burn, they call it. Where the more you find out about a person, the more you come to like them and then love them.

He doesn't need more time to be sure that she's the woman he wants to grow old with. He knows that already. He loves her. And yes, he's obsessed with her. There's no way forward for him without her. And so he's determined to win her round.

He won't allow himself to be burdened by self-doubt and to that end he has already adopted a mantra that he'll keep repeating in his mind:

*Gemma is my own precious gem and she came into my life for a reason.*

# CHAPTER FORTY-THREE

**GEMMA**

I regret drinking so much again last night. This morning, my head feels like it's stuck in a beehive.

I don't look too good either, even after I've showered and dressed. Make-up fails to conceal my red, puffy eyes and taut pale skin.

When I leave the house, I instinctively look to see if John Jackman's SUV is parked outside. It isn't and that's a relief. But the fact that I felt compelled to check ignites a sudden rush of fury inside me.

The bastard must know that he's made me anxious and I suspect he's getting off on that. The bloke who stalked me before clearly did. I could tell from the teasing tone of his voice and the look in his eyes whenever he confronted me. It was as though he relished what he perceived to be a degree of power that he wielded over me.

I tell myself for the umpteenth time that I won't let John

Jackman put me through all that shit again. I'll respond more assertively this time. I've already blocked his number on my phone and I won't respond to any emails he might send me. I'll keep anything that can be construed as evidence, including the messages he's already sent to me. And if he shows up again, I'll threaten to call the police. And, if necessary, I will, just as I did with Sean Kelly.

My mind might well be overloaded this morning, but I still remember to pick up a copy of *Capital Crime* magazine at the newsagent's.

I have mixed feelings about reading it because I know it will bring back all those unpleasant memories and make me feel even more miserable.

The cover alone is enough to cause my heart to swell. There are portrait photographs of five of the people who've been murdered in London's parks and commons and among them is Callum.

I don't look inside the magazine until I'm on the Tube and when I do, a lump cascades into the back of my throat.

Two whole pages are devoted to Callum's murder and the headline reads:

## DEATH OF A DOG WALKER ON
## WANDSWORTH COMMON

My eyes mist over as I stare down at the photos. There's one of Callum and me taken three months before that fateful night. We were out celebrating his birthday at a West End restaurant.

The other photos are of his dog Sampson, a group of police

officers gathered at the murder scene, and a head-and-shoulders shot of Chris Tate, the man who was charged with his murder.

I squint as I read on, ignoring the screech and rattle of the train as it hurtles towards London Bridge.

Journalist Kendra Boyle has written a long, comprehensive feature which includes much of what I told her during her interview with me. But she begins by going back over what happened three years ago when Callum took Sampson for a walk on the common. How he and the dog were bludgeoned with a large stone and left to die. How I discovered what had happened when I went looking for them and came across the crime scene. She includes quotes from me describing what a wonderful man he was and how much I loved him and miss him.

As I continue reading, my chest gets tighter and my eyes become watery and unfocused. But I manage to hold the tears inside me.

A half-page sidebar is given over to Chris Tate. His picture raises goosebumps on my arms. Those small, fierce eyes. The crooked nose that was too big for his face. And that stupid tattoo of his own initials across his forehead.

He always maintained his innocence and Kendra details how he claimed he stumbled across the bodies and didn't raise the alarm because he did not want to be implicated. But he was caught on CCTV fleeing the common and Callum's blood was on his shoes.

She also repeats his claims that as he approached the scene, a man in a hood ran past him, but there was no evidence to suggest that this was true.

Tate's father is quoted as saying that he remains convinced his son was innocent. He told Kendra, 'I know that to his shame Chris was a career criminal. He dealt in drugs and got involved with some unsavoury people. But he was not a murderer. I spoke to him many times after his arrest and before he was killed, and I believed every word he said to me. He did not murder that poor man. Someone else committed that atrocious crime and they've got away with it.'

Kendra also spoke to the woman who was Tate's girlfriend at the time. She said, 'The police did not do enough to trace the man who Chris saw running away from where the bodies were found. I could always tell when my guy was lying because he was hopeless at it, and he told me the truth about what happened that night. He just happened to be in the wrong place at the wrong time.'

I have never been able to shake the feeling that perhaps there was a miscarriage of justice since the evidence against Tate was circumstantial at best. It is possible that Tate arrived at the scene minutes or even seconds after Callum was killed and got close enough to step in the blood that was pooled and splattered everywhere. And given that he was on the common that evening selling drugs, he might well have fled in a panic.

Back then, it was my intention to reserve judgement until the man told his own story in court. But he never got to stand trial and so, to this day, I still don't know the circumstances that led up to what happened.

Or if the person or persons who really killed my fiancé and his much-loved dog have managed to evade justice.

# CHAPTER FORTY-FOUR

When I arrive at the office shortly before nine, my head is still spinning with images from the magazine. And there's a heavy lump in my stomach weighing me down.

Reading the article about Callum has really shaken me up and I'm sure that the relatives of the other victims who are featured are going to be feeling the same. I didn't have time to read their stories on the Tube, but I will later. I feel I have to.

As a journalist, I can tell that a lot of care and effort went into pulling together the special edition. And all credit to Kendra and the rest of the team at the magazine for showing readers why it's no longer safe to venture onto London's open spaces after dark and alone. It seems that not a month goes by when someone, usually a woman, isn't assaulted, raped or murdered. This is made clear on the magazine's introduction page, where it refers to the murder last week of nurse Gillian Ramsay in Richmond Park.

I can see that the magazine is one of the topics of

conversation in the newsroom when I enter. I know that Ryan made a point of ordering in two dozen copies and they're lying around on top of desks or being read and discussed.

Several of my colleagues approach me to ask if I've seen the feature and if so, how I feel about it. One says she admires me for agreeing to be interviewed and another that he can't believe it's been three years since it happened.

When I'm sitting in front of my computer, I find myself wishing that I hadn't agreed to come in on what should have been my day off. My heart isn't in it and I know I'm going to find it hard to concentrate.

And not just because of the memories stirred up by the magazine.

John Jackman's face keeps flashing through my mind, making me feel unsettled and deflated.

I think I need some quiet time to rein in my scattered thoughts and come up with an action plan for dealing with the situation if he doesn't leave me alone. I want to believe that he will now that I've made it clear that I want him to, but my gut is telling me that he won't.

'Good morning, Gemma.'

I look up to see Martin standing there beaming a smile at me.

'Same to you,' I say. 'And thanks again for having that drink with me last night. I really needed it.'

'It was my pleasure. I take it you got home safely.'

A nod. 'Yes, thanks. What about you? Did you get home before Tracy?'

A nod of the head. 'Turns out I could have had a couple more drinks with you. She didn't roll in until almost midnight.'

'That's a shame,' I remark, sensing that he was none too pleased about it.

'Anyway, I came over to tell you that I've read the article about Callum in *Capital Crime* and to say well done for speaking to them about it.'

'Thank you. I just hope it attracts a lot of attention.'

'I'm sure it will. But, changing the subject, has that nutter Sean given you any more grief? I couldn't stop thinking about him last night and what he said to you.'

I shake my head. 'No, but I don't suppose I'll hear from him again unless Alice gives him a reason to. I just hope she's okay.'

I'm about to tell him about what happened when I got home last night with John Jackman. But before I get a chance, Ryan's voice booms across the newsroom.

'Okay, everyone, gather round for a briefing,' he says. 'There's been a significant development in the Larry Spooner story and we need to decide how to handle it.'

There's an almost palpable air of anticipation as we all gather outside Ryan's office.

There are maybe twenty of us in today – reporters, researchers, copy takers and subs. All eager to hear what he's got to say.

He begins by telling us that he's just come off a conference call with DCI Patel, the officer leading the Larry Spooner murder investigation, and Commander Sam Addison, head of the Met's Anti-Corruption Command and Detective Cain's boss.

'I received a call late last night from the Yard's press office,' he says. 'Because we're so invested in the Spooner story, and because it was this paper that he contacted before he was murdered, I was invited to take part in the conference call this morning. Anyway, Patel and Addison were eager to tell me that they're now convinced that Spooner was lying about Cain being corrupt.'

Disappointment floods my insides and it prompts me to respond. 'I don't get it. They've only just started investigating.'

Ryan shrugs. 'Apparently someone has come forward claiming that Spooner told him he was going to spread a false rumour that Cain is a bent copper. His aim was to make life difficult for the detective, who he held entirely responsible for having him banged up for five years for dealing drugs. I didn't know this, but Spooner always insisted that Cain or one of his team planted the drugs on him.'

Ryan pauses there to gauge our reaction and I think Martin speaks for us all when he says, 'This just doesn't ring true, boss. It seems like an easy way out of a difficult situation for the Met. Who is this guy who has come forward anyway?'

'He was one of Spooner's closest friends and, according to Commander Addison, he's not involved in organised crime in any way,' Ryan replies. 'It came out when he was interviewed by DCI Patel in connection with Spooner's murder.'

'And they're just taking his word for it?' I ask. 'How do they know he wasn't paid by the Hagan brothers to say it in the hope it would take the pressure off both them and Cain?'

'I suspect because they want to believe it,' Ryan responds. 'The guy told them that Spooner intended to approach us with some fabricated evidence that would start the ball rolling and that his criminal associates knew nothing about it.'

'Does it mean then that Cain is already in the clear?' someone else asks.

Ryan nods. 'It would seem so. As we know, he's already been interviewed, his electronic devices have been examined and they've not found any link between him and the Hagans. And now they have a bloke who reckons that Spooner's intention was to stitch their man up.'

'Then why was Spooner shot dead soon after he contacted us?' Martin asks.

'I put that question to Detective Patel and she's coming to the conclusion that it was probably a coincidence and his murder had nothing to do with him offering us information. And, let's not forget, we ourselves considered that to be a plausible theory.'

'So where does that leave us?' I ask. 'Do we continue to pursue the story or do we drop it?'

'We stick with it – at least for the time being,' Ryan makes clear. 'Martin is right. It doesn't ring true and the emergence of this so-called close friend strikes me as too bloody convenient. It doesn't mean that Cain won't remain under a cloud of suspicion, but the Met will be able to avoid a huge scandal, and at some point in the near future they might see fit to move him out of the Anti-Corruption Command or even force him to take early retirement. It won't be the first time they've pulled that kind of stroke.'

'So how do we play it?' I ask.

'We move forward on the basis that Spooner wasn't lying and that Cain is corrupt,' Ryan replies. 'Let's see if we can find out who this friend is and speak to him ourselves. And we continue to follow the murder investigation closely and see where it leads us. It could be we eventually conclude that Spooner was about to rope us into some sick act of revenge against an honest copper. And if so, that will be a story in itself.'

I return to my desk with a lot to think about. The story has taken another dramatic turn and we have to wonder now if it involves a police cover-up. It wouldn't surprise me given that a recent report described the Met as 'institutionally corrupt' and said that 'successive Commissioners had failed to ensure the integrity of its officers and the organisation'.

*The Sunday News* has investigated a fair number of police corruption scandals, including several where the top brass was accused of trying to nip in the bud stories that threatened to expose the service's own failings.

And there is no doubt that allegations of corruption against a senior officer in the Anti-Corruption Command would be extremely damaging, regardless of whether they were true or not.

I don't see why we shouldn't continue to approach the story as planned and interview the individuals on the list that's been drawn up.

I've tasked myself with trying to speak to Spooner's mother, who's in a care home. She's his only next of kin and will hopefully shed some light on what kind of man he was. And it's not inconceivable that he took her into his confidence after he was released from prison nine months ago and told her what he was up to.

I pick up the phone to start making some calls, but just then, I'm interrupted by one of the copy takers, who suddenly drops a bunch of flowers onto my desk.

'These were in reception, Gem, and I was asked to bring them up,' she says. 'They were dropped off a short time ago.'

My eyebrows shift up. It's not my birthday, so I jump to the conclusion that they must be from *Capital Crime* magazine as a way of thanking me for contributing to their special edition.

There's a small envelope attached, but when I open it and read the message on the card inside, I feel my breath shorten and my heart spike.

*Happy Tuesday, Gemma. I want you to know that I'm thinking about you. Sometimes you have to fight for what you believe in. And I believe in us. Please let me prove to you that we're a match made in heaven. All my love . . . John xxx*

# CHAPTER FORTY-FIVE

It feels like I've been punched in the stomach and for a while I just sit there without moving.

John Jackman's face pushes itself into my thoughts and I wonder if he seriously believes that I'll react favourably to his message. It's cringeworthy. Patronising. Delusional. But worrying too because it suggests that he's not about to give up on me and has even begun targeting me at work as well as at home.

I bite down on my bottom lip, hard enough to hurt, and feel the dread inching up my spine.

More questions fill my head. What will be his next move? Will he come to my house again? Should I regard his obsessive behaviour as a serious threat? Would it be a stupid idea to meet up with him over a drink in the hope that I'll be able to make him see sense?

The problem is, there are no easy answers. If there were, then situations like the one I've found myself in wouldn't be so commonplace. But they are, thanks to a dating landscape that makes it so easy for men to play the field. Most encounter disappointments along the way, but for some, any form of rejection is hard to swallow and they react badly.

What I don't want is for John Jackman to loom like a spectre in my life for days, weeks or months to come. I've got enough on my plate dealing with the pressure of work and fretting over my best friend's terrifying ordeal at the hands of a controlling, abusive husband.

By now, the pounding in my head is filling my ears and it's so loud that I don't hear Martin approach me from behind. He has to tap me on the shoulder to get my attention.

When I look up, he nods towards the flowers.

'I saw Julie bring them over to you and then when you opened the card, I noticed your face drop,' he says, as he pulls up a chair and sits next to me. 'I'm guessing they didn't come as a pleasant surprise.'

'They're from the bloke who won't take no for an answer,' I tell him.

He nods. 'That was the first thought that jumped into my mind.'

I'm still holding the card, so I hand it to him. 'Take a look at that.'

As he reads it, his eyes narrow to slits and he shakes his head. 'This guy is fucking unbelievable,' he says. 'I was hoping you wouldn't hear from him again.'

'You don't know the half of it. He was waiting for me outside my house when I got home last night. Gave me a right scare.'

'What!' he practically shrieks.

I take a breath and swallow down the saliva that has

gathered in my throat. Then I tell him about the encounter and watch as he screws up his face.

'This is not good, Gem,' he says. 'Surely it's time you contacted the police.'

'We've been through this, Martin,' I reply. 'I'm not convinced they'll want to get involved this early on. They might take the view that it wasn't unreasonable of him to want to see me. And I'm now wondering if they'll even take me seriously. It was only on Saturday when I called them out because Sean turned up at my house to make threats against me. It doesn't look good for me that I'm having to complain about another bloke.'

His eyes widen. It's something that clearly hadn't occurred to him. 'I don't think that should stop you raising the alarm if Jackman is making you feel nervy,' he says. 'You shouldn't have to put up with it.'

'And if it carries on, I won't. But I think it's probably too soon to resort to desperate measures.'

I can see he doesn't want to leave it at that, but I tell him I'd rather not go on talking about it now.

'We have work to do,' I say. 'I can give more thought to it later.' I pick up the bunch of flowers and hold them out to him. 'Meanwhile, you're welcome to take these home and give them to Tracy. She won't have to know that you didn't buy them for her. Otherwise, they're going in the bin.'

He arches a disbelieving eyebrow. 'Do you really think I want them? The bin is where they belong.'

So, that's where I shove them.

The day moves inexorably slowly after that and none of us make much progress.

I'm not able to set up an interview with Larry Spooner's mother because when I contact the care home, I'm told that she's still in shock following her son's death and doesn't want to talk to anyone. But the home's manager does inform me that Spooner went to see her as often as he could and actually visited last Monday evening, two days before he was shot dead.

Other interviews with Spooner's friends and associates are set up and journos are dispatched to carry them out.

Clive continues to tap his colleagues in the Met for information on Spooner, as well as on Detective Cain and the Hagan crime gang. But he doesn't come up with much that we don't already know and it's a bit dispiriting for everyone.

Working up the story is a welcome distraction for me, but whenever I'm not on the phone or in discussion with a colleague, my thoughts return to my own issues.

I have lunch by myself because Martin has to go out on an assignment and I'm in no mood to chat with anyone else.

But my mind continues to reel under a jumble of thoughts, and a riot of emotions runs through me. By 4 p.m. it gets to the point where I find myself consumed by a wave of self-pity and decide that it's probably best if I leave early and go somewhere to chill out. Either home or to a bar or pub.

I'll just have to tell Ryan that I have something personal to sort out. I know that he won't have a problem with it. But as I'm about to go and tell Ryan, my mobile rings.

I don't recognise the number, but I answer it just the same, and when I hear Alice's voice, my heart drops into my stomach.

'I need to see you, Gemma,' she says, her voice laden with emotion. 'And don't worry. I promise that Sean will not find out.'

'Where are you?' I ask her.

'I'm at work and using one of the office phones. Sean has had to go to Maidstone on business and won't be back until much later. So, it will give us a chance to meet up. I know you probably won't want to after all that's happened, but I need to tell you what I've done.'

A jolt of adrenaline spikes through me. 'What have you done?'

'I'll tell you when I see you. Please come, Gemma. There's no one else I can confide in.'

I squeeze my eyes shut and let out a breath because I know that I don't have a choice.

'Okay,' I say. 'Tell me where and when.'

# CHAPTER FORTY-SIX

Ryan is on the phone in his office, so I signal to him that I'm shooting off and he just gives me a wave.

Nobody else asks me where I'm going, and I slip out of the newsroom unnoticed.

Alice and I have arranged to meet at a pub close to her firm's offices in Streatham. I could go by Tube, but I want to get there quickly so I call a cab.

When I'm in the back seat, my whole body feels like it's humming with high-voltage electricity. Something has happened. Something that has triggered another desperate cry for help from my friend.

I can't begin to imagine what surprise she's got in store for me, but it's obviously serious. Given what has already happened, she's taking a huge risk bringing us both together again. How can she be sure that her husband won't find out? Maybe he lied about having a business meeting in Maidstone and is standing outside her office waiting to see where she goes when she leaves there. I certainly wouldn't put it past him.

I try not to acknowledge the sense of panic that is slowly growing inside me.

A number of wretched scenarios are unfolding in my mind involving Sean and John Jackman. Those two men are making it hard for me to relax. To feel safe. To carry on as normal.

I resent them both for twisting me out of shape and draining me of my self-confidence.

And it doesn't help that I've convinced myself that it's going to get far worse before it gets any better.

It only takes me fifteen minutes to get to the pub and Alice is already there. She's sitting at a table on which rest two glasses of white wine.

'I took the liberty of ordering for you, Gem,' she says as I approach. 'I hope that's all right. And thank you so much for coming.'

I lean over and kiss her on the forehead, then remove my coat before sitting opposite her. The first thing that occurs to me is how much worse she looks since we last met. Her skin is the colour of sour milk and the whites of her eyes are webbed with tiny red capillaries.

The pain is raw and visible on her face and it prompts me to reach across the table and squeeze her hand.

'So, what's going on Alice?' I ask her. 'What have you done that has got you so worked up?'

She swallows hard and runs her tongue over her lips before responding.

'I've decided to leave him. I can't take any more. You've been right all along. He's not the man I thought he was. He's a fucking monster and if I stay with him, I will never be happy or safe.'

She pauses to see how I'll react and when I don't because I'm not sure she'll go through with it, she carries on.

'This past week has been an absolute nightmare. After the police came to our house, he accused me of conspiring with you against him and got rough with me again.'

I cock my head to one side and lift my brow. 'Again!'

She puffs out a breath and nods. 'I've not been honest about that, I know. But I've got used to him hitting me when he's angry and I was too ashamed to admit it.'

'So, when he caused those bruises on your arm, it wasn't an isolated incident?'

'No. He gets physical all of the time now. I've been left with bruises on my chest and neck, but I've managed to keep them covered up.'

'Oh, Alice. That's terrible. You should have told me.'

She presses her lips together and nods. 'After he found out that I'd phoned you yesterday, he put his hands around my throat and I thought he was going to strangle me. And then after he called you on my phone, he pulled me into the bedroom and raped me, saying it was time he tried harder to make me pregnant.'

She stops there and sips at her wine, her hand shaking, her breathing laboured.

I squeeze her free hand as tears press against my eyes. The anger I feel is like acid burning me from inside. I didn't realise he'd been so violent towards her and I wish now that I had asked her more questions, pushed her to tell me the truth.

'I can't tell you how sorry I am that you've suffered in silence for so long,' I say. 'You really need to accept that it's time you did something about it. Something—'

'That's why I wanted to see you,' she interrupts me. 'I am doing something about it. And you're the only one who can know.'

I lean forward. 'I'm listening.'

She puts her glass down. 'What I haven't told you before is that a couple of weeks ago, I contacted the domestic abuse hotline. I've been in touch with them since then and today I told them I need to get away from him, but that I have nowhere to go.'

'You could always come and stay with me.'

She shakes her head. 'That wouldn't be possible, Gem. He'd find out and come after me. And you too. But, anyway, my case had already been carefully considered and a plan is now in place. Tomorrow, when Sean is at work, I'll be packing some stuff and moving out. I'm going to a Women's Aid refuge. I've just handed in my notice at work and, unbeknown to Sean, I've been saving money behind his back to help me get by. As soon as I sort myself out, I'll apply for a divorce and make him sell the house, which is now in both our names and no longer has a mortgage. Half will come to me, and then I'll do whatever it takes to move on with my life. But, of course, I can't let the bastard find out where I am or where I'm going.'

Unfortunately, it's a familiar story and the statistics are alarming. I've read that one in four women in England and Wales experience domestic abuse in their lifetime. And, on average, two women a week are killed by a current or former partner. But those figures don't take into account the many women who are too scared to report what is happening to them.

'I'm so very proud of you, Alice,' I tell her as the tears start to flow from my eyes as well as hers. 'And I will always be here for you. Whatever help I can give, I will.'

'I know that, Gem,' she replies, her voice cracking. 'But I should have done this sooner. Before you got drawn into it and were confronted with Sean's dark side. I'll stay in touch, of course, and I'll also make it clear to him that you don't know where I am and that you had nothing to do with my decision to move out.'

## CHAPTER FORTY-SEVEN

We talk for another half-hour before Alice tells me that she needs to go home. And when I exit the pub, I feel emotionally drained.

I now know much more about what she's had to put up with and it's made my blood run cold.

For the first time, she opened up about the physical abuse he's inflicted on her and I'm astounded that she managed to keep it secret for so long. At least she's now found the courage to leave him and I just pray that he doesn't find out before she flees the house tomorrow.

She's already got herself another mobile phone and she's going to call me when she gets to the refuge.

Alice hails a taxi outside the pub, but I decide to walk home. It should only take me about half an hour and I won't then feel the need to go for a run later. The evening is cold, but dry and I'm hoping that some brisk exercise will help to destress me as another shit day comes to an end.

After just ten minutes, though, my head starts to throb

with tiredness and tension. I can't stop thinking about Alice and wondering how the rest of the evening is going to pan out for her. I just hope she hasn't underestimated the guy.

I'm also now having to wonder if her husband will soon pose an even greater threat to me. She says she's going to tell him that I played no part in her decision to leave him and end their marriage. But I strongly suspect that he won't believe her. And if he doesn't, then it scares me to think how he might react.

But it's not Sean who is on my mind as I arrive back in Balham. It's John Jackman.

The thought that he might be waiting for me again is making me tremble with anticipation.

I keep my eyes peeled as I enter my street, but I don't spot his SUV. It's not outside my house or across the road. But he could have parked it around the corner and be watching me from behind a tree or hedge.

My heart accelerates as I approach the house, but thankfully nothing happens and no one appears.

As I go inside, my head is still throbbing soundly and persistently, so I take a couple of paracetamol before I do anything else and wash them down with a glass of wine.

My appetite still hasn't returned, but I know I have to eat something, so I make myself a cheese sandwich and then munch on it while watching the news on the kitchen telly.

There's no mention of Larry Spooner or Elias Cain and I quickly lose interest. My mind is too wrapped up with thoughts of Alice.

It feels like the wind has been knocked out of me and tiredness is tugging at my bones.

I can't be bothered to sit up late immersed in gloomy thoughts, so after a short while, I decide to have a hot bath and then go to bed.

But before I switch off the lights and go upstairs, I check that all the doors and windows are shut and locked. And I have a good look outside to see if anyone is about to pay me an unwelcome visit.

Ten minutes later, I'm standing naked in front of the mirror and the bath is running. I see then that I look as bad as I feel. My face is ashen and drained of blood, and there are shadows beneath my eyes.

But at least I'm not covered in bruises. And, unlike Alice, I don't have to fear being beaten or raped in the coming hours.

# CHAPTER FORTY-EIGHT

## JACKMAN

It's been a long day and he's glad that it's almost over. He's spent the last couple of hours on the sofa drinking whisky and wishing that Gemma was beside him.

He's confident that one day she will be, and hopefully in the not-too-distant future.

In the meantime, he'll just have to imagine that she's here, sharing his house, his life, and proving to him that he was right to persevere.

Naturally, he's as curious as hell to know where she is and what she's doing tonight, but he's determined not to let it get to him. He feels like he's done enough today by sending her the flowers. If she didn't appreciate them, then she surely would have contacted him by now to say so. She still has his number, even though she's blocked it on her phone.

He will therefore take it as a positive sign and press on

with the next step of his charm offensive, which will necessitate another visit to her home in Balham.

Returning his attention to his copy of *Capital Crime* magazine, he rereads the feature about the murder of Gemma's fiancé on Wandsworth Common.

He's so glad she told him about the interview she did with the magazine.

It can't have been easy for her to tell her story. Resurrecting all those memories. Reminding herself of the pain she suffered. It must have been a real challenge.

But she pulled it off admirably.

Inevitably, his eyes are again drawn to the photo of Gemma and Callum that was taken while out celebrating his birthday just months before he was killed.

He remembers seeing it in one of the tabloid newspapers three years ago and thinking how pretty she was and how happy she must have been. The couple had so much to look forward to. A bright, exciting future that was stolen from them.

He then shifts his gaze to the photo of Chris Tate, the man charged with Callum's murder. And instantly his mind takes him back to the first time he met the guy and he recalls why he took an instant dislike to him.

Tate was an ugly bastard with an evil streak. He was cold and callous and it was so annoying the way he laced every sentence with expletives. When the police arrested him for killing Callum, he apparently spat in the face of a female officer.

So, it goes without saying that the man who stabbed Tate to death in prison did the world a favour.

# CHAPTER FORTY-NINE

**GEMMA**

Wednesday morning arrives with rain lashing against my bedroom window.

I place a pillow over my face to shut out the sound, but it doesn't work. Not that it matters anyway since there is no way I'll be going back to sleep.

I can already feel the anxiety crawling into my head, making my heart beat like a triphammer.

It was another bad night. I woke up several times drenched in a cold sweat, worrying that something bad had happened to Alice. That Sean had discovered that she was about to leave him.

I promised her I wouldn't call and that I'd wait for her to ring me when she's settled in the refuge centre. She hasn't yet given me her new number and until she does, it won't be safe to try to get in touch.

She's on her own now and all I can do is pray to God that she's able to release herself from her husband's clutches.

A quick glance at the bedside clock tells me it's 5 a.m. and it reminds me that Callum always used to get up at this time to go to work. I'd get up too and make him tea and toast, and we would sit together in the kitchen for almost a full hour before he left the house.

I miss him so much. I miss his company. His calm, gentle voice that I always found so reassuring. And the way he made me feel good about myself.

I was so lucky to have had him in my life, even though it was for a relatively short time.

In all honesty, I have never really adjusted to being without him. To the solitude. The loneliness. To the fact that everything I'm faced with is a challenge. There were times in the months after he was taken from me that I wished whoever had killed him had killed me too. I'm past that now, but it doesn't mean that I don't have days when it all becomes too much.

Another ten minutes pass before I throw back the duvet and swing my legs over the edge of the bed. As I head for the shower, I tell myself that whatever this new day throws at me, I can handle it. And that's because I know that Callum is still by my side. I might not be able to see him, but I can feel his presence and I can hear his voice in my head. He's urging me to stick with it, for his sake as well as my own.

# CHAPTER FIFTY

Ryan has some significant updates to share as we gather for the editorial meeting at 9 a.m.

'I'll begin with what is shaping up to be another exclusive for us,' he says. 'As you all know, Russell has been beavering away at the story involving the charities that are squandering public funds on meaningless projects and exorbitant pay and bonuses for their directors.'

I've been so immersed in the Spooner story that I had largely forgotten about the other stuff in the pipeline. It's a timely reminder that it takes more than one story to fill the paper.

'You'll recall he attended a press conference in Basingstoke a week ago where the chief executive of one charity responded to the claims by categorically refuting them,' Ryan continues. 'Well, Russell has now got his hands on internal memos that prove that hundreds of thousands of pounds have been wasted. And not only that. We've also been approached by a member of staff at another charity who is prepared to blow the whistle on their financial mismanagement.'

He hands over to Russell, who elaborates on the story that was passed on to him after Larry Spooner called us.

Russell spends five minutes explaining what he has and what needs to be done to get the report together for Sunday's edition.

Then it's back to Ryan, who tells us that Clive, who is working from home today, has managed to come up with new information that should help us move the Spooner/Cain story forward.

'Much to Clive's surprise – and mine actually – he's been given the name of the bloke who's claiming that Spooner told him he was going to make false allegations against Detective Cain,' Ryan says. 'The tip came late last night from another of Clive's contacts inside the Met. The guy in question is one Roy McBride. He was Spooner's drinking pal and he runs a café in Peckham's Rye Lane, close to where Spooner lived and died.'

'Does that mean we can go and talk to him?' I ask, unable to keep the excitement out of my voice.

Ryan nods. 'For sure. But we need to bear in mind that someone – most likely the Hagan brothers – could have paid or put pressure on this McBride to lie to the police in order to stop them digging too deeply into Spooner's corruption claim. And if that is the case, then it appears to be working. Clive has also been told that the Met has already started to scale back on the investigation.'

'I think we all saw that coming,' someone says.

'Indeed, we did,' Ryan responds. 'But for now, we keep on it and, to that end, Clive came up with another lead we can follow up. This one is to do with Cain himself. We know that his wife went missing a year ago, but what we didn't know was that he's been in a relationship with another woman since then. It started about six months ago according to one of his colleagues, but it apparently ended after three months. Clive was given the woman's name and address. She's a Miss Kim Brogan and lives in Rotherhithe. Now, I don't suppose she can tell us much about Cain's job or if he has any links to the Hagans, but she might well add colour to our story if we're eventually able to stand it up.'

'What else do we know about her?' I ask.

Ryan shrugs. 'Only that she works in a casino as a waitress. It's where Cain met her.'

'That's interesting,' I point out. 'His wife's parents told me that Cain was a prolific gambler when he was married to their daughter and he built up considerable debts. That was one of the reasons they were having problems in their marriage. So, it seems he hasn't kicked the habit.'

'And if he is a bent copper, then that could be why,' Ryan responds. 'Maybe he was stupid enough to borrow money from a loan shark working for the Hagans. If so, then it could be that they offered to waive the debt if he agreed to be one of their snouts in the Met. If he went along with it out of desperation, then they would have had him by the bollocks.'

'I'd like a pound for every time that's happened,' Martin chips in. 'It's one of the most common ways that crime gangs lure coppers into their clutches. There was actually a documentary on it a couple of years ago.'

'It's been going on for decades,' Ryan agrees. He then turns to me and continues, 'I'd like you and Martin to follow up both leads, Gem. Go to Peckham and suss out this McBride fella. Then go to Rotherhithe. I'll give you the address of Cain's ex. If she works shifts at the casino, then she might well be at home. If not, you can go on to the casino.'

'Sounds like a plan,' I say. 'I think we should also take the opportunity to drop in on the care home in Camberwell where Spooner's mother resides. So far, she's not been willing to talk to anyone about her son, but if we turn up there, she might change her mind.'

Ryan makes it clear that unless we're able to substantiate Spooner's claim that Cain is on the Hagan gang payroll, then there will be no point pursuing the story with such enthusiasm.

'It's all very well us wanting it to be true because it was this paper the man contacted,' he says. 'But if we can't prove it and the police accept what McBride has told them, then I don't want us to waste time chasing a story that isn't there.'

# CHAPTER FIFTY-ONE

The paper has a contract with a taxi firm and so a car is laid on to whisk us to the three locations.

We head for Peckham first. It's just a twenty-minute drive from London Bridge deeper into South London.

I've still not heard from Alice and I try to push her out of my mind because my insides screw up whenever I think about her. But as soon as we hit the road at half ten, Martin asks me if I've heard from Sean or John Jackman and she's right back inside my head.

I feel my pulse escalate as I bring him up to date with Alice's situation and her plan to leave her husband today.

'Well, that has to be good news,' he says. 'That first step is always the most difficult.'

'You're right,' I tell him. 'I just wish I knew if she managed to keep it from him last night and if she's actually left the house already.'

'It's still quite early, Gem. You just need to be patient. I'm sure she'll contact you as soon as she gets a chance.'

I don't want to talk about it all the way to Peckham, so I switch the subject to how we should handle today's assignments. We know that Roy McBride and Kim Brogan might not be prepared to talk to us. And even if they are, there's no guarantee that what they have to say will be something we can make use of. And that, unfortunately, would be another step towards convincing Ryan that it's probably time to pull the plug on the story.

It happens all the time in our business. You get wind of a story that appears, on the face of it, to have so much potential. You throw everything at it but come to realise that it lacks substance and credibility. It then gets consigned to a filing cabinet and never again sees the light of day.

I don't want that to happen to this story. I'm not yet ready to write off what Spooner told Martin over the phone. And I don't think we should so willingly accept that he was intending to pass onto us a dossier filled with lies about Detective Cain.

That just seems too simple. Too contrived. And too bloody suspicious.

I'm no stranger to Peckham. My parents were living there when my mother gave birth to me and we stayed until I was fifteen. Back then, it had a reputation for being rough and pretty dangerous, and compared to most other parts of London, it still is.

Rye Lane is where everything happens. It stretches for half a mile and is packed with clothes shops, convenience stores, bars, market stalls and cafés.

Roy McBride's café is easy to find. It's at the north end, close to the well-known Nags Head pub.

We're dropped outside and our driver goes off to park up somewhere until we call him.

It's a small establishment with a dozen or so tables and only one of them is occupied by an elderly couple.

There's a woman behind the counter who looks to be in her early twenties, but no one else.

She smiles as we approach. 'Hi there. What can I get for you?'

'Before we order anything, can you please confirm for me that this is Roy McBride's café. We'd like to have a word with him.'

She looks at me quizzically, her brow raised. 'Yes, it is. He's my boss.'

'And is he in today?'

'He is, but he's just popped across the road to get some fags. He'll be back any minute.'

'That's great. In that case, we'll wait for him. And we'll have two Americanos with milk if we may.'

'Of course. Please take a seat and I'll bring them over.'

Only seconds after we're seated, the café door opens and a squat, bullish man wearing jeans and a thick jumper enters. He nods at us as he walks up to the counter and when he reaches it, the assistant points towards me and says, 'Ah, Roy, that lady wants to have a word with you.'

As he turns to face me, I get to my feet and smile at him. Despite the frown that forms on his face, he manages to smile back before stepping straight up to our table.

'Hello there,' he says, in a deep voice with a distinctive South London accent. 'I run this place. Roy McBride. Is there a problem with something?'

'No problem at all, Mr McBride,' I say, taking in his veiny nose and ruddy complexion. 'My name is Gemma Morgan and my colleague is Martin Keenan. We'd just like to discuss a private matter with you if that's at all possible.'

His frown deepens. 'Are you representing the landlord? If you are, then you should know by now that I'm about to settle what I owe on the rent. It's all sorted and the transfer will go through today.'

'That's not what it's about, Mr McBride,' I tell him. 'We're with a national newspaper, *The Sunday News*, and we've been working on the story of the murder that took place near here a week ago. We understand that the victim, Larry Spooner, was a close friend of yours.'

'Yes, he was,' he says, as he adopts a more cautious tone. 'I still can't get over it. But I told the police I don't know who did it or why.'

'Actually, we're interested in what else you told them.'

Just then, our coffees arrive and his assistant places the cups on the table. As soon as she steps away, McBride pulls out one of the other chairs and sits down.

'What are you on about?' he says.

I clear my throat before speaking. 'You may or may not be aware that Mr Spooner got in touch with our paper the night before he was shot. He told us that he worked for a London crime gang and wanted to pass on information about a senior police officer in the Met who is corrupt. He arranged to meet myself and Martin on Thursday morning, but he didn't show because by then he was dead. We ran a front-page story on Sunday, but—'

McBride raises a hand to cut me off. 'No need to carry on.

I know where this is going. But I was under the impression that what I said to the police would remain confidential.'

'And it should have,' I say. 'But it's not uncommon for such things to be leaked.'

He takes a deep breath and lets out an elongated sigh.

'I saw what you wrote in the paper and I tuned in to all the gossip that followed on from it,' he explains. 'I wasn't going to tell anyone what Larry had told me. I thought it best to keep quiet. But my conscience got the better of me and I went to the cops.'

'And what exactly did Mr Spooner say to you?' Martin asks.

He licks his lips with a sharp, pink tongue. 'You obviously know. So, why bother asking me?'

'Well, we would like to hear it from you.'

A pause before he responds.

'Okay, but it's on condition that if you put anything in your paper, then you don't name me. It will cause me a lot of fucking grief if you do.'

'You can rest assured that we won't identify you, Mr McBride,' I tell him.

He shrugs. 'Well, Larry told me he was going to get his own back on the copper who arrested him all those years ago and had him sent down. I already know that it was a Detective Cain because Larry had spoken about him often enough both before and after he was released from prison. He said he'd pulled together a dossier full of fabricated evidence and was going to hand it over to a paper. He didn't say it was *The Sunday News*.'

'And you believed him?' I ask.

He nods. 'Sure, I did. We were mates. I told him that I thought it was a stupid idea, but he was determined. He'd always claimed that Cain stitched him up with the drugs bust. He made me swear that I wouldn't tell anyone. And I'd have kept my word if he hadn't been murdered.'

'I assume you know he worked for the Hagan brothers' crime gang,' Martin says.

McBride gives a short, stunted laugh. 'Everyone around here knew it, but Larry didn't give a toss. He'd been a villain since leaving school and he lapped up the street cred it gave him.'

'Do you know if the Hagans were aware of what he planned to do?' I ask.

'I don't know them, so you'll have to ask them yourself. But I'm pretty sure that Larry wouldn't have told them. It was his secret and I was the only one he confided in as far as I know. And that was because I was the only person he trusted.'

After a pause, I say, 'Are you aware that the police are considering the possibility that you're the one who is lying, Mr McBride? That you may have been paid to come up with this story so that Detective Cain can be cleared quickly of any wrongdoing?'

It was a question that had to be asked and it doesn't surprise me when his eyes ignite with anger.

'That's a fucking outrageous thing to accuse me of,' he snaps, but keeps his voice low. 'I'm not a liar. What I told the cops is the truth. And the detective who took my statement said he believed me. I reckon you're just out to stir things up. In which case, you can both fuck off and don't come in here again.'

## CHAPTER FIFTY-TWO

Having been given our marching orders, Martin and I hurry out of the café.

As we walk away along the street, Roy McBride stares after us from the doorway, his face set in stone.

When we're at the top of the lane and out of his sight, I pull out my phone and call our driver. He tells us he's parked up just around the corner, so we head there.

'What was your take on what McBride said?' Martin asks me.

'I reckon he spun us an out-and-out lie,' I answer.

'Me too. And if he did, then it's likely he was paid to do so and is using the money to clear what he owes on his rent.'

'That occurred to me the moment he mentioned it,' I say. 'And I find it hard to believe that he's not acquainted with the Hagan brothers since his best friend worked for them. He's bound to have been in their company in a pub or at a party.'

'I know exactly what you mean, Gem, but I suppose we

have to accept that we could both be wrong. And even if we're not, I can't see where we can go with this story if the police are prepared to believe McBride and conclude that Cain was targeted with a false allegation.'

The wheels are whirring in my head as we get back to the taxi and I give our driver the address of the care home in Camberwell where Spooner's mother lives.

After we set off, we both continue to reflect on our short conversation with McBride. We can certainly write up a story using what he told us, and promote it as a follow-up to last Sunday's front-page exclusive. It will raise all sorts of questions in relation to Spooner's allegation against Detective Cain and his subsequent murder. But it won't have the same impact as a story exposing a crooked officer working within the Met's Anti-Corruption Command. The same officer who's suspected by many people, including me, of being in some way responsible for his wife's disappearance.

It only takes us ten minutes to get to the Comfort Care Home in Camberwell. Martin stays in the car while I pop into reception. I tell the woman behind the desk who I am and that I would like to see Harriet Spooner if she's up for receiving a visitor. I explain that I've spoken on the phone to the home's manager, Mrs Whyte.

'I'll need to check with her,' the receptionist says. 'She's in the office, so I'll get her.'

Moments later, I introduce myself to Faye Whyte, a tall, middle-aged woman with a friendly face and shiny dark hair.

'I did pass on your request to Harriet, Miss Morgan, but she was in no mood to speak to you or anyone else,' she tells me. 'And I'm afraid you won't be able to see her today as she's about to be taken to hospital for a check-up. You see, since she was told about her son's death, she's been having problems with her breathing. We don't think it's serious, but we do need to be sure as she's almost eighty and very fragile.'

'I quite understand,' I say, and hand one of my cards to her. 'But please let me know if she is willing to have a chat with me. We're just trying to find out more about her son and it seems she's the only family he had.'

'I'll certainly do that and I'm sure she'll be only too happy to talk to you when her head is in the right place. Harriet is a very sociable lady and I know she's going to miss Larry a great deal. What happened to him has devastated her. He came to visit more or less every week.'

'Did you meet him?'

'Many times. All of us here knew that he had been to prison and was not a law-abiding citizen. But he was always very pleasant and polite to us and he adored his mum.'

'Then I look forward to hearing what she can tell me about him,' I say before bidding her farewell.

Our next stop will be in Rotherhithe and the home of Kim Brogan, the woman who is said to have had a brief affair with Detective Cain. We don't know anything about her except that she works in a casino as a waitress and that's where they met.

If she is prepared to talk to us, then we're going to have to be careful what we say. We can't reveal that it's her ex who is the unnamed officer at the centre of the alleged corruption story that's been all over the news. We'll have to give her the impression that we're continuing to look into the case of his missing wife a year after her disappearance. But at the same time, we'll drop in questions relating to his job, his finances and some of the people he associated with when they were together.

Her home turns out to be an end-of-terrace property close to the Surrey Quays Shopping Centre.

Our driver pulls into the kerb across the road and we can't tell from there if Ms Brogan is at home.

'Might be sensible if you go to the door by yourself,' Martin says. 'If she's willing to talk to us, you can call me over.'

'Okay.'

I try to work out in my head what I'm going to say to her as I cross the road and approach the house. But when I'm just yards away from the front door, it's suddenly pulled open and I see a man in a suit standing there.

It takes a moment for me to realise that he's none other than Detective Elias Cain and that his eyes are incandescent with rage.

I stop walking and just stand there, my mouth hanging open, my insides shaking.

'What the fuck are you doing here?' he demands to know.

# CHAPTER FIFTY-THREE

I make steady, unflinching eye contact with the man, but it's several seconds before I find my voice and am able to respond to his question.

'I didn't expect you to be here,' I say, rather timidly.

Detective Cain scrunches his brow at me. 'That's fucking obvious. I got a shock too when I happened to look through the window and saw you walking up to the house. So, answer the question. What are you doing here?'

I take a breath and swallow the saliva that has gathered in my throat.

'I came in the hope that Ms Brogan would be in. I'd like to speak to her.'

Before he can respond, a woman steps out from behind the door, grabbing his attention as well as mine.

'Why do you want to speak to me?' she says.

She looks to be in her late forties and has long light brown hair that hangs free around her shoulders.

The blood rushes to my face and I struggle to think of what to tell her.

'Shall I answer the question for you, Miss Morgan?' Cain says and an ugly smile plays on his lips. 'You want to ask her questions about me because you were told that we used to be in a relationship. Is that right?'

I have no choice but to be honest, so I nod and say, 'Yes, it is. And that really shouldn't come as a surprise to you, Detective. You're a newsworthy subject at the moment and many people, including the readers of my paper, are keen to know more about you.'

'So, you're a newspaper reporter,' Kim says as she throws me a hostile glare. 'Well, you've wasted your time coming here. Me and Elias have been back together for a couple of weeks now. He came to see me today because he's on a day off and wanted to tell me how the press pack and those internet trolls have started to hound him again. It's a disgrace. He's a good man and he's done nothing to deserve it. So, there's no way I'll speak to you about anything. As far as I'm concerned, your lot just like to feed off the misery and misfortune of others. And all you do is spread lies and misinformation.'

She turns sharply and disappears back into the house.

Cain shakes his head at me, his eyes blazing. 'I couldn't have put it better myself. You really are a disgrace, Morgan. You must know by now that what Larry Spooner said about me has been proven to be a lie. I've been told about that friend of his who came forward. But, despite that, you won't drop it and you're still trying to bring me down. Well, you can dig all you want and you won't come across any dirt because there isn't any. And if you were a better journalist and bothered to check your facts you would have known that Kim and I had rekindled our relationship.'

His tone is sneering, condescending, but I don't respond because I feel that I'm on the back foot and I want to avoid saying something that will fuel his anger.

He steps out of the door and towards me, and when he speaks again, there's a sudden gear change in his voice, and it's much lower, presumably so that his girlfriend can't hear him.

'I'm getting really pissed off with you and your paper,' he says. 'First you tried desperately to pin my wife's disappearance on me, then used the anniversary of it to dredge it up again for no good reason. And now you're determined to make something of this Spooner shit. Well, I've warned you before that I'll only take so much before I hit back. And I reckon it's time I did just that.'

Without waiting for me to respond, he strides back into the house. And it's not until after he's slammed the door behind him that I find it in me to move.

Martin is now out of the car as I walk across the road towards him.

My head is fizzing with tension and what just happened has made me feel angry and embarrassed. There was no way I could have known that Cain was in the house, and it's as though a trap was set for me and I walked right into it.

Martin can obviously tell from my expression that I'm not happy. 'Jesus Christ, Gem, are you okay? I didn't realise you were talking to Cain until he stepped outside.'

'I couldn't believe it when he answered the door,' I tell him.

'I'm guessing he was none too pleased. What did he say?'

'Let's get back in the car and I'll tell you. I need to put this place behind me.'

As soon as we're on the move, I begin.

'It turns out the information we were given is out of date. Cain and Ms Brogan are back together and he apparently dropped by on his day off to tell her that we and other media outlets are intent on trashing his reputation again.'

'Ouch! Bad timing.'

'You can say that again. She made it clear that she wouldn't talk to me and he said he was going to hit back at us, whatever that means. Or maybe the threat was just aimed at me.'

'I shouldn't worry about it, Gem. There's not much he can do. We're carrying out a legitimate journalistic investigation.'

'That's not how he sees it. He's already been made aware of what Roy McBride is claiming and he reckons in view of that we should stop chasing what's become a non-story.'

We continue to discuss it on the way back to London Bridge, but we both have to accept that it's so far been an unproductive day. Our story has effectively hit the buffers and it's not clear where we take it from here.

And as if that wasn't bad enough, my latest encounter with Detective Cain has further unsettled me.

Another day. Another threat.

It's reached the point where I'm struggling to play down the sense of unease in my gut.

I can feel my internal dialogue going to work, telling me not to let it get to me. But it already has. And I dread to think what's coming next.

# CHAPTER FIFTY-FOUR

As soon as we get back to the office, we learn that Detective Cain has already been on the phone to Ryan.

'He was furious and said that I was out of order sending you to Ms Brogan's house,' the boss tells us. 'He claims it clearly demonstrates that we're carrying out a witch hunt aimed at destroying him. He wouldn't listen to what I had to say and said he intends to make a formal complaint to the press watchdog and to our own board of directors. He's also told me to expect a call from the Met's media office.'

I wonder if this is what Cain meant when he threatened to 'hit back' at us.

'It was bad luck on our part turning up when we did,' I say.

Ryan shrugs. 'These things happen. And what he alleges is, of course, complete nonsense. After Spooner called us and made the allegation, we had a duty to follow it up.'

I then tell him what the detective said to me and what we got from Roy McBride.

'It's been a disappointing day all round, boss. Even Larry Spooner's mother wasn't able to talk to us because she was going for a hospital check-up.'

Ryan scrunches up his face as though in pain. 'This does mean we now have to consider whether it is worth pursuing the story. It's been effectively shot down by Spooner's mate and I don't think we'll get much co-operation from our own friends in the Met if we keep plugging away at it.'

As much as I hate to admit it, Ryan has a point. The paper's resources are limited, and there are a lot of other things going on that we need to cover.

'The very latest feedback from the rest of the team who are working on this with you is that they're getting nowhere fast,' he continues. 'We're still unable to answer any of the crucial questions that need to be answered. Was Spooner telling the truth about Cain being on the Hagan gang's payroll? Was he really going to hand over a dossier to us, and if so, was it filled with genuine evidence of corruption by a senior officer, or was it going to be just a pack of lies? And finally, was he shot dead because he approached us or was his murder unrelated?'

Ryan leans forward across his desk and puts his hands together in front of his face.

After a few moments, he says, 'I think the way forward is for us to break the story that Spooner, a known criminal, apparently told someone he was going to spread lies about an officer working with the Anti-Corruption Command. We can't name Detective Cain and Roy McBride will also have to remain anonymous. And we won't be able to report that Spooner planned it as a way of getting back at a copper who got him sent to prison.

'Although it will leave a lot of questions unanswered, it will be of interest to our readers who like a good mystery. No other paper has latched onto it yet as far as I know, so we can be the first by posting it online. And then we wait and see if it generates any new leads that we can follow up. If not, we put the story on the back burner for now.'

'It makes sense to me,' I tell him and Martin agrees.

Ryan nods. 'Good. Then I want you to pull the piece together, Gem, and let's get it out there right away. You've got all you need, including direct quotes from the man who Spooner confided in. But I suggest you also include an update on the investigation into Spooner's murder. See if they've made any progress.'

It's an easy enough assignment and I spend the next hour writing it up. The line from the Scotland Yard press office is that the investigation is ongoing, but no arrests are imminent. And they provide me with a quote that makes clear the direction in which they're taking it.

'*We are keeping an open mind as to why Mr Spooner was murdered. But we now strongly suspect that he was the victim of a turf war that has been going on for some months between two rival criminal gangs operating across South London.*'

After I've finished, I send the article straight to the online team and then take myself off to the canteen for a late lunch. But on the way there, I receive a call on my phone from an unknown number.

My heart leaps in anticipation of it being Alice, and when I hear her voice, my entire body freezes.

'I did it, Gem,' she tells me. 'I left the house and I'm now at the refuge.'

I have to bite my lip to hold in a scream of delight. 'Oh wow, Alice. Is everything all right? I've been desperate to hear from you.'

'It's all good thankfully. The other women here have been so welcoming and they've all been through what I've been through. And the staff are really nice. I'll send you a number you can reach me on as soon as I can.'

'So, what's it like there?'

'It's nice. Comfortable. And I feel safe. I've been given my own room and it overlooks a lovely garden.'

'Does Sean know yet?'

'I've left him a long note, but he won't have seen it yet. I explained why I've left him and told him there's no going back, and I want a divorce. I also made it clear that you had nothing to do with my decision.'

'Thank you. What about your parents? Do they know yet?'

'I'll be calling them next. I wanted to settle in before letting anyone know. And I still can't tell you where I am.'

'That makes perfect sense. I'm so proud of you, Alice.'

'I just hope I can manage to hold my nerve and stick with it,' she replies. 'I know it's not going to be easy, but it had to be done. I feel that this is the only option open to me. I will be getting in touch with him by phone soon because there's a lot more that I want to tell him that I didn't put in the note.'

'Well, I'm here for you, Alice, and always will be. You know that.'

'I do, Gem, and your love and support mean the world to me. God forbid Sean contacts you, but if he does then don't hesitate to call the police. It'll take him a while to accept it and he'll be hell-bent on blaming everyone but himself.'

'Don't you worry about me,' I say. 'Just look after yourself and please stay in touch.'

'You can count on it. Right now, you're the only real friend I've got.'

# CHAPTER FIFTY-FIVE

The news from Alice is so welcome and has really cheered me up. But I know that my mind won't be able to rest until I can be reassured that Sean won't react by directing his anger towards me. There is a good chance he will and I have to be prepared for that. But there aren't really any precautions I can take that won't seriously disrupt my life. I'll simply have to deal with it as best I can, just as I'll have to deal with John fucking Jackman if he won't leave me alone.

I have lunch by myself in the canteen because most of my colleagues, including Martin, have already finished theirs and gone back upstairs. But it gives me some alone time to wrap my thoughts around all that's been happening in a bid to make sense of it.

Of course, it doesn't make sense and I'm forced to conclude that I'm merely a victim of circumstance.

After lunch, I return upstairs and learn that my article has been approved and posted on the paper's website. I will now have to wait and see if the story has more life in it, which will depend on whether fresh revelations surface. If not, then there is unlikely to be a front-page follow-up this coming Sunday.

I'm sure that Detective Cain will be breathing a sigh of relief. He still hasn't been officially named as the officer who Larry Spooner accused of corruption and the first anniversary of his wife's disappearance has come and gone. No doubt he'll continue to be vilified by trolls on the internet, but that will eventually die down.

I spend the rest of the afternoon pulling together all the notes that have been drawn up on the Spooner story and dump them into a single file for easy access.

Before I know it, the evening is drawing in and my colleagues are starting to leave the office. It occurs to me that I haven't had a chance to update Martin on Alice's situation. I'm sure he will want to know that she's safely ensconced in a refuge, so I decide to ask him if he wants to go for a drink before he heads home.

But just as I'm approaching his desk, he slams down his phone and spits out a profanity.

'What's up?' I ask him. 'It's not like you to swear.'

He looks up at me and manages a perfunctory smile. 'Oh, it's nothing. Just that Tracy and me were supposed to be going out for dinner tonight. But she just rang to let me know that her agent has arranged a photo shoot in the Lake District and a car is picking her up in a couple of hours. And she won't be back until Friday.'

'That's a bummer. Still, does it mean you can join me for an after-work drink? I can update you on Alice's situation and you can tell me how tough it is being in a relationship with a gorgeous model.'

His smile widens. 'That sounds like a grand idea. The Rose and Crown?'

I return the smile. 'That's what I was going to suggest.'

It turns out that a drink is what we both need to help soften the impact of yet another eventful day.

Even before we get to the pub, Martin opens up about why his relationship with Tracy keeps flitting between good and bad.

'She's becoming more and more obsessed with her job,' he tells me. 'It's as though everything else in her life, including me, is becoming irrelevant. We keep talking about it and I tell her that too often I feel like a spare part, but it doesn't seem to sink in. All she's ever concerned about is the next assignment.'

It feels strange hearing him say such things because all he has ever done is pay her compliments. It makes me wonder if the problems started to arise a while ago, but he refused to acknowledge them.

When we arrive at the Rose and Crown, Martin makes it clear that he's tired of talking about himself. 'I'm probably coming across as a right old whinger,' he says. 'When we go in, I'll switch myself off and you can tell me about Alice and all the other shit that you're having to deal with.'

Once inside, I stump up for a bottle of wine and we take it to a table in the saloon bar. Martin pours the drinks and we clink our glasses before I tell him about Alice leaving Sean.

'That's terrific news,' he says. 'And it's great that she's been given a place in a refuge. She'll be with other women who've also suffered at the hands of abusive partners and I'm sure that it will strengthen her commitment to build a new life for herself.'

'Her husband probably doesn't even know yet,' I say. 'She's left a note for him, but he won't see it until he gets home from work.'

A look of concern crosses his face. 'Then you need to be on your guard, Gem, in case he turns up on your doorstep again. He might think you know where she is.'

'That's also occurred to Alice, so she's told him in the note that I had nothing to do with her decision to leave and I don't know where she's moved to.'

'Well, let's hope he believes her. Now, what about the other nutter who's been giving you grief? The one who insists that he's the love of your life.'

I shrug. 'I don't expect he's given up on me yet. I'll just have to do whatever it takes to convince him that he's wasting his time.'

The conversation then switches to work matters and the next forty minutes is spent trying to come up with ways to keep the Spooner story alive. But we're still racking our brains by the time the wine bottle is empty.

We're both unsure of the wisdom of ordering another bottle because neither of us is up for getting pissed. But then Martin says, 'Tell you what. Since I wasn't expecting to eat in tonight how about I treat you to some nosh here? Then we can have a couple more wines each and they won't go to our heads.'

I'm up for it, partly so that I won't have to cook anything when I get home and also because being here with Martin is helping to keep the negative thoughts at bay.

We share a large pizza and a bowl of fries and that proves

to be just enough for me. After we've finished the food and wine, we decide to call it a night.

Once again, we've enjoyed each other's company, but his parting words set off alarm bells in my head.

'Thanks so much for inviting me for another drink, Gem. It's beginning to feel like I only ever enjoy myself when I'm out with you.'

I really don't know what to make of what he said and it plays on my mind throughout the journey home. Did he really mean it or was it just the drink talking?

It can't possibly be that he's starting to see me as more than just a colleague and friend.

Or can it?

I tell myself not to read too much into it. The poor guy's head is all over the place because he feels that his girlfriend doesn't appreciate him. He's naturally upset. Angry. Confused. And in such an emotionally charged state, he's bound to say things he doesn't mean. Especially with so much wine in his system.

Martin's words stay with me until I enter my street and my thoughts turn to who might be waiting for me there. Sean Kelly maybe. He must know by now that Alice has walked out on him. Or John Jackman perhaps. He must be desperate to engage with me again if he hasn't lost interest by now.

I pick up the pace as I head towards my front door and each intake of breath feels sharp in my lungs.

But for the second night running neither of those men confront me and as soon as I'm inside, I twist the key in the lock. And that's when I realise that I'm standing on an envelope.

I pick it up and see just my name scrawled neatly in big back letters. No stamp or address, which tells me it was hand delivered.

I wait until I'm in the kitchen before I open it and as I read the note that's inside, my head starts to spin.

*Hi there, Gemma. I can't get you out of my mind and unless I can see you again, I don't know what I'll do. Tomorrow night at 7 p.m. I'll be waiting for you at the wine bar where we had our first amazing date. Please, please, please come along and have just one or two drinks with me. Let's talk in a civil way about our situation. I feel this is the only way we can sort things out and move forward with our lives.*

*All my love,*
*John xxx*

# CHAPTER FIFTY-SIX

John Jackman's note keeps me awake for most of the night as I agonise over how to respond to it.

I'm faced with a real dilemma. Should I just ignore it or go along to the wine bar in the hope that I can persuade him to stop harassing me?

On the one hand, it will give me an opportunity to look into his eyes and really get my message across. When he confronted me on the street the other night, I was too shocked to fully articulate my feelings.

But, on the other hand, going on what will effectively be a third date might encourage him to believe that all is not lost. That there's still a chance he can win me over with his steely determination and ridiculous expressions of love.

I know that if I stay in bed, I'll drive myself crazy thinking about it. So, even though it's only 5 a.m., I get up, slip on my dressing gown, and go downstairs to make myself a cup of tea.

I check my phone while drinking it and thankfully there

are no messages or emails to make me feel any worse than I already do. My body is numb and my mind is in utter disarray.

The TV news provides only a brief distraction, but there is one story that grabs my attention and sharpens my senses. It's about a man who was jailed for life yesterday for murdering his wife. The woman went missing three years ago and he'd told the police and her family that he had no idea what had happened to her. But when new evidence came to light, detectives reopened the case and dug up the back garden of his house, where they found her battered body.

It makes me think of Detective Cain and I wonder yet again if he did something like that to his own wife. I recall the police did search their small back garden but found nothing. But if he did kill her, he could well have dumped her body somewhere else.

I just wish they had put more effort into solving the mystery of her disappearance. But at the same time, I understand that it often comes down to a question of resources. In the UK, someone is officially reported missing every ninety seconds, and that means the police have no choice but to prioritise which cases to doggedly pursue.

Even after I finish my tea, my mind is still in overdrive as I go upstairs to get ready. Before showering, I check myself in the mirror and my reflection makes me wince. My face is drawn and red veins are spoiling the whites of my eyes.

The shower perks me up a little, but I'm still not back to my old self even after I'm dressed.

It's quite early, so I make myself coffee and toast. But when I start tucking into it, my doorbell rings, causing my stomach muscles to contract. I'm pretty certain that at this time in the morning it won't be someone that I'll be glad to see.

And I'm proved right even before I reach the door when the letter box flaps open and a familiar voice bellows through it.

'It's me, Gemma. Sean. Don't pretend you're not in. I need to talk to you and I won't go away until I do.'

Anger flares inside me and I shout for him to back away from the door. I'm prepared to listen to what he has to say, but no way am I going to let him into my home.

Through the peephole, I watch him step back along the path and when he's about five yards away, he stops and clamps his arms around himself.

I throw caution to the wind then and open the door. Much to my surprise, I'm not nervous. Just furious. And determined not to let the bastard succeed in intimidating me again. This is the third time he's come here and it's in spite of being warned not to do so by the police.

'I know what you want from me, Sean, but I'm going to have to disappoint you,' I tell him. 'I haven't a clue where Alice is and if I did know, I wouldn't tell you.'

He pumps out his chest. 'You're lying. I know you are. This is all your fault and you've got what you wanted.'

The anger swells inside me. 'Oh, grow up, Sean. Alice has left you because you've been mistreating her. I had nothing to do with it. I was shocked myself when she called yesterday to tell me she'd walked out. I didn't think she had it in her. But she refused to say where she was going and she didn't give me a phone number that I can reach her on. But she did say she'll ring you at some point.'

He shakes his head and when he speaks again, his voice is high-pitched and filled with menace. 'You're taking me for a fucking fool and that's a mistake. Alice and me were happy until you started messing with her mind. And now she's alone and I bet she's wishing she hadn't listened to you. So, just tell me where she is and I can go and talk some sense into her.'

'For the final time, I really don't know,' I say. 'And she doesn't want you to know because she's scared of you. She wants you out of her life and I can understand why.'

He starts moving towards me but stops abruptly when I raise my hands.

'You come any closer and I'll call the police again,' I yell at him. 'And I will make sure that this time they arrest you. There's no way you'll be able to convince them that you didn't come here to threaten me.'

I can sense him turning it over in his mind and for several long seconds he just stares at me with a look of feral rage on his face.

Then he shakes his head again and says, 'You underestimate me, Gemma Morgan. I warned you more than once to stay out of our lives. Well, you chose to ignore that warning and, irrespective of whether or not I'm able to mend my marriage, I'm going to make sure that you suffer big time for what you've done.'

He turns abruptly and walks away then, and I don't go back inside until I see him get into his car and drive off.

# CHAPTER FIFTY-SEVEN

It beggars belief that I've been threatened yet again. It's the second time within twenty-four hours and the third or fourth time in less than a week.

Is it any wonder that it feels like my world has been turned on its axis?

I sit in the kitchen for a while with my heart booming in my ears. I briefly contemplate calling the police, but I know that if I do, I will have to wait for them to arrive. And then I'll be told once again that there's nothing that they can do other than to issue Sean with another pointless warning.

*Be strong*, I tell myself. *You faced up to the prick, and despite what he said, you may well have convinced him that you don't know where his wife has gone.*

Before I leave the house, I make up my mind not to involve the police even though a nagging voice questions the wisdom of that decision.

But Sean Kelly's latest rant is not the only thing occupying my thoughts during the journey to work. There's also John

Jackman's note and whether or not I should take him up on his invitation to join him for a drink tonight.

As soon as I walk into the newsroom and see Martin at his desk, my mind flips back to what he said to me outside the pub last night.

I stopped thinking about it after I read John's note, but suddenly his words are ringing in my ears.

'*It's beginning to feel like I only ever enjoy myself when I'm out with you.*'

He probably won't even remember that he said it and I'm certainly not going to remind him. There are more important things for me to worry about.

'Good morning, Martin,' I say as I approach him. 'How are you today?'

He looks up and pouts at me. 'I'm still recovering from a bit of a hangover. After downing over half a bottle of wine with you, I went home and knocked back Christ only knows how many brandies.'

'Oh dear. You shouldn't have bothered coming in.'

He shakes his head. 'Too busy, and anyway I didn't fancy spending the day at home.'

'Well, hopefully it will wear off soon.'

I'm eager to share with Martin the latest developments in the drama that is now my life, but it will have to wait until lunchtime.

Before then, we're both busy. First, there's the editorial meeting, where Ryan informs us that there are no updates on the Larry Spooner story.

'His murder is still being vigorously investigated, but they're no longer looking into his claim that Detective Cain is corrupt,' he says. 'They're happy to accept that Roy McBride is telling the truth about Spooner making it up.'

'So, what next for us, boss?' I ask him.

'I've been thinking about that and I want you and Martin to pull together a feature for Sunday on organised crime in London,' he replies. 'Use Spooner's murder as the peg to hang it on and drum up some more on his background. How did he get involved? What did he do for those he worked for? Maybe his mum can help you there if you eventually manage to talk to her. And include a segment on whether the police are winning the war against the crime gangs.'

'We'll get cracking on it right away,' I say.

Ryan gives me the thumbs up. 'Great. If it turns out as well as I hope it will, then we can spread it across the centre pages.'

The rest of the morning is spent making phone calls, going through our files and searching for information online.

When lunchtime comes, Martin and I retreat to a quiet table in the canteen. But instead of talking about the feature, I tell him about Sean's visit to my house and the note that John Jackman pushed through my letter box.

I'm not sure which of the two incidents shocks him most, but it's the note he wants to talk about after I show it to him.

'I can't believe you're actually giving serious consideration to seeing the guy again,' he says. 'Why the hell would you do that?'

'Because it might offer me a chance to bring this madness to an end sooner rather than later,' I respond. 'I'll be able to spell out to him in no uncertain terms that I'm not interested in a relationship with him.'

'But you've already made that perfectly clear. You've sent him messages and told him to bugger off when he turned up outside your house.'

'I know, but he still won't leave me alone. So, maybe the only way to make him see sense is to explain to him that he's causing me a lot of grief. Encourage his empathy, in other words, and point out that if he wants me to be happy, then he needs to leave me alone.'

Martin clucks his tongue. 'Surely having a cosy drink with him in a wine bar would be rewarding his behaviour.'

I shrug. 'He might well see it that way, but it might also do the trick. Look, I've not made up my mind yet, but the more I've thought about it, the more I'm coming round to believing that I should seize the opportunity. It'll be in a public place, so I'll be perfectly safe, and if he makes me uncomfortable, I'll just walk out. But I hope it won't come to that.'

He drinks some of his juice as he thinks about it. Then says, 'Believe it or not, Gem, I'm beginning to see where you're coming from. I actually suspect a lot of women have done the same thing as a last resort. And perhaps it works more often than not.'

'Exactly, and it isn't as if I think John Jackman might be a raving psychopath who will do much more than make a nuisance of himself. He struck me as a nice guy. The perfect gentleman. I just didn't feel that he was right for me.'

'Even nice guys develop obsessions that make them behave out of character. You read about it all the time and their stories are always popping up on Netflix.'

When we finish our lunch, Martin asks me if talking about it has helped me to make up my mind.

'I need to give it some more thought this afternoon.'

'Well, if you do decide to go, I'll be coming along as your wingman,' he says. 'I'm by myself again tonight and I've got nothing else to do. I'll aim to get to the wine bar before seven and keep a protective eye on you. And don't worry, I'll make sure he doesn't realise what's going on.'

'You don't have to do that, Martin. It's a public place and not much can go wrong.'

'It's better to be safe than sorry, Gem. And besides, how do you know he won't follow you home afterwards if he doesn't succeed in charming you into giving him another chance?'

Martin's thoughtful offer bolsters my self-confidence and, in the middle of the afternoon, I tell him that I intend to accept John's invitation. I give him the name and address of the bar and send him John's photo from the dating app.

It doesn't mean I feel perfectly relaxed about it or that I'm convinced it's the right thing to do. But I do believe it's worth a try.

# CHAPTER FIFTY-EIGHT

I make a point of leaving the office at half four so that I can be home by half five. I need time to mentally prepare myself for my 'date' with John Jackman.

Martin assures me that he will be in the bar when I arrive and that affords me a degree of comfort. It doesn't stop me wondering if I'm about to make a huge mistake, though, and my inner voice keeps repeating the same questions. Am I being naïve? Will I be able to convince him that he will never be a part of my life? And is his Mr Nice Guy image just cover for a cold, manipulative womaniser who can't accept rejection?

As if on cue, my heart speeds up when I enter my street. Looking for men lurking behind trees and in the shadows has become an unfortunate habit. But, yet again, I manage to get inside my house without having to deal with any nasty encounters.

The first thing I do after removing my coat is to go into the kitchen and pour myself a glass of wine, which I drain in four gulps.

I'm sure that I've drunk more in the past week than during the whole of the previous month. I remind myself once more that it's something I will have to keep an eye on.

For a while after Callum's murder, I turned to the bottle far too often just to help me get through each day. But I eventually came to realise that it was nothing more than a destructive form of self-therapy and cut back.

The problem is, my body is already rigid with tension and I feel a tightness in my stomach, a fierce apprehension. I need to pull myself together before I go to the wine bar. It means stamping on my emotions, forcing them down, so that I'll be able to present myself as strong-willed and confident.

I don't bother to shower and I make very little effort with my face. Plus, I see no reason to dress to impress. Jeans, jumper and an old leather jacket will suffice.

By half six, I'm on the sofa and psyching myself up with another glass of wine when my phone rings.

Unknown number.

'Hello,' I say.

'Can you talk, Gem,' Alice replies and I'm not at all surprised that it's her.

'Of course. I have to go out in about fifteen minutes, though.'

'I won't keep you that long.'

'How are you?' I ask her.

'I'm okay. Getting ready for my second night here.'

'Any problems?'

'Not so far, but I did have to cut short a phone call I had earlier with Sean. It started off well enough and he pleaded with me to come home, but when I insisted that we were over, he lost it. Started swearing and making threats. And he told me he'd been to your house and you'd threatened to call the police.'

'I did. He doesn't believe you haven't told me where you are.'

'Well, I made it clear to him again. But you know what he's like. The only truth is his truth. I'll call him again tomorrow and hopefully he'll have calmed down by then. I wanted to tell him that I'm going to consult a lawyer, but I didn't get the chance.'

'I'm sure that will please him.'

'He doesn't think I have the guts.'

'Well, you have, Alice, you've just got to stick with it.'

'I intend to and I'm so sorry he hassled you again. But you've got my blessing to have him arrested.'

I don't tell her about the overt threat he made because I don't want her to feel guilty or even be tempted to go back to him for my sake. So, I just tell her that I can handle the situation and then switch the conversation back to her new life in the refuge centre.

We talk for ten more minutes, but I make a point of not telling her what's been happening with John Jackman or that I've arranged to meet him again. I don't want to burden her with my problems. Before the call ends, she gives me her new number and I promise not to share it with anyone.

'We'll get together soon, Gem,' she says. 'Meantime, just look after yourself and let me know if he contacts you again.'

'I will.'

Conversations with my best friend always serve as a sobering reminder that she's facing a much harder time than I am.

I leave the house at ten to seven with adrenaline searing my senses. It's a calm, quiet night outside and not as cold as it has been of late. It makes me wish I was out jogging instead of going somewhere I don't want to go to have a drink with someone I don't want to meet.

It's another example of how my life has gone wildly off course due to the actions and threats of three men who seem intent on drowning me in a sea of anxiety.

As I approach the wine bar, my heart rate triples and I have to pause to regulate my breathing. The nagging voice returns, telling me that I'm being stupid, reckless, and that I should turn around and go back home.

But once again I choose to ignore it and stride towards the entrance with my shoulders pushed back and my head held high.

# CHAPTER FIFTY-NINE

The place is only about half full, so I spot John Jackman the moment I walk in.

He's sitting at the same table we occupied on our first date. He's wearing a dark suit with a light blue open-neck shirt and looks confident, sure of himself. But unlike the moment when I first laid eyes on him, I don't find him at all attractive.

When he sees me, he stands up and waves me over.

As I cross the room towards him, I find the voices and bursts of laughter of the other customers strangely comforting. And so too the presence of Martin, who is perched on a stool at the bar. Our eyes briefly meet, but we don't acknowledge each other.

I can feel the colour infusing my cheeks as I approach the table and I have to swallow down the rock in my throat.

John moves quickly to pull a chair out for me, but I'm glad he doesn't attempt to embrace me or kiss me. He probably knows that if he did it would make things more awkward than they already are.

'You look stunning, Gemma,' he says, and I flinch as his gaze sweeps over me.

I sit down and respond with a faint smile, then notice that there's a bottle of wine on the table along with two glasses.

'Is the wine okay with you or would you prefer something else?' he asks me.

'It's fine,' I reply, and manage to maintain steady eye contact with him.

He fills the glasses while I struggle to make myself comfortable on the chair.

'Cheers,' he says.

We raise our glasses but we don't clink them together. I take a sip from mine and notice then that his features are taut with anticipation.

'I really am grateful to you for coming here, Gemma,' he says. 'I trust it means that you do believe that there's a glimmer of hope for us. You can't possibly know how happy that makes me. I was beginning to think that I'd already lost you.'

His choice of words sparks a surge of anger in me, but I repress it and slowly shake my head.

'That's not what it means, John, so please don't build your hopes up,' I make clear, pitching my voice low so that the other customers can't hear me. 'I came because I want to get through to you that we do not have a future together. I want you to understand that and stop bothering me. Please.'

He responds with a broad smile. 'But you haven't given us a chance. And that's all I'm asking you to do. Let's get to know each other better. Share a few more evenings out. Go to the cinema, the theatre. For a long walk. I'm certain that if we continue seeing each other, then you'll soon feel about me the same way I feel about you.'

I swallow down my irritation and keep my voice measured and calm. 'That is never going to happen,' I tell him. 'I've already explained to you that I don't believe there's a connection between us. You need to accept that and move on. I'm sure it'll be only a matter of time before you meet someone else. Someone who does want to enter into a relationship with you.'

'But I don't want to move on and you're the only woman for me,' he responds. 'Meeting you was the best thing that has happened to me in years. I know it sounds corny, but it truly was love at first sight. Fate brought us together, Gemma, and I don't—'

'Please stop there, John.' I lower my voice even further to a hard-edged whisper. 'Whatever you think or say is not going to make me change my mind. I've thought long and hard about it and although I think you're far more attractive and interesting than all the other guys I met through the dating app, I don't think we're a match.'

He frowns, as though confused. 'Then why did you bother coming here? The truth is, I didn't expect you to. And I made myself believe that if you did it would mean that you were having second thoughts about what you'd done and said to me.'

'Then I'm sorry you thought that. I came to try to reason with you and to stop you harassing me.'

He leans forward and reaches across the table to grab my hand. His grip is uncomfortably firm. 'Don't say that, my love. You don't mean it. I know you don't. You're just scared of commitment. But I promise that if you give me a chance, I'll prove—'

I pull my hand away and slam down my glass, spilling wine over the table. 'That's it,' I snap through gritted teeth. 'I've had enough of this. I should have known that coming here would be a waste of time.'

I rise quickly to my feet, but so does he, and before I can turn and walk away, he moves around the table to block my path.

'No, Gemma. Please don't go,' he pleads, loud enough to draw the attention of everyone in the bar. 'I'm so sorry if I offended you. Just sit back down and let's talk. I've got much more I want to say to you.'

'No. This is going nowhere and you should know that if you carry on stalking me after tonight, then I'm going to the police. And I will also spread the word online that women should steer clear of you. Now, will you please move out of my way?'

His face hardens and I see fire in his eyes. He opens his mouth to respond, but before the words come out, Martin steps up behind him and taps him on the shoulder.

'Get out of the lady's way, you plonker,' Martin says to him.

John spins around and responds with, 'What the fuck has it got to do with you?'

Martin doesn't flinch. Instead, he turns to me and says, 'Go round the other way, Gem. And then let's leave this place before things get out of hand.'

John looks from Martin to me, confusion distorting his features. 'I don't fucking believe it,' he yells as I step away from him. 'You didn't come here by yourself, did you?'

'Just let it go,' Martin tells him, raising his voice. 'You're scaring her.'

He faces Martin again and for a moment I fear he's going to lash out, but he doesn't.

'And who the fuck are you? The boyfriend I didn't know she had? Did you come here together so that you could humiliate me? Is that it?'

Martin doesn't answer and instead turns his back on John and moves towards the door, where I'm about to join him.

John stays where he is, his angry eyes moving between the both of us as two burly members of staff approach him.

'Calm down please, sir,' one of them says. 'We're not prepared to tolerate such behaviour here.'

By now, Martin and I are close to the door and before we step through it, I look back over my shoulder and see that John has fallen silent. He seems completely oblivious to what the two men are telling him, and as he continues to stare at me, his eyes fierce and unflinching.

And then, before I turn away, he mouths a single word that I don't need to be a lip reader to understand.

'Bitch.'

# CHAPTER SIXTY

As we step out onto the street, my face is burning, my heart pounding, and when I speak, my voice trembles with rage and shock.

'Well, that was a big fucking mistake,' I say. 'I just hope I haven't made things much worse for myself.'

Martin places a hand on my back and I try not to imagine what might have happened if he hadn't been there. 'At least you left him in no doubt that he's fighting a losing battle,' he replies.

Before crossing the road, we both look back to see if he's emerged from the bar yet, but he hasn't.

'I'll walk you home,' Martin says.

'There's no need,' I reply, the phlegm ratting in my throat. 'I haven't got far to go. You should head back to your place.'

He shakes his head. 'No way am I letting you go by yourself. I want to be on hand just in case he follows you.'

'Do you think he will?'

'Probably not, but it's best to be safe.'

We're about to turn a corner, and before we do, I look back again and I'm relieved to see that there's still no sign of John.

'I'm sure that once he's calmed down, he'll regret what just happened,' Martin tells me. 'He clearly didn't expect you to react the way you did.'

'And I didn't expect it to be over in just a couple of minutes. But as soon as he started speaking, I realised I'd wasted my time and there would be no reasoning with the guy.'

Martin has never been to my house, so I lead the way and when we get there, my nerves are in tatters.

'Thanks so much,' I say to him. 'I'm not sure I would have known how to have handled it if you hadn't been there. Shall I call you a taxi?'

'There's no hurry. I'll come in and wait for a bit if that's all right. Just so that I'm here if he shows up.'

His voice is calm and reassuring, and I'm comforted by the fact that he's offered to stay for a while.

Once inside, we remove our coats and I take him into the kitchen, where I open the fridge and point to the wine. 'I assume you would prefer this to a hot drink,' I say.

'Absolutely. I had a gin and tonic in the bar and I only managed to get through half of it.'

We go into the living room with the wine bottle and two glasses, and sit next to each other on the sofa. It feels weird to me because it's been so long since I've had a man in my house.

'Nice place you've got here,' Martin comments, but I only respond with a curt nod because there's a thickening in my throat and my gut is fighting waves of nausea. 'It's really got to you, hasn't it?' he says.

'Nothing like that has ever happened to me before,' I tell him. 'It was so embarrassing, as well as disturbing. And I actually thought he was going to hit you when you confronted him.'

'I did too. And part of me wishes he had so that I could have had the pleasure of smashing my fist into his face.'

I can't help but smile. 'You did yourself proud, Martin, and I'm really grateful.'

'I'm just glad I was there.'

I take a long, shaky breath, wishing my heart rate would return to normal, and my mind starts dialling through what happened in the bar.

'Do you really think he believes that you're my boyfriend and we set him up to humiliate him?' I ask.

He shrugs. 'Who knows? I suppose it might have looked like that to him. But, so what? If he now thinks you're with someone else, he's more likely to leave you alone and accept defeat.'

His phone rings then, taking him by surprise, and he wrestles it from his pocket.

After glancing at the screen, he says, 'It's Tracy. I'd better not answer it here because I'll have to explain what I'm doing in another woman's house while she's away.'

He lets it ring out, then puts it back into his pocket.

'Now I really feel guilty,' I say.

He shakes his head. 'Don't be daft. It's not a problem. I just think it's probably best if I explain things to her when she's back tomorrow.'

I drink some more wine, hoping it will ease my nerves, and then get up to look through the window.

'There's nobody out there,' I say. 'John lives in Brixton. I should imagine he's on his way there by now.'

Before sitting back down, I top up our glasses with more wine.

'Why don't you take tomorrow off?' Martin suggests. 'Do something to take your mind off this and all the other stuff you're dealing with. I'll explain things to Ryan and crack on with the organised crime feature.'

'Being at work takes my mind off it,' I tell him. 'And please don't mention any of this to Ryan. I don't want him or anyone else to know about it.'

There's a weighty silence between us for almost a minute before Martin breaks it with, 'I'm happy to stay here for as long as you'd like me to, Gem. But if you want to go to bed, I'll make a move.'

I'd be more than happy for him to remain here all night, in the spare room of course, but it wouldn't be right. We're close, but not that close. And he does have a girlfriend.

'You should go,' I reply. 'I feel safe here, and even if John does turn up, I won't be letting him in. We could both do with an early night.'

He uses his Uber app to summon a cab and while we wait for it to arrive, I thank him again for being there for me.

'You went above and beyond tonight, Martin, and I won't forget it.'

The cab arrives within five minutes and before he leaves the house, he gives me a hug and I put my arms around his waist. It feels good, comforting, and once again it occurs to me how nice it would be to switch places with Tracy.

* * *

After he's gone, I go and make myself a hot chocolate in the hope that it will help me to sleep. I sit in the kitchen to drink it and run through in my head all that happened this evening.

Turns out my inner voice was right when it tried to persuade me not to go to the bar. How I wish I had listened to it.

John's response to what I told him was most certainly out of order, but despite that, I do feel a smidgeon of sympathy for him. I just wish I could have explained to him that Martin is not my boyfriend and that we didn't go along to try to humiliate him.

I could send him a message or email to point that out, but I'm sure it would be a bad idea.

No, I'll just let it be and hope that he starts looking elsewhere for the love of his life.

I finish the chocolate and go upstairs. My bed beckons, but when I eventually slip beneath the duvet, it still feels as though my heart is trying to break its way out of my chest. So I know that it'll be a while before I'm able to drop into the icy embrace of oblivion.

## CHAPTER SIXTY-ONE

**JACKMAN**

He's been home for over an hour now and the fury that's engulfing him is still all-consuming.

He's angry with Gemma Morgan, but also with himself for being stupid enough to believe that inviting her for a drink would be a good move as part of his charm offensive.

It backfired spectacularly and his dreams of a future with her have been shattered.

But perhaps that's a good thing because he's discovered that she's not the woman he thought she was. This evening in the bar, she revealed her true colours. She's cold, vindictive, manipulative.

There's no question in his mind that she must have known that agreeing to join him for a drink would make him believe that his persistence had paid off. That she was still interested in having a relationship with him.

But, instead, it seems that she accepted his invitation so

that she could cruelly put him down, label him a stalker and humiliate him in front of a room full of people. She even threatened to make him an object of derision on the internet.

And, to top it off, she turned up at the date with another man. Most probably someone she's been seeing all along. Another guy from the dating app. The prick she dumped him for.

He can only assume she did it to get her own back on him. To punish him for going to her house, for sending her those messages, for expressing his undying love for her.

When the pair of them rushed out of the wine bar, he was tempted to follow. He held back because he knew he would probably do something that he'd come to regret.

But that doesn't mean he's going to let her get away with what she's done.

He had offered her his heart and soul and he would have gone to the ends of the earth to have made her happy. And not just for her sake, but for his own too.

What happened to her fiancé Callum was a tragic event. But she was the real victim. And after he was matched with her on the dating app, he saw an opportunity to ensure a better and brighter future for both of them.

But the bitch has scuppered that well-intentioned plan and left him feeling hurt, disconnected and miserable. What makes it much worse is that he hasn't suddenly stopped loving her because of it. And he's as sure as he can be that he always will.

And that means he'll have to decide what to do about it.

# CHAPTER SIXTY-TWO

**GEMMA**

I'm up early again on Friday morning and move around the house in a sleep-deprived mist.

It was another not very comfortable night during which my mind kept replaying what happened in the wine bar.

I briefly consider taking the day off as Martin suggested, but the prospect of sitting around doing nothing leaves me cold.

At the office, I'll have plenty to keep my brain active. Pulling together a feature on organised crime in London is right up my street. It's an issue that has always intrigued me because the activities of the various gangs have had such a detrimental impact on the capital. So many crimes can be attributed to them – murders from shootings and stabbings, drug peddling, people trafficking, corruption, fraud and grand-scale money laundering.

Our article will benefit from having Larry Spooner's

murder to hang it on. The investigation into it is progressing. Speculation as to who did it is rife on social media. Was he shot by a rival gang as part of a turf war? Or was he killed on the orders of his own gang leaders who found out that he was about to expose a corrupt copper on their payroll?

All the elements are there to make it a riveting centre-page spread this Sunday.

I try to focus on it on my way to the office, but it's not easy because so many other thoughts are dancing around in my head. The encounter with John Jackman in the bar. The threat from Sean Kelly, who believes I persuaded his wife to leave him. The not knowing if one or maybe both of them will be waiting outside my house again when I return home this evening.

And, of course, I can't ignore the possibility that Detective Cain will do more than just complain about our handling of the Spooner story and his wife's disappearance.


I'm one of the first in the newsroom and waste no time getting started by checking my emails and the stories that have come in overnight.

There are two that broke after the morning-paper deadlines. A young man was stabbed to death outside a nightclub in Camden and a woman was raped and beaten by two men who broke into her home in Stratford.

Why do most days seem to start with such sad, shocking news? I ask myself. And how long will it be before moving to London comes with an official health and safety warning?

Martin arrives slightly later than he usually does and comes straight over to my desk.

'Did you manage to get a good night's sleep?' he asks me.

I shrug. 'Four hours at the most, but it was enough.'

'And I take it that Jackman didn't turn up uninvited.'

'If he did ring the bell, I didn't hear him. But I'm sure he didn't.'

'Then fingers crossed that you've seen the last of him. What about the other loony? Your friend's husband.'

'I forgot to tell you that she spoke to him yesterday and told him that I don't know where she is. Hopefully it will now sink in and he'll stop pestering me.'

I'm not convinced he will, though, and that's why I know I'm going to find it hard, if not impossible, to relax.

At the editorial meeting, Ryan informs us that Detective Cain has lodged a formal complaint with the press watchdog, accusing us of invading his privacy and seeking to undermine his professional integrity. And the document he's submitted mentions me by name.

Ryan tells me not to worry and offers his backing, then adds, 'He wants to scare us into staying away from him. And we will, but only if nothing else comes to our notice that suggests he's not the honest cop he wants everyone to believe he is.'

Ryan goes on to say that Cain is still being targeted by online trolls who refuse to accept that he had nothing to do with his wife's disappearance.

'The interview he did with us and several other papers obviously hasn't convinced them that Mrs Cain just walked out on him,' he explains.

As soon as the meeting ends, me and Martin get to work

on the organised crime feature. It's a real team effort. We discuss the shape it will take and the facts and figures that will be included. He picks the brains of various people over the phone while I begin typing it up.

Mid-afternoon, he draws my attention to news of a forthcoming BBC documentary on the criminal gangs who are operating in London's prisons. It'll reveal that thousands of inmates are linked to well-established organised crime syndicates and that gang-related violence in the prisons has reached an all-time high.

'Take a look at the list of cases that will get a mention,' Martin says. 'It includes the guy charged with murdering your Callum.'

I tense as I read the name Chris Tate.

There is no picture, only a few paragraphs describing how, three years ago, he was pushing drugs on behalf of a South London gang when he was charged with the murder of an innocent dog walker on Wandsworth Common. While on remand in prison, he got into a scrap with a villain who worked for a rival gang and was stabbed to death.

The documentary will use it as one of several examples of how the various gangs have been waging war for years in the prisons and the authorities have failed to get things under control.

'I wasn't wrong to show it to you, was I?' Martin asks me. 'I did wonder if I should.'

I smile and shake my head. 'Not at all. I've grown used to coming across such things. But I don't think we'll refer to Tate in our piece, although I will include a line on how organised crime has infiltrated our prisons.'

We continue working on the feature for the rest of the afternoon and it's almost finished when I leave the office at the end of the day. Tomorrow morning we'll knock it into shape and pass it to Ryan for approval.

My mind is reeling when I arrive home, but I still remember to steel myself for any unwelcome surprises as I approach the house.

There are none, thank God, so I'm indoors just after eight and still in one piece.

I've already decided to go for a jog before I settle down. It will do me good and hopefully release the tension that has built up inside me.

Thankfully, it's still dry outside when I set out fifteen minutes later. The streets are quiet and soon my heart is beating faster and I can feel my stress levels start to drop.

I keep it up for about half an hour and it's all going well until I'm heading back home.

That's when I suddenly hear footsteps behind me, but before I have time to stop or turn around, I receive a sharp blow to my upper back that sends me flying forward.

I instinctively raise my hands to shield my face as I fall heavily onto the pavement. I manage to roll onto my side and a cry erupts from my throat.

Then I look up and a cold panic tightens in my chest when I see a figure looking down at me.

Black Puffa jacket with the hood up. Black face mask like those we all wore during Covid. And black gloves.

There's no question in my mind that it's a man.

I open my mouth to scream, but he stops it coming out

by kicking me hard in the stomach. The pain is excruciating and it forces me to shut my eyes.

Before I can open them again, more blows are raining down on me. My head. My face. My chest. My shoulders. He's punching, kicking, grunting like an animal.

I try to fight back by lashing out blindly from my position on the ground. I grab his leg. His sleeve. But all I manage to do is rip off one of his gloves.

Pain and sheer terror quickly render me helpless and I fear that I'm about to die.

But then, just as suddenly as it began, the beating stops and I'm conscious of my attacker fleeing the scene.

Seconds later, I know why, when I hear loud voices approaching.

## CHAPTER SIXTY-THREE

'Oh my God. We saw you being attacked. But you're safe now. My husband is calling for an ambulance. And the police.'

My head and body are throbbing and my vision is blurred, but I can hear the woman's voice. She's kneeling on the pavement next to me, her hand resting gently on the top of my head.

'The bastard ran away as soon as he heard us,' she continues. 'Can you speak to me?'

I take a breath that turns into a cough and utter something that even I don't understand.

'Don't worry,' the woman says. 'Just try not to move.'

I hurt all over, especially across my chest and back where he kicked me. He used his fists on my face and head, but I managed to deflect most of the blows with my hands and arms.

I'm a right mess, I know, but I also know that I'm lucky. Very lucky. If this woman and her husband hadn't seen me being attacked, then he might still be laying into me.

My mind is too scrambled to make any sense of it, but I'm

already wondering if it was a random attack. Or was I targeted for a reason by someone who wanted to hurt me?

Or kill me!

The woman is speaking to me again, but I'm no longer listening to what she's saying. My pulse is hammering against my temples and I feel like I'm going to be sick.

I do manage to cling to consciousness, though, and after what feels like an eternity, I hear an approaching siren.

The police arrive first. Two uniformed officers. Both male. They quickly assess the situation, including the extent of my injuries.

'Are you able to sit up?' one of them asks me.

By now, the shock has worn off slightly and my brain is less foggy. I tell him that I can and the two of them set about easing me into a sitting position. The pain eats into me and I cry out.

'An ambulance will be here soon,' the same officer says. 'Am I right in assuming that you were jogging when you were attacked?'

I nod. 'Yes. He . . . he came at me from behind. Pushed me onto the ground and started kicking and punching me.'

'So, it was definitely a man?'

'I'm certain of it. He was . . . he was all in black and wearing a face mask.'

'We've had a description from the couple who disturbed him. Fortunately, they live close by and were on their way home. They're also convinced it was a man.'

'I need to thank them.'

'There'll be time for that. Now, I don't suppose there's any way you can identify your attacker?'

I shake my head and it ignites an explosion of pain. 'I didn't see his face. And I don't know who it was.'

The officer is helping to support me with one hand on my shoulder. He now uses his other hand to dab at my forehead with a tissue.

'It's a cut,' he says, and I see blood. 'But I think you were lucky. Your injuries could have been much more serious. We will do . . .'

His voice is suddenly drowned out by the sound of another siren.

Within minutes, a paramedic takes his place and quickly concludes that my injuries are not life-threatening.

'But we will need to get you to hospital,' he tells me. 'Are you able to stand up or will you need a stretcher?'

'I can stand, I think.'

He helps me to my feet, but it's a struggle and every part of my body screams with pain.

'We'll come to the hospital shortly,' the police officer tells me. 'But first we'll take a statement from the couple who scared your attacker off and check to see if he's left any evidence behind. We'll also be assigning the case to a detective.'

It takes two paramedics to get me to the ambulance, and on the way, I get a chance to thank the couple. They look to be in their late fifties and they both wish me well.

In the ambulance, I learn that I have a swollen face, black eye and cut forehead, plus bruises and swellings to other parts of my body. But I won't need any stitches in the head wound apparently. My lungs feel like they're on fire and I'm having to blink back hot tears.

The paramedic asks me if there's anyone who needs to be contacted and I tell him no, at least not right now.

It makes me think of my mobile phone and I shove my hand in my pocket to see if it's still there. It is, which comes as a relief.

'Did your attacker steal anything from you?' the paramedic asks.

'No, but maybe he would have if he hadn't had to run away. I had my phone with me, but I never take my purse when I go running.'

I'm taken to St Thomas' Hospital and whisked into the emergency department, where I'm given medication to ease the pain. I have to strip off so that I can be examined and some X-rays are taken of my head and chest. But no broken bones are found and they're confident that I haven't suffered any internal injuries.

It's then that I get to see myself in a mirror and my bloated and bruised face makes me shiver. The cut on my forehead is just over an inch long but is no longer bleeding. There's a dark, ugly patch beneath my right eye and my bottom lip is swollen. But at least my features are still intact.

I'm told that I will have to be kept in overnight, though, and I'm asked again if anyone needs to be informed.

I would like to let Martin know, but Tracy's back home with him tonight, so I don't think it would be a good idea. Instead, I give them Ryan's name and tell them I will ring him myself.

I do that before I'm moved to the ward and he's naturally shocked and worried after I explain what happened.

'But it could have been much worse, so there's no need to

panic,' I tell him, even though I'm struggling to stop myself from panicking. 'It's highly unlikely I'll be in tomorrow, though, so Martin will have to finish the feature we're working on.'

'Don't you worry about that, Gem,' he replies. 'Just get better. I'll come and see you first thing.'

'There's no need.'

'Of course, there is. I'd come now if you'd let me.'

'But the police will be here soon to ask me more questions and then I expect the doctors will give me something to help me sleep.'

'Well, you take care.'

'I will. I'm in good hands.'

'Do you want me to let your parents know?'

'Absolutely not. There's nothing they can do and it will likely cause my mum to have a heart attack.'

I'm moved to a private room instead of a ward to make it easier for the police to speak to me. And while I wait for them to arrive, I have a good cry, the tears burning and streaming down my cheeks.

A nurse comes to console me and with her help, along with a couple of sleeping tablets, I eventually manage to drop off.

But just three hours later, at four o'clock on Saturday morning, I'm nudged awake again so that I can be interviewed by the police.

# CHAPTER SIXTY-FOUR

'I'm Detective Sergeant Fenwick, Miss Morgan,' he tells me. 'I've been assigned to try to find out who attacked you. I'm sorry I couldn't get here any sooner and that we've had to wake you up. I needed to go to the scene first and be briefed by the uniforms who attended. Are you feeling up to answering some questions?'

He's fortyish and well over six feet tall, with narrow features and scruffy brown hair. There's a uniformed officer standing behind him. Female, and about ten years younger.

'I'm fine to talk,' I tell him. But that's not strictly true, because my throat is tight and I'm struggling to get air into my lungs.

He begins by asking me if I live alone and what I do for a living. When I tell him I'm a print journalist, it piques his interest and he wants to know which paper I work for. I suspect he's wondering if I've written something that upset someone.

'What I know is that you were out jogging when you were

attacked from behind by a man wearing a black hood and mask,' he says. 'After you fell to the ground, he started to beat you. But he fled when a couple who were passing by saw what was happening and shouted at him.'

I nod. 'I hate to think what he would have gone on to do to me if they hadn't been there.'

'I gather you're not able to describe the man.'

'That's right. I keep reliving it in my mind, but his face was covered up and it was dark. And it all happened so fast.'

'Well, for your information we'll be viewing street-camera footage in the area and I'm sure he'll be on it. The spot was close to your home, I understand.'

'Yes. A couple of hundred yards at most.'

'And do you regularly go out running around the streets in the evenings?'

'As often as possible. But nothing like this has ever happened to me before and I've been doing it for years.'

The detective makes a thoughtful sound in his throat. 'We don't know, of course, if it was a random attack by someone who wanted to rob you or just hurt you. Or if you were picked out for any other reason. Do you know of anyone who might want to cause you physical harm, Miss Morgan?'

And this is when for him it becomes more than just a run-of-the mill street assault.

'As a matter of fact, I can name three men who I'm sure would be delighted to know that I'm in hospital having been beaten to a pulp,' I say. 'The first threatened me only yesterday. The second lost his temper with me on Thursday night and called me a bitch. And the third has accused me of trying to get him sacked from his job.'

DS Fenwick's eyebrows draw together and he looks at me incredulously. 'Are you being serious, Miss Morgan?'

'I'm being deadly serious,' I respond. 'In fact, the first one of them I mentioned also threatened me a week ago and I reported him to the police. So, there will be a record of it.'

He flicks a glance at his uniformed colleague and then back at me.

'Let us hear it then, Miss Morgan,' he says. 'Please explain to us why you're so unpopular.'

I begin with Sean Kelly and tell him about the threats he made to me on the two occasions he came to my house. I recall that it was a PC Matlock who responded to the call so I give him her name.

I then explain the situation with John Jackman and what transpired at the wine bar.

'I don't want to believe that it was him who attacked me, but it could have been,' I say. 'He's roughly the same build.'

'So what about the third man?' he asks.

'Well, he happens to be one of your colleagues on the Force. Detective Chief Inspector Elias Cain.'

His mouth drops open and he's momentarily lost for words. Then both he and his colleague seem completely nonplussed when I tell them that the detective turned on me and my paper after we published the story last Sunday about Larry Spooner's corruption allegation.

'I read that story,' he says. 'So, are you telling us that it was DCI Cain who Spooner named in the call to your office?'

'That's exactly what I'm saying.'

I've let it out without thinking and now I remember that

his identity has been kept secret from most of his colleagues in the Met, as well as the public at large.

Whoops!

More questions are fired at me, thick and fast, and the grilling lasts another half an hour. When it's over, I feel hollowed out, but not in the least bit guilty for suggesting that one of the three men I've mentioned might have attacked me or got someone to do it on their behalf.

Detective Fenwick assures me that all three will be questioned and be asked to account for their movements last night. But before he goes, he tells me that a black leather glove was found at the spot where the attack took place and asks me if I know anything about it.

'It must be the one I pulled off the guy when I grabbed his wrist,' I reply.

He gives a thoughtful nod. 'Well, it's been bagged up and will shortly be delivered to forensics. If we're lucky, there might be one or two fingerprints on either the inside or outside. Or both.'

# CHAPTER SIXTY-FIVE

My head refuses to empty after DS Fenwick has gone and I'm unable to get back to sleep. My whole body continues to ache and I can't get comfortable.

I'm given tea and biscuits by a nurse and more medication to reduce the pain.

A doctor eventually comes to check on me and gets me out of bed to see if all my parts are functioning. My limbs and back are still sore, but I don't find it that difficult to walk along the corridor.

The doctor is pleased with how quickly I'm recovering from the beating, but I won't be discharged until the X-rays have been examined by a radiologist and they're sure I'm fit enough to go home.

I'm sitting up on the bed when, at 7 a.m., I'm told that I have visitors. Minutes later, Ryan and Martin enter the room and the shock is evident on their faces when they see me.

'You should have phoned me last night, Gem,' Martin says. 'I would have come straight here.'

'I only had time to make one call and I knew that Ryan would let you know,' I reply. 'And it's not as if I was on death's doorstep. No bones were broken and the swellings are already starting to go down.'

Martin shakes his head. 'That's not the point. You shouldn't have had to deal with it by yourself. I can't believe it happened. Who do you think did it?'

'No idea. His face was covered up. But I did manage to rip off one of his leather gloves and the police are going to see if he left any prints on it.'

A guilty look suddenly flashes on Martin's face and he says, 'I've told Ryan that you've been having problems with a couple of blokes, Gem, and that one of them made threats against you. I'm sorry, but it just came out.'

'Don't worry about it,' I respond before turning to Ryan. 'Martin was the only person I confided in because I didn't want it blown out of proportion. But in view of what has happened, I was going to tell you this morning. And I've already gone through it with the police.'

Ryan pats me on the shoulder. 'Whatever trouble you've been going through, Gem, you've done a bloody good job concealing it. But, look, could the guy who threatened you be the one who attacked you?'

'I don't know. The police are going to speak to him, along with the other two.'

'Two! For fuck's sake, Gemma, what's been going on?'

And for the second time this morning, I tell my story of the three men who, for different reasons, have been making me feel so ill at ease.

Ryan already knows that Detective Cain has been critical

of me and that he believes I want to damage his reputation. So, it's what he learns about Sean and John that makes his eyes pop out.

'I can see why you've been so unsettled by it,' he says. 'One guy stalking you while another one threatens you. I just wish I had known.'

I shrug. 'There was nothing you could have done. They were my problem to deal with and they came out of nowhere just when the Spooner story broke, which meant that Detective Cain was added to the mix.'

Ryan pulls in a heavy sigh. 'This is the sort of story we'd be drooling over if it didn't involve one of our own. There's a high-ranking copper who might be corrupt. An abusive husband who fears losing control of his wife. A stalker obsessed with someone he's only just met. And, of course, a decent, attractive woman who appears to have made enemies of all three.'

I smile weakly. 'I appreciate the compliment, Ryan, but don't even think of asking me if I'm prepared to let you put it out there with my name on it. Because I'm not.'

He pats my shoulder again. 'Fear not, Gem. That didn't even enter my mind.'

'Yeah, right!'

Martin then tells me that he'll finish off the organised crime feature and Ryan confirms that it will run across the centre pages.

'You don't have to worry about any of that, Gem,' he says. 'Just worry about yourself.'

'I will, boss.'

Ryan then expresses concern about how safe I'll be after I leave the hospital.

'We can always find you somewhere else to stay,' he tells me. 'A hotel maybe.'

It's something that hasn't yet occurred to me and there's a sudden tightness in my chest. But I decide to play it down.

'I'll be perfectly safe at home,' I tell him. 'I can't let what's happening turn me into a scared rabbit.'

They both have to leave after an hour to work on tomorrow's paper and I promise to let them know if and when I'm discharged.

But I'm not left alone for long. Another nurse comes to take me to the bathroom, where I use the loo and have a shower.

After that, I'm by myself for a while and I just lie there on the bed, white noise filling my mind.

At one point, I have a sudden, intense flashback of the masked man aiming punches at me and it takes my breath away.

My head continues to ache despite the medication and I feel so painfully lonely and helpless. I blink away tears that well up, but they keep on coming.

It's not until four o'clock that I'm given the all-clear and told that I can go home. Nothing untoward showed up on the X-rays and the doctors are confident that I will bounce back pretty quickly.

Just as I'm getting ready to leave the hospital, DS Fenwick pays me another visit. He wants to see how I am and bring me up to date with the investigation into the attack.

'It didn't take me long to trace and interview the three men whose names you gave me,' he says. 'They all denied it was them who attacked you and they appear to have concrete alibis. Detective Cain was at a female friend's house in Rotherhithe and she confirmed that to us. Sean Kelly was working late at his office and he was with several colleagues. And John Jackman was in his local pub by himself between eight and ten. I had someone check the CCTV there and he's on it.'

'But any one of them could have paid someone to do it for them.'

'That is possible. Or it could mean that you were attacked by a total stranger.'

'Then why be so brutal about it? He knew I was out jogging and so I wouldn't have had much of value on me.'

A shrug. 'You must know yourself, Miss Morgan, that women are assaulted on our streets every single day for no good reason. And those out running by themselves in the dark make for easy targets.'

'What about the glove I snatched?'

'It's still with forensics. These things can take time. And please bear in mind that if your attacker does not have a criminal record, his prints won't be on the database.'

He then asks me if anyone is picking me up to take me home and when I tell him I was about to arrange for a taxi, he offers to give me a lift.

On the way home in an unmarked police car, he takes the opportunity to go over some of the ground he's already covered, but most of the questions relate to what Larry Spooner said to us and the conversations I've had with Detective Cain. That doesn't surprise me since it's obviously a hot topic inside the Met.

When we arrive at my house, there's no danger of me being

confronted by anyone, and Fenwick gets out of the car to watch me walk up to my front door before getting back in and driving away.

Once inside, I go straight upstairs and start to fill the bath. I pour in some Epsom salts before shedding my badly stained running top and leggings.

I intend to have a long, hot soak in the hope that it will soothe my sore muscles and help to destress me.

I feel bereft, empty of everything, and my mind almost hurts from exertion. Try as I might, I can't ignore the gnawing fear that's growing inside me. If my attacker was not one of the three men who have been causing me so much angst, then who was he? And will he strike again?

If it was a random attack by a vicious predator who was prowling the streets, then he just got lucky when he saw me jogging. But what if he wasn't? What if it was a pre-planned assault by someone who'd been following me for some time, and seized the opportunity when it came to cause me harm?

These are among the questions that are making it so hard for my mind to settle, and even after thirty or so minutes in the bath, my nerves are still as taut as guitar strings.

When I get out, I dry myself off, slip on my dressing gown and make myself a cup of tea. I then send a text to Ryan and Martin to let them know that I'm home, feeling much better and about to go to bed. I also give them the news that Sean Kelly, John Jackman and Detective Cain are no longer potential suspects in the attack because they all have alibis that the police have checked.

They both reply within seconds to tell me that they're thinking of me and will call tomorrow.

I pop a sleeping pill and wash it down with the tea. Then, before going upstairs, I decide to check all the downstairs doors and windows to make doubly sure they're all locked.

And that's when I notice that another hand-delivered envelope is lying on the doormat. It wasn't there when I arrived home so it must have been put through the letter box while I was in the bath. And I don't doubt that it's from John Jackman because yet again my name is written on it in neat black letters. Fear clutches at my stomach because it means he knows that I'm back from the hospital.

I tear it open with trembling fingers and find a get-well card inside. The inscription reads: *Wishing you a speedy recovery.* Beneath it, John has scrawled a message:

*I heard from the police that you were attacked in the street and spent the night in hospital. I'm so sorry, Gemma. But why tell them that you thought that it might have been me who did it to you? I would never harm you even though you've treated me so cruelly.*
   *Love always,*
   *John xxx*

# CHAPTER SIXTY-SIX

**JACKMAN**

He's only had a few snorts of coke, but he feels as high as a kite.

He took a huge risk driving to and from Gemma's house in this state to deliver the get-well card, but it was worth it. He wanted her to know that he hasn't lost interest in her and that he's none too pleased that she sent the police to his home.

He'd been tempted to ring her doorbell and confront her, but resisted because he knew it would have been a mistake. He's already made plenty of those lately.

The first was convincing himself that he and Gemma must have been matched on the dating app for a reason. The second was to allow himself to fall in love with her against his better judgement. And the third was to walk into the trap she set for him at the wine bar.

He's been so fucking foolish, so misguided. And not for the first time it's all gone wrong because he listened to his heart rather than his head.

And now he's at risk of slipping back into his old habits and becoming the drug-addled pisshead he used to be.

The first significant warning sign was going to a dealer he knows earlier today and purchasing a gram of cocaine. It's the first time in almost two years that he's resorted to drugs to stop his mind from imploding. It's made him realise that he needs to get a grip and regain control of his emotions before he's once again at the mercy of the demons that have created so many problems for him throughout his life.

## CHAPTER SIXTY-SEVEN

**GEMMA**

The ringing of my phone snaps me awake at eight o'clock on Sunday morning.

I'm amazed that I actually managed to sleep for so long – at least six hours after eventually dropping off – and I put it down to pills and pain medication.

It's Ryan on the line and he gushes an apology when he realises that he's woken me.

'I've been up for so long myself that it didn't occur to me to check the time,' he says. 'But I'm so glad you managed to get a good rest. How are you feeling?'

'Still pretty poorly, but I reckon that's a result considering what happened.'

I don't bother to tell him about the card that John Jackman slipped through my door, and when he kindly offers to come and see me, I tell him not to bother as I plan to spend most of the day in bed.

'In that case, I'll let Martin know,' he replies. 'He said he was hoping to drop by.'

'Thank you. How's the paper looking?'

'Really good. And your feature is a belter.'

'I'll check it online so that I don't have to go out.'

'Just so you know, we and several of the other papers are mentioning the attack on you. But don't worry, the police haven't released your name, so it's not out there, and it goes without saying that we won't.'

I tell him that all being well I'll be coming to the office tomorrow and he says not to worry if I'm not up to it.

After we end the call, it takes me just minutes to pull up the story of the attack online. It's included in several news feeds and not much is made of it because it's the type of crime that happens far too often and I wasn't beaten to death.

*The Sunday News* version is more or less replicated on the other sites with a similar headline.

## SAVAGE ATTACK ON FEMALE JOGGER

A woman was attacked and badly beaten last night while jogging along a street in Balham.

Her identity hasn't been revealed, but it's known that her attacker fled when two people saw what was happening and called out.

The victim, in her late twenties, was rushed to hospital, where she was treated for a number of injuries. It's understood the attacker was wearing a hood and mask.

I'm so used to reading and writing stories about victims of crime that I can barely believe that this one is about me.

I have a quick look at the organised crime feature, but decide I would rather read it in the actual paper. If I walk to the shop, it will give me a chance to get some fresh air into my lungs and see how well my battered body can function.

I don't bother to shower, but I do cover the cut and bruise on my face with a thick layer of make-up. And I put on a hat to conceal my unwashed hair.

It's a dull day outside, the colours muted and pale, and when I start walking, the pressure hurts my thighs and back. And there's a dull, deeply embedded ache behind my eyes. But within an hour I'm back home and grateful to sit down.

I'm really pleased with what Martin and me pulled together and I'm sure the feature will appeal to our readers. After skimming through the rest of the paper, I make myself a sandwich for lunch. Having skipped breakfast, I'm feeling quite peckish.

While eating it I get a surprise call from the manager of the care home where Larry Spooner's mother resides.

'I'm ringing to tell you that Harriet is back from hospital, Miss Morgan, and she's happy for you to drop by for a chat at any time,' she tells me.

'That's good news,' I reply. 'Would tomorrow morning be okay?'

'I'm sure it would. Make it after ten and give me at least an hour's notice. I'll make sure she's ready for you.'

'Thanks. And can you tell her that I'm looking forward to meeting her?'

I fire off a message to Ryan to let him know and make it

clear that I want to interview her myself. He responds by saying that's fine and suggests I go straight there from home rather than coming to the office first.

I know full well that talking to the woman might prove to be a waste of time, but whatever light she can shine on her dead son could well be useful when it comes to writing more stories about him.

I spend the next couple of hours sitting on the sofa feeling swamped by a sense of isolation. I even contemplate calling my parents, but decide not to because if I do, I might let slip what's happened and I don't want them to know.

Instead, I close my eyes and imagine Callum sitting beside me with his arm around my shoulders. He's telling me not to worry, and promises not to let any more bad things happen to me. The sound of his voice in my head is so welcome, so comforting, that I find it easy to believe that he's communicating with me from beyond the grave.

My phone rings again just as I feel myself starting to doze. This time it's Alice and her voice is pitched high with concern.

'Oh God, Gem. I'm so glad you've answered. I've only just been told what happened to you on Friday and I didn't know if you were still in hospital.'

'I came out yesterday and I'm doing all right,' I tell her. 'In fact, I've just been for a walk.'

'How badly hurt are you?'

'I've got a black eye and a few bruises. The guy, who was wearing a mask, would have carried on beating me if a couple hadn't spotted him and caused him to run off. How did you find out?'

'I rang Sean to tell him that I'm going to consult a lawyer.

And he was in a rage because the police had been to see him. He said you told them that he might have been the person who attacked you.'

'I gave them several names and his was one of them. And since he had already threatened me, I had no choice but to. But he told them he was at work at the time.'

'Having the cops come calling really upset him. And his mood took another nose dive when I insisted yet again that I wouldn't be coming back. He started threatening me and said he's going to do whatever it takes to find me and when he does, he'll make me wish I had never been born.'

'The man is charm personified,' I say.

'He was when we first got together, but now he's a fucking animal.'

We're interrupted by another call I have come through and when I see it's the number that DS Fenwick gave me, I tell Alice I have to go.

'Hi there, Miss Morgan,' he says and begins by asking me how I am.

'Improving all the time,' I tell him. 'I've been out for a walk and I hope to go to work tomorrow.'

'That's great news. I'm ringing you with another update.'

'Go on.'

'Well, so far, your attacker has not shown up on any of the street cameras in that area, but we do believe we know who he is.'

My heart thunders in my chest and I hold my breath.

'Several fingerprints were found on the glove you snatched from his hand,' he continues. 'We came up with a match on the database. A character named Aaron Gallagher who lives quite close to you in Tooting. He's certainly a nasty piece of work, with form for theft and burglary, and he once did a short stint in prison for assaulting a man in a pub.'

'The name's not familiar to me,' I say. 'Has he been arrested?'

'Not yet. We went to his house, but he wasn't there. His neighbours told us that he lives alone but hasn't been seen since Friday. It could be he's done a runner because he feared his glove would lead us to him.'

'So, what next?'

'We'll keep looking. And if I may, I'd like to send you his prison mugshot. Come straight back to me on whether you recognise him or not.'

The photo comes through on my phone seconds later and shows a man in his thirties or forties with a blunt, square face and bald head. I'm certain I've never seen him before and say as much when I respond to the detective.

Afterwards, I type the name Aaron Gallagher into Google and come up with a few matches. But none of the individuals live in London or look like the guy in the photo.

I then phone Ryan to pass on the name to him, along with the mugshot. He says he'll get someone to see what information they can dig up on him.

The image of the man who attacked me stays in my mind throughout the rest of the day and gives rise to many more questions. But I don't have any of the answers, because as far as I'm concerned, he's a stranger and why he wanted to hurt me is a complete mystery.

# CHAPTER SIXTY-EIGHT

Last night, I dreamt of Callum. He was lying beside me in our bed, telling me to stay strong, that he will always be there to protect me. His voice was soft, his body warm, and the feel of his lips on mine made me cry.

When I woke up, my face was wet with tears, along with the pillow beneath my head.

The dream was so vivid that it's encouraged me to have more belief in myself. To view whatever lies ahead as a challenge and not a threat.

That doesn't mean I can simply will the anxiety out of my mind, though. It's still there this morning, making it hard for me to be positive about the future.

I feel like a dead woman walking as I go from room to room getting ready to leave the house. But at least my movements are not restricted in any way and I'm no longer in pain.

I've showered and dressed and covered the bruise and cut on my face with make-up. I've also had tea and toast for breakfast and caught up with the news on the television. But throughout the morning ritual, the photo of the man who attacked me has kept popping up in my head, sending a hot flush through my veins.

Aaron Gallagher.

All I know about him, apart from his name, is that he has a criminal record, lives in Tooting and was stupid enough to leave his glove at the scene of his crime. He must have been aware when he realised his mistake that prints can be lifted from leather surfaces. And maybe he panicked and fled his home knowing the police would soon turn up.

I just wish I knew why he carried out such a brutal attack on me. And whether he would have beaten me to death if that couple hadn't arrived on the scene.

I wait until just after nine before sitting down to make some calls. The first is to the care home where the manager tells me that she's spoken to Harriet Spooner who is happy for me to come by any time after ten. I then ring Ryan to let him know that I'm well enough to do the interview and that afterwards I'll come to the office.

Next, I call Martin, who sounds relieved to hear from me.

'Are you sure you feel up to working today?' he says. 'It seems too soon. I'll be happy to go and see Spooner's mum.'

'I feel better and I need to keep busy,' I tell him. 'The woman has agreed to see me and it's all arranged.'

'What do you expect to get from her?'

'I'm not sure. But her son's murder is still a hot topic and so it won't hurt to find out more about the guy.'

'Best of luck then. Meanwhile, Ryan tasked me with coming up with more info on the bloke who's believed to have attacked you. Aaron Gallagher.'

'And what have you got?' I ask, then hold my breath until he answers.

'Nothing other than what you've already been told,' he says and I feel a jab of disappointment. 'He's a petty criminal who hasn't made much of an impact on the London crime scene. And the cops are not prepared to give out his full address. But I'll keep plugging away.'

I then call Alice to find out if she's had another conversation with Sean.

'Not yet,' she replies. 'But I will have to ring him again soon. I've just discovered that he's transferred all the money out of a joint bank account.'

'The bastard.'

'I can manage for now, but it's got to be sorted.'

A thought occurs to me and I say, 'Have you by any chance heard of a man named Aaron Gallagher?'

She responds after a beat. 'No. Who is he?'

'The man who attacked me. The police found his fingerprints on the glove I pulled from his hand. He's a known criminal apparently, with a record. I asked if you knew him because he also lives in Tooting.'

'What's his address?'

'The police haven't given it out.'

'Try to find out. If he lives near our house, I can ask around. I may have moved out, but I can still get in touch with the few people I know in the area.'

The final call I make is to summon a taxi to the Comfort Care Home in Camberwell, where Larry Spooner's mother is waiting to speak to me.

\* \* \*

When I get there, the manager warns me not to expect too much from Mrs Spooner.

'Harriet is a lovely lady, Miss Morgan, but she suffers from various health problems, including a mild form of dementia,' she says. 'She often gets confused and has frequent lapses of memory, particularly when it comes to remembering recent events. So, you'll have to bear with her.'

'That's not a problem.'

One of the carers shows me to Harriet's room and when we enter, she's sitting on an armchair staring out the window.

'Your visitor is here, Harriet,' the carer tells her. 'It's Miss Morgan from the newspaper.'

Harriet immediately turns and when she sees me, her face breaks into a smile. 'You're the reporter who wants to write something about my son,' she says, her voice low and croaky.

'That's correct, Mrs Spooner.'

'Then come and sit next to me. And call me Harriet.'

The room is quite small and as well as the armchair, it contains a single bed with bedside cabinet, a wardrobe, chest of drawers and dressing table.

The carer pulls out a chair from under the dressing table and places it in front of the armchair. 'I'll leave you two to get acquainted then,' she says and steps out of the room.

Harriet is a diminutive woman with a bush of grey hair and wrinkles carved into her face. She's wearing a thick jumper and a pair of loose trousers, and on her lap rests a framed photo of her dead son.

'Thanks for seeing me,' I say as I perch myself on the chair. 'And let me start by offering my condolences. I'm so sorry for your loss.'

324

'It still hasn't sunk in,' she responds and holds up the photo for me to see. 'Larry should not have died before me. He had so much of life to look forward to. And despite what people say about him, he was a good person who sadly made the mistake of following in his father's footsteps. You see, my late husband never walked a straight line and Larry chose to go down the same path. That's why he ended up in prison. He mixed with the wrong people. People like the Hagan brothers, who encouraged him to do bad things. The reason I agreed to speak to you, Miss Morgan, was so that I could tell you that. And I do hope you include it in whatever you write about him.'

'I'll be sure to do so,' I say. 'How much do you know about what happened to him?'

She rolls out her bottom lip and a deep frown settles on her forehead. 'He was either stabbed or shot while walking home from the pub. I can't remember what they told me. All I know is that I will never see him again.'

Tears gather in her eyes and she draws in a tremulous breath.

'Are you aware that he contacted my newspaper just before he was killed?' I ask her.

She nods. 'I have been told. I gather he was going to reveal something about someone and there's speculation that it could be the reason he was murdered.'

'Were you aware that he was planning to do something like that?'

She shakes her head. 'He would never tell me what he got up to in his job and I didn't really want to know. So, I can't divulge any secrets because he didn't share them with me.

But I can tell you that he would read stories to me and remind me of all the good times we had as a family when he was growing up. I really looked forward to his visits. He came whenever he could after he got out of prison.'

'Do you know if he was in a relationship?'

'He was before he went to jail. I can't recall her name, but I know they were together for quite a long time and I had hoped they would get married.'

It doesn't take me long to realise that I'm not going to get much out of Harriet, but I persevere for a while and I learn that her son had once dived into a lake to rescue a young girl who was drowning. He was a big fan of Millwall Football Club and as a boy his ambition was to be a magician.

I then recall that Spooner had visited his mum on the Monday evening, two days before he was shot on the Wednesday night.

'Can you recall how he was when you last saw him and what you talked about?' I ask.

She smiles. 'I certainly can. He told me that he was going to give up the life he'd been leading and get a proper job. I was so pleased. But we couldn't talk about it for long because he was in a hurry and had to go somewhere. I wasn't expecting him that day anyway and it's come back to me now that he dropped by because he wanted to leave a package with me. I'd completely forgotten about that until now. He said he was going to come and pick it up on the Thursday, but that was the day the police arrived to tell me he was dead.'

I lean forward, my interest aroused. 'What was in the package, Harriet?'

'I have no idea. He put it in the drawer over there and I

think he said that if he wasn't able to pick it up, then he wanted me to ask one of the carers to post it for him.'

'So, you don't know who it's meant to go to?'

'He didn't tell me. At least I don't think he did. My memory is not what it used to be, I'm afraid.'

She suddenly hauls herself up off the armchair and crosses the room to the chest of drawers.

'I think he put it in the top drawer,' she says, and pulls out the drawer. After rummaging inside, she tugs out a brown padded envelope. 'Here it is,' she announces, clearly pleased with herself. 'If you hadn't come here today, it would probably have been in there for months. I hardly ever use that drawer. It's full of tops I no longer wear.'

She squints at the address on it and I notice that it also has several postage stamps.

Having read it, she turns to me and says, 'You did tell me that you work for *The Sunday News*, didn't you?'

'That's right.'

She holds the envelope out for me. 'Well, would you believe it? Larry wanted this sent to your paper.'

I feel a shot of adrenaline as I take it from her and see that it's addressed to the editor of *The Sunday News*. And in large capital letters is the address of our London Bridge office building.

I can barely contain my excitement. 'If it's okay with you, Harriet, I'll take it with me and hand it over to the boss myself. It'll save one of the carers having to post it.'

She's already back in the armchair and she waves a hand at me. 'Yes, please do. I'm curious as to what's in it, but I'm sure that if Larry had wanted me to know, then he would have told me.'

I don't stay for long after that because I'm desperate to get outside to open the envelope. No way will I be able to wait until I'm at the office.

I call up a taxi and once I'm in the back, I carefully tear it open.

Inside, there are three photos that make me draw a sharp breath and a sheet of A4 paper inside on which has been typed four allegations against Detective Cain. On the back of each photo has been written a time and date. And sellotaped to one of them is a small computer memory stick.

There's also a typewritten note addressed to the editor, which I have to read twice.

*I planned to hand over this dossier to your paper so that I could explain how and why I pulled it together. I wasn't going to identify myself for obvious reasons and my name doesn't appear anywhere in here.*

*If you've received this in the post, then it means that I'm dead. I'm guessing my pal Roy McBride grassed me up. He's the only person I confided in and I wish I hadn't.*

*I found out six months ago that DCI Elias Cain was on the Hagan brothers' payroll and I set out to get my own back on him for something he did to me some years ago. The bastard has been working for them for about three years.*

*It started after they got one of their sex workers to approach him one night in a casino. She lured him into bed and they were secretly filmed having it off and the tape was used to blackmail him. I managed to get my hands on it because it was on a phone that I borrowed* from someone who was in on it. Cain has been paid well and it's helped him to settle his gambling debts.

Check out the stuff I've pulled together. There's enough on the memory stick to bring the cunt down and I've printed some of it off.

Mr Anonymous

# CHAPTER SIXTY-NINE

When I walk into the newsroom, I'm immediately the centre of attention. All eyes turn towards me and I'm quickly surrounded by concerned colleagues who are surprised to see me and want to know how I am.

I answer their questions and explain that I'm feeling rough, but not incapable of doing my job. But I don't allow myself to be drawn into any long-winded conversations because I'm eager to tell Ryan what I've come up with.

When I finally get to my desk, I shake off my coat and take the padded envelope from my bag.

I've already noticed that Ryan is in his office and on the phone, and I've been told that Martin is in the library searching through files.

The excitement is building inside me and as soon as I spot Ryan putting his phone down, I rush over to his office and let myself in.

'I see you got a warm welcome out there,' he says with a smile. 'And it's good to see you looking like your old self.'

'Not so much of the old, boss,' I tell him as I close the door behind me.

'So, how did it go at the care home?' he asks.

It's my turn to smile as I hold up the envelope. 'Much, much better than I expected because I came across this.'

He looks puzzled. 'What is it?'

'The dossier that Larry Spooner was going to hand over to us,' I say. 'And it changes everything in respect of the corruption story.'

I sit opposite him and place the envelope on the desk in front of me.

'It's probably best if I'm the only one to handle this stuff so as not to contaminate it with so many prints,' I say.

I then explain how, through an extraordinary stroke of luck, it came into my possession. And that I opened it even though it's addressed to the editor because I suspected what was inside.

'It proves that Spooner did gather up various pieces of incriminating information against DCI Cain over a period of six months,' I tell him as I remove the contents of the envelope. 'He then put them all together in here and intended to hand it over to us. His aim, as he explained to Martin over the phone, was to expose Cain as a bent copper for personal reasons. But fearing his gangster paymasters might be tipped off before he was able to deliver it, he took the precaution of leaving the envelope with his mum. He planned to pick it up from her room before heading for the meet with us in Covent Garden on the Thursday morning.

'The envelope is stamped and addressed to the paper, and

his mum was supposed to arrange for it to be posted if he didn't show up to collect it. But she forgot that it was there.'

It's a lot for Ryan to take in and his eyes grow to the size of small saucers as I read out the note from 'Mr Anonymous'.

'Blimey, Gem, this is pure gold.'

'Now take a look at the photos and what he's laid out on that sheet.'

Detective Cain features in all three photos. Two of them appear to be images taken from a secretly filmed video clip. One shows him lying naked on a bed while a young woman, also naked, fondles his erect penis. In another, he's sitting on top of the bed next to the woman and they both appear to be smoking cannabis joints. The dates and times written on the back of the photos reveal that the images were recorded early one evening just over three years ago. And back then Cain was still with his wife.

The third photo was apparently taken just four months ago and shows two men standing next to each other on a quiet street. One of the men is Cain and the other is someone who Ryan and I recognise as gang leader Charlie Hagan. The photo was taken from a distance, most likely by Spooner himself, but you can clearly see Hagan handing what looks like a small envelope to the detective.

'I suppose it's reasonable to assume that this is Cain taking a bribe,' Ryan says.

We turn our attention then to the sheet of A4 paper on which has been listed four allegations against Cain.

- *He tipped the brothers off about a raid that was going to take place on one of their clubs.*

- *He sabotaged court proceedings against a member of the Hagan gang by leaking information that was integral to the prosecution's case.*
- *While working with the Major Crimes Unit, he destroyed evidence that would have led to a gang member's conviction for attempted murder.*
- *And since he's been with the Anti-Corruption Command, he's protected other coppers on the gang's payroll who have come under suspicion.*

'Do you think that this stuff could have been fabricated?' Ryan asks as I slip the memory stick into his computer.

'I reckon it's highly unlikely,' I reply. 'Spooner obviously put a lot of effort into it. He must have followed Cain on occasion and since he was on the inside, he would have presumably been privy to some, if not all, of the services Cain was providing.'

The memory stick contains the video clip of Cain having sex with the woman back when his wife was still with him. It lasts for thirty or so minutes and includes the pair smoking cannabis at the end of the session.

And there are several more photos of Cain together with one or both of the Hagan brothers.

In addition, there's a document that lists the same allegations on the A4 sheet, only this one contains far more details, including names, dates, times and locations.

'We need to get all this copied before we show it to the police,' Ryan says. 'They're not going to be happy. But what does surprise me is that Spooner went to so much trouble to pull it together. He took a huge risk and must have known that it wouldn't just bring down Detective Cain. There's enough here, assuming it can be proved to be true, to put the Hagans themselves behind bars.'

'Well, I'm not sure that Spooner would have cared about that,' I say. 'According to his mum, he was going to give up his life of crime and go straight.'

At that moment, the office door opens and Martin steps in without knocking.

'Is it okay to disturb you guys?' he says.

'Sure thing,' Ryan responds. 'I was actually just about to come looking for you. We've got—'

But Martin cuts him off and says to me, 'I've just heard that the police have collared the bloke who attacked you, Gem. Aaron Gallagher. I don't know the details, but he's apparently in custody and soon to be questioned.'

His words snatch my breath away and I'm only half conscious of Ryan saying, 'Close the door, Martin. We've got some news for you too.'

# CHAPTER SEVENTY

Hearing that Aaron Gallagher has been arrested hits me like a blow and a flash of heat spreads through my body.

This is another huge shock, but a welcome one, and I feel extremely relieved because it means I don't have to worry that he'll be looking to attack me again at some point. It should also mean that I will soon know why he did it and if I was a victim picked at random.

'How did you find out?' I ask Martin.

'From one of my contacts on the Force,' he replies. 'I rang her last night to see if she knew anything about the guy and she said she'd make some enquiries. She just got back to me to say he was arrested early this morning. But she doesn't yet know the circumstances.'

'It's certainly a result, Gem,' Ryan says. 'The detective who interviewed you will no doubt be in touch soon with the good news. Let us know as soon as you hear from him.' Ryan then turns to Martin. 'Pull up the other chair, mate. It's now our turn to surprise you.'

Martin listens in stunned silence as I tell him about the envelope and how it came into my possession. I spread the photos and documents across Ryan's desk and warn him not to touch them.

It's not easy for me to relay all the details this time because there's so much going on inside my head. But Ryan is there to help and it takes only about fifteen minutes to put Martin in the picture, which includes showing him a short extract from the explicit video clip.

After he's taken it all in, he expels a puff of air, and says, 'So, Roy McBride lied when he told the police and us that Spooner was planning to spread a pack of lies about Cain. The only thing that's fake about that porno clip is the woman's screaming orgasm.'

Things move rapidly from then on. I take it upon myself to copy the photos, documents and contents of the memory stick, while Martin begins to research the claims that Spooner makes.

Ryan gets straight on the phone to the police and arrangements are made for them to come and pick up the dossier and speak to me.

He then brings the editorial team together to brief them.

'We won't run anything online until we know how the Met intends to react to it all,' he says. 'But we will delve into the claims that are made and build up a more extensive profile of Detective Cain. If all goes well, everything will be in place to make a massive splash on Sunday.'

It's all very exciting, but before long my brain is aching with the effort of thinking.

* * *

Three plain-clothes police officers from the Met's Anti-Corruption Command – all colleagues of Cain – arrive within the hour. They spend the next hour speaking to Ryan and myself in his office, where I hand over the envelope and its contents and show them a segment of the video featuring Cain having sex.

I explain how I came across the dossier and make it clear that I'm the only person who has handled it apart from Spooner's mother.

The officers are made aware that everything has been copied and they're not happy about that. But short of launching a tricky legal bid to seize it, there's not much they can do.

Ryan is given the name of a senior officer who will act as a contact point between the Met and the paper and we'll be told as soon as possible what action, if any, is going to be taken.

Soon after the officers leave, I receive a call from Detective Sergeant Fenwick, who wants me to know about Aaron Gallagher's arrest. He's surprised to learn that I already know.

'I'm afraid we haven't got anything out of him so far,' he informs me. 'We've told him about the glove and that we've got him bang to rights. But he's been told by his lawyer to go down the no-comment route for now.'

'Where did you find him?' I ask.

'His car was flagged by a number plate recognition camera in Putney. We did some checking and found out that it's where his sister lives. So, uniforms were sent to the house and, sure enough, he was there.'

'Thank goodness for that.'

'I'll keep you abreast of events, Miss Morgan. But instinct tells me that it won't be long before the guy opens up. He's a nervous wreck and clearly doesn't want to make things even worse for himself.'

At four o'clock, Ryan calls me into his office to thank me for turning things around on the corruption story.

'Coming across that dossier was a stroke of luck, boss,' I say.

He shakes his head. 'Doesn't matter. You played a blinder by returning to work so soon after the attack. And now I want you to go home and rest. We've got a busy week ahead of us.'

I'm already limp with fatigue and my thoughts are muddy, so I'm more than happy to leave early.

By the time I get home, my head is falling in and out of a fog, but I'm still alert to the possibility that someone might be waiting for me. Nobody is, though, and relief floods through me.

Soon after I get settled on the sofa with a bowl of chips and a glass of wine, the full weight of the day's events suddenly hits me. I suddenly lose my appetite and feel a headache bloom.

The remaining chips are quickly binned and I swallow a sleeping tablet with what's left of the wine.

Then I go upstairs to bed in the hope that a wave of blackness will soon engulf me.

# CHAPTER SEVENTY-ONE

A crack of thunder wakes me from what was a reasonable night's sleep. Six or seven hours maybe. And it was nightmare-free.

As the morning progresses, I allow myself to believe that the tide might well be turning in my favour. The man who attacked me is in police custody. The detective who keeps questioning my journalistic integrity could soon find himself behind bars. And I've heard no more from my stalker or my best friend's husband who keeps threatening me. Could it be that they've both decided to leave me alone?

I'm also feeling much better in myself. The cut on my forehead is now barely noticeable and it takes just a dab of foundation to make the bruise under my eye disappear.

As soon as I'm ready I practically rush into work so that I can get there early.

There's still a high level of excitement in the newsroom and very few of my colleagues have taken the day off despite it being a Tuesday.

At the first editorial meeting, Ryan tells us that he's had a conversation with none other than London's Police Commissioner.

'He's told me that Detective Cain has been suspended from duty while the contents of Spooner's dossier are being assessed. And he wants us to hold fire on publishing anything until they've decided if there's a case to answer, which he reckons will be within twenty-four hours. It's a reasonable request under the circumstances, so I've agreed to it. Meanwhile, we plough on with pulling things together.'

It's a busy day, but I do find time for a short lunch break with Martin. And it's then that he breaks the news that he and Tracy have decided to call it quits on their relationship.

'We were up most of the night talking about it,' he tells me. 'We both agreed that it's run its course, which is why things have been so difficult between us lately. We clearly want different things in life.'

'I'm really sorry to hear that,' I say. 'How do you feel about it?'

He shrugs. 'Not as bad as I thought I would. It was going nowhere and I now realise that we probably fell out of love with each other a while ago.'

It strikes me that he's bearing up extremely well and I wonder if it's really hit him yet. Maybe one or both of them will have second thoughts when it sinks in.

The news is a surprise to me and I feel a mixture of emotions. It is of course sad that it seems not to have worked out for them, but part of me is pleased that it might give me an opportunity to get to know him better.

'Why don't we have another after-work drink and you can tell me all about it,' I say.

His eyes light up and he nods. 'I'd like that.'

And so at least I now have something to look forward to at the end of what promises to be an intense day.

My task is to add to what we already know about Detective Cain and to start working on a background piece. There's already a wealth of information on file about his career and his missing wife. But I want to find out more about his private life. Has he got more skeletons in the cupboard? Is he addicted to gambling? How often does he take drugs? And was he regularly unfaithful to his wife?

I'm still in the process of building a list of where to go and who to speak to when, at five o'clock, DS Fenwick rings me again.

As soon as he starts speaking, I feel the muscles knotting in my stomach.

'The good news is that we've finally got a confession out of Gallagher,' he tells me. 'He's admitted that he actually went to Balham on Friday evening with the aim of attacking you as you were arriving home from work. But he got delayed by traffic and after parking several streets away, he arrived just as you were setting off on your jog. So, he followed you and picked his moment to launch his attack.'

'But did he say why he wanted to hurt me?'

Fenwick pauses before answering. 'He claims he was paid a sum of money by a friend of his to hurt you as punishment for something you had done.'

The shock takes my breath away and it's a moment before the words come out. 'Who paid him then? Has he said?'

'He claims it was the man who's been giving you such a hard time, Miss Morgan. Sean Kelly. A patrol should be arriving at his house in Tooting about now.'

# CHAPTER SEVENTY-TWO

It feels like I've been gut-punched, and when I come off the phone, I sit at my desk without moving for several minutes. The anger is burning in my chest and my hands are trembling. But I suppose I shouldn't be surprised.

After all, plenty of men become monsters when they don't get their own way and he's obviously one of them. Not content with abusing his own wife, he apparently decided to turn his anger on me because in his warped mind I'm responsible for her leaving him.

I recall what he said to me when he was waiting outside my house as I returned from a jog.

*'If you don't stay away from my wife, I'll take matters into my own hands. And, believe me, you won't be left with just a few bruises.'*

But it seems the bastard was too much of a coward to do his own dirty work.

I'm sure that the tension must be radiating off me in waves as I cross the newsroom to Ryan's office.

The news naturally comes as a shock to him as well and he wants to know more about my relationship with Sean and Alice. He knew nothing about them before I was attacked and I find it uncomfortable explaining how I got dragged into their marital mess.

'Go home, Gem,' he says when I'm finished. 'You need to get your head around all this crap and you won't be able to do that here.'

'I'm planning on going for a quick drink with Martin first.'

'That's a good idea. Take him with you when you go. He's got troubles of his own, so you'll be good company for each other.'

'Then he's told you that he's broken up with his partner.'

He nods. 'Soon as he came in this morning. From what I gather, it's been a long time coming.'

There's one thing I need to do before leaving the office and that's to phone Alice. She answers promptly. 'I was going to call you later, Gem. I've been wondering if there's any news on the bloke who attacked you.'

'Actually, that's why I'm ringing,' I reply. 'He's been arrested.'

'That's good. Let's hope they lock him up for a long time. Do they know why he did it?'

I take a deep, stuttering breath and say, 'He's claiming he was paid to do it, Alice. By Sean. The police have gone to arrest him.'

I hear her gasp. 'Are you serious?'

'Yes, I am. The guy, Aaron Gallagher, told them that Sean wanted me punished for what I did to him.'

'My God, Gem. That's terrible. We both know my husband is a nasty bastard, but I can't believe he would do that.'

343

'The guy has described Sean as a friend apparently. Are you sure you've never heard of him?'

'I'm positive. I know very few of his friends. He could be someone who works for Sean's debt collection agency or even one of the blokes he plays snooker with.'

'Well, the police will want to tell you what's going on. Will they know how to contact you?'

'I'll get one of the support workers here to get in touch with them.'

'And if I hear from the detective, I'll pass on your number.'

Alice starts to respond, but then suddenly breaks down and sobs loudly into the phone.

'Are you okay?' I ask her.

Seconds pass before she can get the words out. 'No, I'm not. This . . . this is all too much, Gem. I'm so sorry for what he did. It's all my fault. I shouldn't have told you what he was doing to me.'

'Don't say that, Alice. This is down to him.'

'Look, I have to go, Gem. I feel sick. But I'll call you if I hear anything.'

And with that, she ends the call.

I tell Martin what Sean has allegedly done before we head for the Rose and Crown. I feel it's only fair that he knows where my head will be when we sit down for a drink.

His reaction is predictably one of shock and outrage.

'So, a guy who abuses his wife blames you because she decided to walk out on him. And then he pays someone to give you a hiding. It's fucking unbelievable.'

'He warned me to stay away from Alice,' I say. 'I took the

threat seriously and called the police. But, other than that, there was nothing else I could do.'

'At least he's come unstuck, Gem. So, let's go and drink to the fact that he no longer poses a threat.'

An hour later, and we're on our second bottle of wine. But I still find it impossible to relax. Too many thoughts are tumbling through my mind and I keep losing track of what we're talking about.

We both try to focus on the positives – Aaron Gallagher's arrest and the fact that Sean Kelly's involvement in the attack on me has come to light. And there's the discovery of Larry Spooner's dossier exposing Detective Cain as a corrupt copper.

But it's not enough to boost our spirits and we both struggle to suppress our emotions. There's a moment when I think Martin is about to cry while talking about breaking up with Tracy. Instead, he pinches his eyes shut to stop the tears from falling and hurries off to use the loo.

It's coming up to half six when we decide to call it a day, but just as I stand up from the table, my phone rings.

The hairs on my neck stir when I see that it's yet another call from DS Fenwick.

'I'm sorry to bother you again, Miss Morgan, but there's something I need to ask you,' he says.

'That's not a problem,' I reply. 'What is it?'

'I wondered if you know how I can get in touch with Sean Kelly's wife, Alice. I'm aware from what you told me that she no longer lives with him, but the number I've got for her is not working.'

'That's because she's got a new phone and she's moved to a Women's Aid refuge. I can give you her number and I've already told her what Sean is believed to have done. Are you going to tell her that you've arrested him?'

'Actually, Miss Morgan, we didn't get a chance to arrest him. I'm afraid the news that I need to pass on to his wife is that he's no longer alive. Officers who called at their home found him dead inside.'

# CHAPTER SEVENTY-THREE

I try to speak, but it's as though the words are sticking to the back of my throat. So, I just hold my phone to my ear with a trembling hand and listen to what else the detective has to tell me.

'It appears that Mr Kelly may have suffered a fatal head injury as a result of falling down the stairs,' he says. 'We believe it happened sometime this morning while he was alone in the house. But it has yet to be determined exactly how long he'd been lying at the bottom of the stairs.'

'It was an accident then?' I manage to utter.

'That's the assumption. There's no sign of a break-in at the house and it seems that nothing has been disturbed. But what I've told you is for your ears only at this stage, Miss Morgan. Please keep it to yourself and hold off on contacting Mrs Kelly until I've broken the news to her.'

After I've sent him Alice's number, I sit back down and say to Martin, 'I need another drink before I go. Would you mind getting me something stronger than wine? A vodka. Double.'

'What's wrong, Gem?' he asks, concern pulling at his features. 'Who was that?'

'I'll tell you when you've got the drink. I need to wrap my own head around it first.'

As I wait for him to return to the table, the blood pounds in my head and my heart feels like it's being squeezed by an iron fist.

In my mind's eye, I see the steep spiral staircase in Alice's house. I've walked up and down it enough times to know that a fall could cause someone serious damage. Alice told me that she stumbled part of the way down it once, twisting her ankle and bruising her chin. Although I now have to wonder if she did actually trip or did Sean have something to do with it.

When Martin arrives back with my vodka, I see that he's got himself a whisky.

'Come on then, Gem,' he says. 'What's happened now? Who phoned you with more bad news?'

I take a sip of vodka before responding. 'It was the detective. He told me that Sean is dead.'

As I tell Martin all that I know, I sense from his expression that he's trying hard not to smile.

'Well, look at it this way,' he says. 'The guy got his comeuppance. Fate made sure that he didn't get away with what he did to both you and his wife.'

Martin then goes on to remind me that hundreds of people in the UK die each year as a result of falling on stairs and thousands more are injured.

I'm not interested in facts and figures, but I do wonder if he's right in saying that Sean got what was coming to him.

And I'm not sure how I feel about it. Am I sad or glad? Maybe I won't know for sure until I've fully processed what has happened.

When we're out on the street, I decide to take a taxi to Balham rather than mess about on the Tube.

While we both wait for cabs to come along, it occurs to me that I haven't asked Martin if he and Tracy will carry on living together for the foreseeable future.

'She's already planning to move out at the weekend,' he tells me. 'She's going to live with a friend in Chiswick. The tenancy agreement on the flat is in my name and I'll stay there for the time being.'

We manage to hail two taxis at the same time and give each other a hug before going our separate ways and I realise how grateful I am to have this wonderful man in my life.

On the journey home, a sense of unreality consumes me. It feels as though I'm trapped in a never-ending nightmare and the pace at which things are happening is scary.

Sean's sudden death is the latest in a series of events that have knocked me for six. It follows the attack on me, the threats, my dating disaster and the pressure of working on an explosive story that has already involved the loss of a life.

And, of course, there's poor Alice, my best friend, whose life has been shattered by her abusive husband. The late Sean Kelly.

I'm desperate to speak to her, to find out how she is, to be a shoulder for her to cry on if she feels the need to cry.

I've made up my mind to call her when I get home because I'm sure that DS Fenwick will have contacted her by then.

But it turns out there's no need because as soon as I close the front door behind me, my phone rings and it's her.

'The detective told me that you know about Sean,' she says when I answer. 'I can't believe he fell down the stairs. It's crazy.'

'I'm really sorry, Alice. How do you feel about it?'

'To be honest, I'm not sure whether to laugh or cry. I know that sounds horribly callous, but he put me through hell and what he did to you was depraved. He deserved to die and I said as much to that copper.'

I can understand her reaction, but I wonder if it will change when reality sets in.

'So, what will you do now?' I ask her.

'I don't know. There's nothing to stop me from going home and I will, but not yet. And I suppose it will be down to me to sort the funeral. He lost touch with his parents years ago. And Christ knows what will happen to his business.'

'You can count on me to help. You know that.'

'I do. And what's your reaction, Gem? Are you relieved that he's gone?'

'Of course, I am. But I wouldn't have wished him to die like that. And I would like to know for certain if he paid that man to attack me.'

'The police are convinced the bloke is telling the truth. The detective told me that Aaron Gallagher did work part-time for the agency. He was called in to collect debts from those who kicked up a fuss.'

'And did the detective tell you exactly what Sean told him to do to me and how much he was paid?'

'He didn't want to, but I got it out of him. He said Sean

gave him several hundred quid to give you a good hiding. Bad enough to put you in hospital, but not to kill you.'

I sigh. 'Then it's hard not to conclude that the bastard is where he belongs.'

We talk for another ten minutes and agree to meet up soon.

'It's safe for me to come out of hiding now,' Alice says. 'And my brute of a husband won't be around to stop you and me from staying friends.'

When I come off the phone, I take a moment to think about what we just said to each other. It was a strange but honest conversation during which we both expressed our true feelings. It's made me realise that there's a glimmer of light at the end of the tunnel.

# CHAPTER SEVENTY-FOUR

On Wednesday morning, my mind dwells on the dream I had last night.

It took me back to the last conversation I had with Callum. It was just before he left our flat to take Sampson on that ill-fated walk across the common. He told me they would be gone for no more than an hour.

'When I get back, let's open a bottle of wine and a big bag of crisps and get stuck into a new series on Netflix,' he said.

'Anything you fancy?'

'You mean apart from my soon-to-be wife?'

I smiled at him. 'Yes, that's what I mean.'

He laughed as he placed the lead on Sampson's collar. 'I thought we had already established that you're in charge of the remote. So, you can choose. But please don't pick anything that's too cheesy or depressing.'

He then took me in his arms and kissed me on the lips. Our last kiss. The last time I looked into his eyes. The last time I was really happy.

The dream takes my mind off all the other stuff that kept me awake for most of the night. And it stays in my head all the way to the office, helping me to beat off the pessimism that's threatening to overwhelm me.

As soon as I'm at my desk, I put in a call to Alice to see how she is. And I'm pleased to hear that she's okay and that DS Fenwick has already visited her in the refuge to explain in more detail what they think happened to Sean.

'He had bruises all over him apparently, including a big lump on his head that they believe was the fatal blow,' she says. 'He probably fell from the very top of the staircase. I asked the detective if he knew why Sean wasn't at work when it happened and he told me that he did go in but then told his colleagues he was going home because he felt unwell. Aaron Gallagher claimed he last saw Sean on Sunday when he was paid for attacking me. '

Alice adds that she's been told that she can go home whenever she's ready to.

'I don't think I can face it yet,' she tells me. 'Maybe if I go in a day or two you can come with me.'

'Of course, I can,' I say. 'I'll ring you later.'

Things start to unfold then at a frantic pace. We learn that the Met has launched a full-scale investigation into the corruption allegations against Detective Cain. Officers have concluded that the evidence provided in Spooner's dossier is far more convincing than they'd expected it to be. They plan to carry out a major search of Cain's home and look into every aspect of his life. It means we can run a story online so long as we don't identify him.

We're also told that café owner, Roy McBride, has confessed to lying when he said that Spooner told him the information that he was going to pass to us had been fabricated.

'I'm told that the cops put a lot of pressure on him,' Ryan says when we're together for the editorial meeting. 'He now claims that Spooner did tell him that the dossier contained genuine information and so he grassed to the Hagan brothers in return for dosh to help keep his café afloat. It's presumed that they arranged for Spooner to be shot. Afterwards, they got McBride to spread the story that Spooner made it all up. He's been charged with perverting the course of justice.'

'What about the Hagans?' someone asks.

'They're being questioned but are denying everything, and they're lawyered up,' Ryan replies. 'But the police are now convinced they did arrange for Spooner to be topped. Whether they will ever be able to prove it is another matter. Probably not.'

Martin and I are told to crack on with the feature on Cain, and Ryan wants me to try to get a statement from the man himself.

I call his private number from Ryan's office and put it on speaker.

To my surprise, Cain answers and, before I can get a word in, says, 'I can guess why you're calling, Morgan. I heard that you're the one who instigated all this bollocks after laying your hands on Spooner's fake dossier. You must be really pleased with yourself. Well, you won't be after I'm cleared and then set my lawyers on you and your fucking paper.'

He hangs up then and Ryan immediately regrets not having recorded it.

Soon after that, DS Fenwick gets in touch with another update.

Aaron Gallagher has been charged with causing grievous bodily harm to me and remains in custody.

So, all in all, it proves to be yet another eventful day. At the end of it, I ask Martin if he wants to go for another drink, but he's got some stuff to sort out with Tracy.

That's fine with me and I head straight home. I actually start to look forward to a long evening chilling out by myself. For the first time in what seems like ages, I feel ready to relax. I'm not being threatened or intimidated, and I'm hoping now that I can soon put this painful period in my life behind me.

And the optimism continues to grow, right up to the point when I walk into my kitchen and turn on the light.

That's when I see that one of the glass panels in the back door is broken.

Dread floods my body, but before I can react, I hear movement behind me. As I start to turn, an arm is wrapped around my neck and a hand that's grasping a large knife is thrust in front of my eyes.

'Good evening, Gemma,' a familiar voice whispers into my ear. 'Did you really believe that I would just let you walk away after all the pain that you caused me?'

# CHAPTER SEVENTY-FIVE

'If you scream or try to get away from me, Gemma, I will cut your throat.'

I freeze as he holds me tightly against him and his boozy breath causes my nostrils to flare.

'Stay calm,' he continues. 'I'm going to take my arm away and hold onto your hair. And then you're going to walk steadily into the living room, where you're going to make yourself comfortable while I spell out some home truths. And be aware that this knife will be barely an inch from the back of your head the whole way. All I need is an excuse to plunge it in.'

My ears pound with a deafening beat as John Jackman takes hold of my hair before removing his arm.

As he pushes me out of the kitchen and into the hallway, he says, 'In case you're wondering, I've been here for over an hour. I called your paper first to check that you were there. I'd already recced the house and so I knew to approach it over the back wall. And then getting in here was easier than

I expected it to be because you made the same mistake that so many people make, which is to leave the key to the back door in the inside lock.'

His words send a rush of terror through me, making it hard to breathe, but somehow, I manage to speak.

'Why are you here, John? What do you want?'

'We've got some unfinished business, Gemma,' he responds calmly. 'I didn't want to do this, but you gave me no choice after the way you and that bloke treated me in the wine bar. You not only signalled the end of our relationship before it had properly got started, but you also totally humiliated me and I'm not going to let you get away with it.'

'But that's no reason to hurt me, John. You must realise . . .'

'There's more to it than that,' he interrupts me sharply. 'A lot more. And it goes way back to the day your now dead fiancé screwed up my fucking life.'

A wave of panic and confusion sends a tremor of alarm shooting through me.

Before I can ask him what he's talking about, I'm in the living room and being pushed down onto the sofa. He's already placed a chair from the dining room in front of it and now he lowers himself onto that.

Then, suddenly, he's facing me, knife in hand, his face dark and intense.

He's wearing a black hoodie and jeans, and a pair of blue latex gloves, which I assume is so that he doesn't leave any prints behind.

'Keep your mouth shut and let me do the talking, Gemma, and don't interrupt me. I've got a lot to say and I don't want to hang around too long because there's somewhere I need to be.'

I feel a cry in my throat, but I'm too scared to let it out. He's sitting about four feet from me and he could stab me in the blink of an eye.

'I'll start where it all began,' he says, and his voice is disturbingly calm. 'It was that night three years ago on Wandsworth Common when both our lives were ravaged by what happened.'

All I can do is stare at him as the blood roars in my head.

'You see, it wasn't Chris Tate who killed your fiancé, Gemma. It was me.'

# CHAPTER SEVENTY-SIX

I feel my mouth open, but say nothing. I can't speak. Can't move. I just sit there staring at John Jackman.

'Back then, I also lived in Wandsworth and at the time I was into drugs,' he says. 'I often went onto the common in the evenings because my dealer hung around there – his name was Chris Tate. I was sitting on a bench minding my own business and waiting for him to turn up when your fella walked by with his bloody dog, which wasn't on a lead. It came right up to me and started barking and growling. I waved it away, but it refused to move, so I stood up and kicked it.'

By now, a cold numbness has enveloped me and my pulse is beating high up in my throat.

'Anyway, your fella then came over and started shouting at me. I told him to fuck off and pushed him when he got too close. He pushed me back and we got into a scrap. We ended up falling on the grass and my hand landed on a large stone. I grabbed it and hit him with it. First on the face and then on the side of the head.

'I didn't realise he was dead until I tried to get him to move and couldn't. It wasn't my intention to kill him, but he was to blame for not keeping control of his dog. I knew it would look like I murdered him, so I scarpered, but not before I used the same stone to stop the mutt from barking at me. I was running from the spot when I passed Chris Tate, but he didn't recognise me because my head was covered.'

His words are like ice sliding down my spine and when I try to speak, he jabs the knife at me.

'I told you not to interrupt. I haven't finished telling my story.'

He pumps out his chest, his gaze eating into me like acid while I sit there cloaked in a red mist.

'Even though I didn't mean to kill him, I've struggled to live with the guilt and it broke my heart when I watched you give a grief-stricken interview with a TV reporter,' he goes on. 'But I didn't have the courage to give myself up, not even after Tate was charged with Callum's murder. And it came as a relief when he was killed in prison because it meant that there wouldn't be a trial. But at the same time the guilt became more intense, and I found it hard to live with myself.'

There's a question I need to ask and I can't keep it in despite his threat.

'But why the hell did you contact me on the dating app if you knew who I was?'

To my relief, he responds with a shake of the head. 'When I saw your photo, it was a real shock. But I felt compelled to meet you out of curiosity. I wanted to see how you were coping. When we shared those messages with each other, I became even more curious and I convinced myself that one way to assuage my guilt would be to do whatever I could to make you happy. And then we met and from that moment I knew I wanted to spend the rest of my life with you. But then you rejected me. I sincerely believed that if I didn't give up, I'd eventually win you over. But you weren't prepared to give us a chance, so it's your fault that it's come to this. First your fella fucked up my life and now you have.'

Everything inside me has turned cold and my heart is banging against my ribs.

'Why did you come here, John?' I ask him. 'What are you going to do with that knife?'

His eyes are bulging now, nostrils flaring, and I try to brace myself for what's to come.

'I'd have thought that was obvious, Gemma. I didn't come to the decision lightly. I took today off work to think it through, and as you've probably guessed by now, I've had quite a bit to drink. But the thing is, you're in my head and in my heart, and I now realise that there's no way I can move on with my life knowing that you're alive but not with me. I won't be able to function if I have to keep wondering where you are and who you're with.'

He gets quickly to his feet and pushes back his chair.

'Get up, Gemma,' he says and I do because I know that if he intends to kill me, I need to give myself a fighting chance.

But he doesn't move, just stares at me, the knife gripped in his hand.

I stare back, but I don't move either because I fear that he'll strike out if I do.

I still can't believe what I've been told. The revelations have shaken me to the core. I can feel sweat beading on my forehead and my heart is banging against my ribs. All I can do is stand in the middle of the room as a riot of emotions tears through me.

'This is all your own fault, Gemma,' he repeats. 'It didn't have to be like this.'

His words send another cold rush of blood through my veins and I feel vulnerable, helpless, defenceless.

I throw a glance at the door that leads into the hallway and wonder what will happen if I dart towards it. I'm not sure I would even make it. And if I did, what then? No way would I be able to get out of the house. I'm trapped in my own home with a man armed with a knife who wants me dead.

'I've agonised over what to do, Gemma, and I've decided that this is how it has to be. You've done too much and now you know too much. And, as I see it, this is the only option open to me. I'm sorry.'

Panic seizes my chest, making it hard to breathe, and as he takes a step towards me, I'm overwhelmed by a gut-churning wave of terror.

There's only one thing I can do and so I throw myself to the side and rush at the door. But I manage only two steps before I collide with the chair that shouldn't be there and stumble face forward onto the carpet.

I roll onto my side and, looking up, I see him standing over me, his legs astride mine. He's shaking his head and clenching his jaw.

'I'll make it quick,' he says. 'Just close your eyes.'

'Please stop it, John,' I plead with him as I hold up my hands. 'You don't have to do this. And it won't make your future any more bearable. You must know that.'

He's leaning down towards me, aiming the knife at my chest, but he suddenly stops. His demeanour shifts, and a frown digs into his face, as though he's questioning what he's about to do.

'This is not who you are, John,' I say, desperation in my voice. 'You're essentially a good person. I could tell that when we met. You've convinced yourself that you want to kill me, but in truth you don't.'

His eyes continue to stare into mine and his breathing becomes increasingly heavy.

I fight the urge to hit out by reaching for his hand or shoving my knee up into his groin. It would surely encourage him to act instinctively and not to hesitate.

'You can kill me, John, but I'll still be in your head,' I say. 'And if you're already ravaged by guilt, it will only get worse. You might not like me now, but you've said that you love me. Imagine then how you'll feel if you're standing there watching me die.'

I'm screeching now, but I can see he's listening. Taking it in. Wondering if he really does want to go through with this.

He shakes his head again, slowly. 'I just wish you had given me a chance, Gemma. I know it would have worked out. We could have . . .' He chokes on his own words and tears glisten in his eyes.

Then he stands up straight and I watch the emotions chasing across his face. Confusion. Regret. Shock. He's fighting with his conscience. I'm sure of it. He clearly didn't think this through. The consequences. His true feelings. The fact that murdering someone he loves is going to be harder than he thought it would be.

Suddenly, he throws out a long sigh, and says, 'You're right, Gemma. This is not what I want to do. I just convinced myself that it was what I needed to do. But I can see now that it won't solve anything. Even if you no longer exist, my life will still be fucked up. And that's not because of you. It's because of the mistakes I've made.'

He holds up the knife and stares at it for a few moments, as though trying to work out why it's in his hand. And then he drops it onto the floor.

'For once in my life, I'm going to do the right thing. I hate myself enough as it is and killing you will only make me more unhappy.'

'What now then, John?' I ask, my voice low, brittle.

He lifts up his head, as though he's proud of himself. 'I'm now going to leave here and go home. And when I get there, I'll decide whether to end my own life or wait for the police to come and get me.'

I wonder if he means it. That he's now seen the light. Or is he playing with me? Dragging this out because he's enjoying it?

I see he's about to move so I hold out my hand. 'Please can you help me up before you go, John? My back hurts and I'm not sure I can manage by myself.'

He steps forward as I roll onto my side. He then reaches for my hand and pulls me up.

It happens so fast that he doesn't see me retrieve with my other hand the knife he dropped on the carpet.

And a second later he cries out in pain when I thrust it deep into his stomach.

# CHAPTER SEVENTY-SEVEN

I release my grip on the knife and step back. Despite what I've done, I feel strangely calm.

John remains standing, like a drunk who has lost his bearings. His face is screwed up, mouth open, eyes fixed on me.

I sense he wants to say something but is unable to speak.

'You killed the man I loved and allowed another man to go to prison and die there,' I tell him. 'You've got what you deserved.'

His eyes roll upwards in their sockets before his legs give way and he collapses onto the floor with a loud thud.

I stare down at him, my pulse beating high up in my throat, and I have to resist a dark, seductive urge to pull the knife out of his stomach and thrust it into his heart.

Instead, I'm content with watching the life ooze out of him while feeling not a scintilla of guilt.

Who knows if he really was going to walk away without killing me. And if he had, would he have actually taken his own life or given himself up to the police?

I very much doubt it.

He moves his head and his swollen tongue pokes between thin blue lips. Then his eyes close, his features relax, and I feel a deep sense of satisfaction when he takes his last breath.

I can't move for almost a minute and when I do, it's to prepare things for when the police arrive. I don't want them to know exactly what happened here.

I have to convince them that I didn't mean to kill the man who came here to kill me.

# CHAPTER SEVENTY-EIGHT

The police have no problem believing what I tell them. After all, Jackman did break into my house with the intention of murdering me.

There's the broken window in the kitchen, the knife he brought with him, the latex gloves, his shoeprints on the grass, and the mess I made to make it look like I struggled with him.

I show them the note he put through my letter box several days ago and the get-well card, plus the various creepy text messages. And I suggest they contact DS Fenwick who knows that Jackman had been stalking me and I felt threatened by him.

'He was waiting for me when I got home,' I tell them. 'He grabbed me around the neck and told me that if he couldn't have me then he was going to make sure that nobody else could. When he came at me with the knife, he made the mistake of thinking it would be easy. But I put up a fight. I managed to knock the knife out of his hand onto the floor.

We both lurched towards it, but I reached it first and as I stood up, he threw himself at me and the knife went into him.'

The detective in charge acknowledges that it appears to be a clear case of self-defence.

I briefly consider telling him what Jackman did to Callum, but decide not to. It would serve no useful purpose other than to make the police wonder if I killed him deliberately as an act of revenge. And I don't need things to get more complicated than they already are.

I have to leave the house so that the detectives and forensics team can do their job.

The police arrange for a car to take me to a hotel. By the time I get there, it's almost midnight – too late to let people know what has happened.

That has to wait until Thursday morning, when I call Ryan, Martin and Alice, who are all completely floored by the news.

I don't go straight home because the scene-of-crime officers are still there cleaning up. Instead, I head for the office and, on the way, DS Fenwick calls me to offer his sympathy.

'I've been fully briefed on what happened last night, Miss Morgan, and I can't believe how lucky you were,' he says. 'I don't know anyone else who has gone through what you've gone through in such a short space of time. But it shows yet again that the world moves in mysterious ways. Two of the men you were threatened by are now dead. And the third is set to spend the rest of his life in prison.'

'What are you talking about?' I ask him. 'Do you mean Detective Cain?'

'That's right. I've just learned that he's about to be charged.'

'So, it's been proved that he is corrupt?'

'Not yet, but I'm sure that's only a matter of time. No, the charge DCI Cain faces is one of murder.'

# CHAPTER SEVENTY-NINE

An official statement is released by the Met just before I arrive in the newsroom and the level of excitement it generates is off the scale.

Some of my colleagues find it more interesting than the story I have to tell.

The charge of murder against Cain follows the discovery of what remains of his wife's body in the cellar of their home. It turns out that when it was searched a year ago by police after she went missing, they didn't do a proper job.

This time, while looking for evidence to prove that he's corrupt, they were more thorough and uncovered a hole in a partition wall behind a tool cabinet. Cain had put her in there after covering her naked body with vinegar and baking soda to conceal the smell of decomposition.

Off the record we're told that he's confessed to killing her. It apparently happened during a fierce argument after she found out that he was in hock to the Hagan brothers. He's claiming that she slapped his face and in response he pushed her. She fell backwards, hitting her head on the side of a table and died instantly. But he pretended she left him, for fear of being accused of murder.

So, the mystery of his missing wife is solved at last, but it will have to be determined just how much of what he's saying is the truth.

It's not long before attention turns to me and the grilling begins in earnest. News of what happened to me is already being covered online and this time my name is included in the reports.

I feel obliged to give an exclusive interview to the reporter who is writing it up for *The Sunday News*. I describe it as a terrifying experience. I also make a point of saying that what happened should serve as a warning to all women who look for love via dating apps.

The day ends early for me on strict orders from Ryan, who insists I join him and Martin for a drink in the Rose and Crown. In the event, a dozen more of our colleagues come along. They want to let me know how pleased and relieved they are that I killed the man who tried to kill me. And they want to congratulate me on being the person responsible for bringing down a detective who is not only corrupt, but also a murderer. I smile and thank them, but I find it all very stressful. I don't regret anything I've done but I am struggling to contain my emotions.

Eventually, I receive a call from the police informing me that I can return home. The forensic officers have finished and they've cleaned the place up as best they can.

Martin won't let me go by myself and comes with me. When we get there, I'm amazed at how tidy it is and even the blood has been cleaned from the carpet.

'Your ordeal is over, Gemma,' Martin tells me. 'Those vile men who made you miserable are out of your life. Things can now return to how they were.'

It all gets to me then and I break down in a paroxysm of tears.

Thankfully, Martin is with me and when he puts his arm around my shoulder, I realise that at last I feel safe again.

# EPILOGUE

Three days later, I'm with Alice at her house in Tooting. She's moved back and we're sharing a bottle of wine as we talk for the first time about everything that has happened to us.

The secret I'm carrying of what really happened to John Jackman is a heavy burden, so I decide to share it with her, safe in the knowledge that she won't tell anyone else. I even reveal that it was Jackman who killed Callum.

What I don't expect is for her to respond with a secret of her own.

'I'm glad you've confided in me, Gemma, because I've been dying to tell you about something I did,' she says. 'You see, Sean didn't fall down the stairs here. I pushed him.'

It all comes out then. How she came home that morning thinking he'd be at work so she could pick up things she wanted to take to the refuge.

'I didn't want him or anyone else to know I'd been here, so I wore a coat I borrowed and covered my face with a scarf,' she says. 'I was upstairs riffling through drawers when I heard the front door open. As I stepped out onto the landing, I saw him and he saw me. He came rushing up and I knew he was going to hurt me, so, as he got close, I lashed out and pushed him. He went flying. All the way down the staircase.

'He was badly hurt and couldn't move. His head was swollen and his arms were trapped beneath him. But he was still conscious and begged me to call an ambulance. There was no way I was going to do that. Instead, I got a cushion and held it over his face until he stopped breathing. And then I left and went back to the refuge. It didn't even occur to the police that I'd been here.'

'I don't think either of us should regret what we did,' I tell her. 'We were each given an opportunity to save ourselves and we took it.'

We both have a good cry then, but we shed tears of joy because now at last we can look forward to the future.

When Alice regains her composure, she says, 'I just hope I can meet someone who will treat me right and who I'll want to start a family with.'

'I hope so too eventually,' I say. 'But I've come to the conclusion that for the foreseeable future I'd rather be by myself. I'm not ready to embark on another relationship and I certainly won't be making use of any dating apps.'

'What about this Martin bloke you keep mentioning?' Alice says. 'It sounds to me like he's ticking all your boxes.'

I smile at her. 'Right now he's just a friend. But who knows? He might eventually become something more.'

## THE END

# ACKNOWLEDGEMENT

I would like to say a special thank you to Amy Mae Baxter, my new editor at Avon/Harper Collins. She was closely involved in this book and her input has been invaluable. She's a true professional and a joy to work with.